When I wake up in the middle of the night, Dex isn't

I tiptoe into the kitchen to get some milk, then look around
for him. I hear voices outside, so I move the blinds to the side
to take a peek. Dex is talking to a man I've never seen before.
His hand is around his neck, squeezing.

I gulp.

Would Dex kill him? What did the man do?

Finally, he shoves the man and then points to the gate.
Next, Dex turns to Arrow, says something to him, and then
punches him in the stomach.

Why did he do that?

I get back to bed before they can notice me.

An hour later, Dex slides back into the sheets and pulls
me into his arms, hugging me. He even kisses the top of my
head.

I feel safe with him, but I feel like there's a side to him I
obviously don't know.

What the hell is he hiding?

Which Dex is the real Dex?

Praise for the first
Wind Dragons Motorcycle Club novel

DRAGON'S LAIR

"Chantal Fernando knows how to draw you in and
keep you hooked. *Dragon's Lair* is a bike book un-
like any other . . . [with] a heroine for strong-willed
women and an MC of hot bikers."

—Angela Graham, *New York Times* and *USA Today*
bestselling author

ꙮ Wind Dragons MC Series ꙮ

DRAGON'S LAIR

CHANTAL FERNANDO

G

GALLERY BOOKS

New York London Toronto Sydney New Delhi

G

Gallery Books
An Imprint of Simon & Schuster, Inc.
1230 Avenue of the Americas
New York, NY 10020

First Gallery Books trade paperback edition April 2015

GALLERY BOOKS and colophon are registered trademarks of Simon & Schuster, Inc.

For information about special discounts for bulk purchases, please contact Simon & Schuster Special Sales at 1-866-506-1949 or business@simonandschuster.com.

The Simon & Schuster Speakers Bureau can bring authors to your live event. For more information or to book an event, contact the Simon & Schuster Speakers Bureau at 1-866-248-3049 or visit our website at www.simonspeakers.com.

Manufactured in the United States of America

10 9 8 7 6 5 4 3 2 1

Library of Congress Cataloging-in-Publication Data is available.

ISBN 978-1-5011-0618-7
ISBN 978-1-5011-0624-8 (ebook)

To Ari.

You've been with me since the beginning.

And you're still here.

This one is for you.

ACKNOWLEDGMENTS

ABBY ZIDLE and Gallery Books—A huge thank-you for loving the Wind Dragons as much as I do!

Ari at Cover It! Designs—Thank you for everything. You know how much I love you.

To my agent, Kimberly Brower—Thank you so much for all that you do for me!

To my sister Tee—Thanks for all your help with the boys while I was writing this book. If it weren't for you, it would have taken me a much longer time to finish it.

Rose and Tash at *Forever Me Romance*—I can't thank you guys enough! You are both amazing, wonderful people, and I appreciate all the time and effort you put in to help me. Love you both!

Kara Brown, Stephanie Knowles, and Stephanie Felix—Thanks for your help.

JC Emery—I love our daily sprints. Thanks for everything!

Kitty Kats Crazy About Books—A big thank-you to you.

Readers: Please note that this is *not* a dark romance. This e-book is the updated rereleased version of *Dragon's Lair* and contains new material.

I hope you enjoy it!
Love, Chantal Fernando

People will love you. People will hate you. And none of it will have anything to do with you.

—Abraham-Hicks

PROLOGUE

WALK home from school and stop in front of my house, sitting down on the lawn. I don't want to go inside. I like school and fifth grade, and I wish I could stay there all day. Everyone else can't wait to get home, but not me. My mother is always criticizing me, telling me what's wrong with me every time she sees me.

Sit up straight, Faye.

Ninety-eight percent is not one hundred percent.

A lady would never dress like that.

I know I'm not perfect, but she never likes to point out what I'm good at.

I'm smart—I get good grades, and my teachers always tell me how well I'm doing. I love learning new things every day.

Boys tell me I'm pretty, but my mother doesn't ever tell me this.

"What you doing sitting out here alone, Fairy?"

I look up, staring into the handsome face of my neighbor Dex. He sits down next to me and stares at the sky in silence. "Did you get locked out or something?"

I shake my head. "No, just wanted a little peace and quiet before I go inside."

"Hmmm," he says, turning to look at me, then glancing at my house. "You'd tell me if you were in any trouble, wouldn't you?"

A few years older than me and a hell of a lot cooler, I liked being around Dex. He was the most popular boy I knew and always looked out for me. He spoke to me like I was his equal, not like some stupid kid. He never spoke down to me like my mother did either. Instead, he joked with me, teased me playfully, and told me that I was smart enough to be anything I wanted to be. He said he was just next door in case I ever needed anything, or if I was ever in any kind of trouble. I was always happy that I'd been born in this house, because it was right next to his and he'd always been a part of my life.

"Yes," I mumble. It's not like I was in any real trouble. I just never felt comfortable at home, so I avoided it when I could.

Dex reaches into his pocket and pulls out a Snickers bar. "Halves?"

I nod my head and smile.

My mother doesn't give me chocolate, and Dex knows that. He always shares his with me.

My mouth waters as he breaks the chocolate bar in half and hands me the biggest piece.

"Thanks," I say, taking a big bite.

"Eric's playing video games at home, if you want to go and hang with him," he says, standing up.

"Where are you going?" I ask him, not wanting him to leave.

He looks down at me with his piecing blue eyes and grins. I'd always liked his eyes. They were such a beautiful color and were usually smiling.

Friendly.

Warm.

"I'm going to meet some of my friends."

He points to the boy and two girls walking up the street. "Either go inside or go to my house, but you can't just sit here alone, it's not safe."

His friends call out to him. He had a lot of friends, I'd noticed.

A lot of them were female.

For some reason, I didn't like that. I didn't like to share him.

I was ten and Dex was fifteen, so he definitely led a different life than I did. Even though he was older, he always had a little time for me. It made me feel special.

"See you around, Fairy," he says to me with a grin before he walks off to meet them.

I sigh and stand up, slowly walking to my front door.

When I get there, I turn around to see Dex standing on the street, staring at me. He motions for me to go inside. I know he won't leave until I do. I don't know what he thinks is so dangerous about sitting outside my house, but I know he's just trying to protect me. As soon as I'm inside, I close the door behind me and peep through the blinds.

The second my door closes, he turns around, putting his arm around one of the girls.

I narrow my eyes and turn away.

Dexter Black doesn't know it yet, but one day he's going to be mine.

 **ONE**

I STARE at the old motel in apprehension, taking in its brown brick exterior and dirty windows.

Not the Hilton, that's for sure.

Feeling sorry for myself is a foreign concept. I normally consider myself a strong woman. I need to be one, with the parents I was given and the career I want in the future. I have a strong will, and I'm not afraid to open my mouth and say what's on my mind. I don't mince words or back down. I find humor in awkward situations and try to make the most of my life.

But I guess there's a first time for everything, because here I am, tail between my legs, feeling more than sorry for myself. Kind of pathetic, really.

I'd have thought sixty dollars would have gotten me a better room than this, but I was wrong.

It has been known to happen.

I check in at reception, paying for one night and trying not to stare at the mold on the wall. The bored-looking girl at the counter hands me my key, then I drag my feet to my room, taking one bag with me. Inside are my toiletries, clothes, and a few valuables—including my purse, passport, and food.

Unlocking the door, I walk in and check out the room. A small bathroom, a couch, a bed, a fridge, and a TV. Eh, it could be worse. I put my bag on the couch and take off my sandals. Placing them neatly in the corner, I pull out a plastic container and open the lid.

Reaching inside, I decide on a piece of apple. As I munch on the cut fruit I contemplate my life. I have five thousand dollars saved, a growing belly, and no clue what the hell I'm going to do. My entire life, I'd had a plan. I always knew exactly what I was going to do, and how I was going to do it. But now? I had no plan. It was a scary thought, especially under the circumstances. One thing I know for sure is that I need to keep moving. One night here, and then I'm going to keep on driving. I want to get as far away from my old life as possible. That shit does not need to catch up with me.

I take a long shower, then take my time rubbing moisturizer into my skin. I have cherry-blossom lotion that I use every day without fail, and tonight is no exception. It gives me a little comfort, a little sense of normalcy. I brush my teeth, comb my wavy auburn hair, and climb into bed. Wishing I had brought my own sheets, I ignore the musty smell and fall asleep.

This is my life now, and I can't afford to complain.

Literally.

~

Another night passes and then I'm back on the road, heading farther north. I actually enjoy the drive; it's nice being away from the city. Before it gets dark, I check into another sketchy motel and all but collapse onto the bed. Driving at night isn't safe—there are animals that cross the roads. After a good night's rest, I spend the next day looking for a job—applying anywhere and everywhere. I'm not fussy; I'll do just about anything right now. Beggars can't be choosers. I'd never had to use that saying before in my life, coming from a fairly wealthy family. But just because my parents had money didn't mean we were happy. Far from it, actually. A quiet knock at the door makes me groan. I'd just gotten comfortable. I force myself to get up, expecting housekeeping. I open the door slightly, just enough to see who it is through the chain lock.

My jaw drops, and panic instantly sets in.

Definitely not housekeeping.

Unless they decided to hire a hot-as-hell, angry biker.

"Open it, or I will," he demands, his eyes blazing. I consider my options for a few seconds before I slide open the lock. He could just break down the door if he wanted to, so there really is no point. I open it and take a few steps back as he enters.

Crystal-blue eyes narrow on me. A muscle ticks in his jaw as his gaze rakes over me, checking to make sure I'm okay. He's wearing worn, ripped jeans and a long-sleeve black T-shirt that accentuates his muscular build. He looks good; he always did though.

"Just in the neighborhood?" I ask, hope filling my voice.

"What the fuck, Faye?" he rasps, gripping the doorframe.

I take another step back. I don't know what he's capable of right now. The old Dex would rather cut off his arm than hurt me, but do I really know him now? I don't even know how the hell he found me.

Does he know? Of course he does.

Nothing gets by Dexter Black.

He bangs the door behind him, the noise making me flinch.

"Pack up your shit," he demands, eyes searching the crappy motel room, which is now looking considerably smaller with his hulking presence. "We're leaving." He doesn't look happy with what he sees. In fact, his scowl deepens. He crosses his arms over his broad chest and stares me down, waiting for me to move.

"I'm not going anywhere," I say, putting my hands on my hips and glaring at him. He's not the boss of me. Yes, he's a badass, sexy man with whom I had one night of hot, passionate sex, but that doesn't mean he gets to tell me what to do. I might have liked him bossy in bed, but this right here is a different story.

He takes a deep breath, as if calming himself. "I've been looking for you for two days. I'm trying not to lose my fuckin' temper here, Faye, but you're pushing me. I don't think I've ever been this patient in my fuckin' life."

This is him patient?

"I'm not going anywhere," I reply, lifting my chin up. "And you can't make me."

We stare at each other, the tension building.

I can actually feel the moment before he snaps.

His fists clench, and the tightness in his jaw looks almost painful.

I step back into the frame of the open bathroom door as he loses it.

He picks up the TV and throws it into the wall. The crashing sound makes me jump, but he doesn't stop there. He punches the wall several times, then slides the few glasses off the table in one smooth movement.

More crashing.

There goes my deposit.

He turns and points his finger right at me.

I gulp.

My eyes widen as he grabs my bag and starts packing anything of mine he comes across. I walk up to him and try to grab it away from him, but one deathly look has me retracting my hand.

"Temper tantrum over?" I ask, trying to keep my voice steady.

He looks down at my bare feet, then at all the glass scattered on the carpet floor. "Don't move."

I do as I'm told as he brings me a pair of my shoes. I slide them on and look up at him.

Why does he want me to go with him? What good can come from it? What I need to do is move on with my life and settle down somewhere quiet and safe. Somewhere without sex-on-a-stick bikers and their douche-lord cheating brothers. Somewhere where my parents aren't around, and I can be myself.

"I just want to be left alone, Dex," I say, tears forming in my eyes. I'm tired, so fucking tired. My life isn't meant to be like this, and I hate the fact that he's seeing me this vulnerable.

I hate it.

I'm not this weak—not usually.

And he's the last person I'd want to see me like this. He's strong. Nothing touches him. I have no idea how he would handle me if I broke down right now, which I'm seriously close to doing.

"No, you thought running was going to solve your problems. You thought *lying* was going to solve your problems. You're lucky my dipshit brother mentioned that you left, and that you were pregnant, or I wouldn't even know I was going to have a fuckin' kid!" he yells, losing his composure.

Talk about kicking me when I'm down.

"I really don't need your shit right now," I mutter, looking down at the floor, feeling like the worst person in the world. Because he's right, I probably wouldn't have told him. I can't say what I would have done.

"You would have gone on, wouldn't you? Your whole life without telling me," he says in disbelief. "Don't you think I deserved to have heard this from you?"

I think about lying, but in the end I don't. I deserve his judgment over this. "Do you really think you could give this kid a good life?"

Wrong thing to say, but I needed to say it because that was my rationalization for leaving without a word. His eyes turn cold and hard. "I guess you're going to find out now, aren't you?"

"How do you know this kid is even yours?" I ask, lifting my chin up. Why am I poking the dragon? I have no idea.

"I know because the condom broke that night, and you hadn't had sex with Eric in a while," he says, staring straight at me. "Or anyone else."

"The condom broke?" I gape, my eyes flaring.

Well, that explains things doesn't it?

And who is he? The sex police? I hadn't had sex with anyone else, but how did he know that?

He watches me under his lashes but ignores my comment.

"Grab your shit, Faye. You have five minutes or we leave without it," he says, sitting down on the bed. I grit my teeth but do as he says, taking my few belongings and packing them back in my bag with efficient ease.

"I'm ready," I say, avoiding eye contact. He takes the bag from me and hikes it on his shoulder, then holds the door open. I walk out and wait for him to lead me to his car. He walks down toward the parking lot, and I follow, a few steps behind.

"What about my car? It has some of my stuff in it," I ask him.

"Rake will drive it home," he says as he opens the door to a black four-wheel drive. He grips my hips and lifts me up onto the seat. My breath hitches at the contact and flashes of our night together enter my mind.

Him braced above me as he grinds into me, sweat dripping down his body.

Me on all fours in front of him, his fingers digging into my hips as he thrusts.

"Faye," he says, snapping me out of it.

"Huh?"

"What were you just thinking about?" he asks, his voice a low rumble.

"Oh, nothing," I mutter embarrassment coloring my cheeks.

"I'll bet. I said Rake will handle your car, so don't worry about it."

"Rake?" I ask, my brows furrowing in confusion. I watch as Dex lifts his head toward the side of the building. I follow his line of sight and see a man leaning against the wall, smoking a cigarette. He walks over and stands next to Dex.

"So this is what the fuss is all about," the man named Rake says, checking me out and not being subtle about it.

"I'm Rake," he says, grinning at me. He's a good-looking man. Blond hair, curling around his face, green eyes, and a panty-dropping smile. He has a lip ring and an eyebrow ring—both suit him perfectly.

"Faye," I say, managing a small smile.

"I have to drive your car home," he says. "You owe me, Faye." Another grin, and then he's off.

Dex sends Rake a look I can't decipher, then turns to me.

"You okay?" he asks, scanning my face. His expression softens as he looks over me.

"Yeah. Thanks for asking," I tell him, clearing my throat. He grunts in reply, closing the door and heading to the other side. When he pulls out of the parking lot, he turns to me.

"You know, I thought you were one of the good ones. I never thought you would do something like this, trying to keep me in the dark about my own kid."

With that parting shot, which I feel deep in my bones, he drives me back home.

Back to the place I'm trying to escape.

Back to where my child will have no future.

TWO

ANOTHER A. Well done, Faye," my professor says, smiling down at me.

"Thank you, sir."

"Are you ready for the mock trials next week?" he asks.

"I am. I can't wait to get into the courtroom," I tell him.

He smiles. "You're going to be a great lawyer, Faye."

My heart warms at the compliment.

"Thank you, Professor. I'll see you next week," I say, walking out of the classroom and humming to myself.

I get into my car and pull out of the parking lot, deciding to drop by and see my boyfriend. I'm halfway through my law degree, with only two years left. Eric is the same. We've been together since we were in ninth grade, much to my mother's dismay. My parents are big on caring about what others think, and I'm a constant source of embarrassment for them. What they don't know is that I'm one of the good ones. I don't smoke, I don't drink, and I've never touched drugs in my life. I'm studious and care about my future. I'm ambitious and goal-oriented. Eric is ambitious as well, which is what I like about him. After we graduate, we're going to start our own law firm, get married, and buy a house. We have a plan.

I've wanted to be a lawyer ever since my mother planted the seed in my head at a young age. I don't know when her dream became mine, but it did. There isn't anything else in life I could imagine myself doing now that I chose this route. Law keeps me, and my mind, busy. I don't have time for anything else except my career, and Eric of course. Considering he lives next door, it makes things a lot easier.

I pull into my driveway and check my makeup in the rear-view mirror. Wide hazel eyes stare back at me, lined in black kohl. My nose is straight and splattered with freckles, my lips plump and covered in pink gloss. Satisfied with my appearance, I slide out of the car and walk next door to his familiar house. The front door is unlocked, which isn't unusual for Eric's house, so I don't think anything of it. I'm always going in and out of his house, and his mother is social too—always having her friends over. I walk down the hall, checking my phone messages as I make my way to his room. My eyes are still on my phone as I enter, glancing up only when I hear a noise.

I gasp.

This is the moment I know will change my life forever.

I stare in openmouthed shock as a naked Eric pounds into a woman from behind. They are both facing away from me, enjoying themselves at the same moment I'm finding it difficult to breathe.

My chest tightens.

My carefully structured world collapses.

I'm a good girl. I've never cheated, never even held hands

with another man. I'm not perfect by any means, but I know, *I know*, I don't deserve this shit.

Eric was more than my boyfriend—he was my friend. I've known him for as long as I can remember. This is more of a betrayal than anyone could imagine.

I close my mouth and then open it. Shock overrides my system. Never once did I suspect something like this from him. Never.

Anger soon replaces my shock.

"You fucking bastard!" I yell, taking two steps back, my hands on my face. Eric stills, then pulls away from the woman, turning to look at me with wide eyes. He starts shaking his head, as if *he* can't believe this is happening.

I can't believe this shit.

"Faye . . ." he says, reaching his arms out. For me? He has to be kidding.

"You weren't meant to be back until later."

Seriously? So this is my fault for finishing class early?

The woman rolls onto her back and sits up, pulling the sheet to cover herself. I gasp as I get a view of her face. Trisha. A friend of mine. In fact—one of my only female friends, at least that's what I'd thought. The knife currently embedded in my back throbs with the intensity only a double betrayal can cause. I swallow hard, trying to retain composure. I just didn't understand.

I didn't fucking understand.

Trisha breaks eye contact, as if ashamed. And she should be. I swallow, casting one last look at the man I thought I'd spend my life with. My friend. My partner. My neighbor. As a little girl I played video games with him and his brother. I held hands with him when we hit high school. I shared my first kiss with him. The first time we made love.

And it obviously meant nothing to him.

"You two deserve each other," I say softly, turning and running out of the house like a hellhound is after me. I can hear Eric call out my name, desperation in his tone, but I couldn't care less, and why should I? If he didn't want me, he should have told me. I would have handled it fine, and we could have still been friends. But now?

He's dead to me.

What does a girl do when she finds her boyfriend cheating on her? Well, after she's cried herself sick for two days, she forces herself to get her ass out of bed. She plasters a smile on her face and reminds herself that people break up and relationships end every day. Life isn't over. Change is good. She deserves better, and things happen for a reason. Then she gets dressed up, paying special attention to her appearance, and goes out.

And that's exactly what I did.

I don't need Eric. Screw him.

What I need is a little fun.

There's a bar I've seen but never been to. Knox's Tavern, it's called. It's meant to be "the place to be," so why not check it out.

I get out of my car, smoothing down my dress, and start to feel a little nervous. I close the car door and stare at the entrance.

I'm going into a bar. By myself.

I've never done anything like this before. I'm usually not one to frequent bars or clubs, and I'm usually hanging out with

Eric, studying, or attending events organized by the university.

Why am I here again? Oh, right—my boyfriend is a lying, cheating bastard.

I need change, and I need it now.

I walk inside.

The place is packed. My eyes scan the small dance floor before they land on the bar. I plop down on a stool, smiling at the men sitting near me. The place is swarming with attractive men and women. A good pickup place, then. There are blond twins serving at the bar, both muscled and drop-dead gorgeous. I stare at them for as long as I can until someone notices, then I turn away, blushing.

Eric who?

"What can I get you?" one of them asks.

"Umm . . ." I mutter. "Strawberry daiquiri, please."

That's the only drink I can remember the name of. I tried one once at a friend's eighteenth. God, I'm so boring. And predictable.

Next time I should order a shot of tequila—that should make the night more interesting.

The bartender smiles at me warmly, then turns to make my drink. I fight the urge to fan myself—he really is a delicious-looking man. I pay for my drink and sip it slowly, enjoying the people-watching. When I see what other women are wearing, I start to feel more confident in my black romper and wedges. I'm not showing too much skin at all. Still, to get out of the house I had to wear a cardigan over the romper, or my parents would have complained, and then I would have had to hear another lecture from my mother on how a proper lady should act. I left the cardigan in my car.

"Can I buy you a drink?" a man asks me.

I smile at him. "No, thank you, I'm still struggling to finish this one."

He grins. "How about a dance, then?"

I'm about to decline when I think—why the hell not? He looks to be about my age and is good-looking, in a preppy kind of way.

"Just a dance?" I ask with an arched brow.

He chuckles. "Just a dance. I won't propose to you, I promise."

I smirk at that and put my hand in his.

Two songs later, I return and order another drink.

A water this time—I know, I'm such a party animal. My dance partner gives me his number with an invitation to join him tonight, one I respectfully decline. Like I said—it was just a dance.

I sit here for another hour, declining the few drink invitations I get but feeling flattered all the same. None of the men really interest me, and I wonder for a moment if it's because I'm picky, or if it's because of Eric.

"Can I get you another drink, gorgeous?" the bartender asks me.

I can feel myself blush. "No, thank you."

"What's a pretty thing like you doing out here alone?" he asks. "I'm Ryan, by the way."

I smile. "Faye."

"Nice to meet you, Faye. If you need anything let me know," he says sincerely, not in a sleazy way.

I nod my head and thank him, then return to my people-watching.

When everyone starts to get really drunk, and a fight breaks out between a couple of bikers, I decide it's time to head home. I question why I feel a little disappointed. Did I want to pick up someone tonight? Do something spontaneous for once? I wasn't sure. What I did know was that none of these men make me want to step out of my comfort zone and take a chance on them. Maybe coming here tonight was a mistake? I shake my head. No, it wasn't. I did something I've never done before. I experienced something new, no matter how insignificant it would seem to someone else. And I had a little fun. Fun that I deserved.

As I walk to my car, a spring in my step, a man standing next to a gorgeous black Harley stops me in my tracks. He's wearing dark jeans, low on his narrow hips, a black T-shirt, and a battered leather jacket.

I know just who he is.

And I'm seriously surprised to see him. I thought he'd left the city for good.

I'd never forget those piercing blue eyes and thick, dark messy hair.

That smirk.

Those lips.

I haven't seen him in five years. Five years that have been *very* good to him. In fact, he seems to have gotten even sexier with age.

Dex.

I've had a crush on Dex for as long as I can remember. A silly, childhood crush. He was the local bad boy, but to me he was sweet and patient. Everyone at my school was scared of him, but not me. I knew the real Dex, and he was kind to me, always looking out for me. He might have been rough around the edges, the black sheep of his family, but he was sweet inside.

At least he used to be.

The Dex standing in front of me is all man, nothing boyish left in his appearance.

My heart races as his lips curve into a smile that I know, firsthand, has broken many hearts.

When he left, I was disappointed. He hadn't even said good-bye.

He nods his head at me, a slight imperceptible move. He then starts to walk toward me, his gaze roaming my body, slowly. When he grins and reaches out his hand to me without a word, I don't think. I just take it. He pulls me into his body for a hug that brings back a million memories. I lay my cheek against the cold leather of his jacket and smile.

"Long time no see," I say, breaking the silence. I inhale deeply, taking in his scent. *Something that I will never admit to another person.*

"Look at you, all grown up," he says in a low husky voice that gives me shivers. My body is on the curvy side. I have smallish breasts and a narrow waist but flared hips and solid thighs. Oh—and a huge ass. I don't like it, but the way he is staring at me lets me know that he does.

He likes what he sees.

A heck of a lot.

And it makes me feel good. Confident.

"I could say the same," I reply breathlessly, boldly checking him out. Is that an eight-pack under there? I want to let my hands wander over his stomach to feel what's there.

If only.

His laugh is throaty. "Like what you see, do you?"

I step away from him, clearing my throat.

I've always liked what I've seen with him; that was the problem. "I'm surprised you recognized me."

He grazes his teeth over his lower lip. "It was the hair, dead giveaway."

I swallow hard. "Oh."

"It's only been a couple of years, Faye, how could I forget you?"

"Oh," I repeat.

Very articulate, Faye.

"Who are you here with?" he asks, eyes darting to the bar. "Not that it matters."

"No one," I reply, shrugging my shoulders a little sheepishly.

He frowns. "You came here alone? It's not safe, Faye; this bar gets some unsavory characters."

I roll my eyes. *Like you?* I wanted to say. "I was only here for a little while, and I drove. I'm fine. I deserve to have a little fun now and then, you know."

He gives me a slow-spreading devilish smile. "Yes, I suppose you do. What are you doing right now?"

I arch my brow. "I *was* going home."

He grins crookedly. "And now?"

I lick my lips and dart my eyes away from his before replying. "And now I'm going wherever you are."

He laughs softly. "You always did like following me around, didn't you?"

I purse my lips and look at my car. "I can always go home, you know."

I take a step toward my car when he pulls me closer against him. "I don't think so, babe. You aren't going anywhere."

"Is that right?" I ask a little breathlessly. "I'm grown up now, and there won't be any following. I can walk away as easily as I can stay."

It was bold, telling him I was going wherever he was. His reply, however, made me angry. I used to follow him around as a kid, but now I'm a woman and I won't be panting after any man, especially one who doesn't want me, even if he is Dexter Black.

He studies me, looking thoughtful. "I didn't mean it like that."

I nibble on my bottom lip, the tension between us rising as we watch each other in silence, our bodies pressed against each other.

"Are you single?" he asks, licking his lips and studying me.

I nod. "I am."

"Good," he mutters under his breath, gaze roaming my face intently.

"Want to get out of here?" he finally asks in a low tone.

My eyes flare. "You just got here."

"I've found what I'm looking for," he says, squeezing my hand gently.

Do I want to go with him? With the way he's looking at me, I know what he wants. He's never looked at me like this before. Then again, he probably only saw me as the little girl next door. I'm now a woman, and he's seeing that. He wants me. And damn if I don't want him too.

My gaze lowers to his lips. I'd really like a taste of them. This is Dex. I might not know him completely anymore, but

I know that he would never hurt me. I swallow hard as I think about having sex with him, a fluttering in my chest at the possibility. I squeeze my thighs together. If there was one man in this world I wanted—it was him.

I make my decision.

Fuck the consequences. I don't owe Eric anything anymore. I'm a single woman. And I find myself wanting Dex, badly.

Don't regret anything that makes you happy.

"Okay," I reply on a shaky breath.

"You sure?" he asks, rubbing his hand down my arm. "'Cuz I want you pretty fuckin' bad right now. I can't even think straight."

I shiver at both his gravelly tone and his admission.

"Trust me, I'm sure," I say with more confidence in my tone. The feeling is mutual.

He leans down and kisses me, catching me off guard. At the first taste of his lips, a moan escapes me. His lips are soft, and he tastes like mint. His hand cups the back of my neck as he pulls me in, kissing me deeper. My tongue reaches out to touch his, inciting a moan from deep in his throat. He pulls back before I want him to, staring into my eyes, looking almost surprised.

"Fuck," he whispers.

"What?" I ask breathlessly, wanting his lips back on mine.

"Get on, babe," he demands huskily, leading me to his bike. "We need to get out of here, now."

"I've never been on a bike before," I admit, staring at it. I couldn't help but feel excited at the thought of straddling his bike, my arms wrapped around him, my cheek pressed to his back.

His answering smile makes my pulse race. "You'll love it, trust me. Just hold on to me and enjoy the ride."

I nod and touch the seat with my hand, watching as he pulls off his leather jacket. "Here," he says, putting it on my shoulders. "You'll freeze otherwise."

I slide my arms into the sleeves and zip it up. It's big on me, but deliciously warm and smells just like him. He looks at me in his jacket, licking his bottom lip again, an almost possessive look flashing in his eyes. He shakes his head then, his jaw tight.

Did I just imagine that? It's probably my wishful thinking.

He puts a helmet on me. I don't breathe as he places it on my head, I just stare into his eyes. He touches my cheek with a gentle finger before turning away. I release the breath I was holding and get on the bike, wrapping my arms around his stomach. I can feel his taut, rock-hard abs properly now under his thin T-shirt. Definitely an eight-pack.

We ride for about half an hour, finally pulling up to a hotel. Spending all that time pressed against him has left me achy . . . and wanting. Never once in my life did I think I'd have a chance with Dex. I'd locked him away in my "never going to happen" fantasies, but here I was. And I was going to make the most of it.

As we walk inside, I realize something.

"My car . . ."

I just left it there, completely captivated by Dex. I didn't even think.

"I'll handle it," he says, in a low husky voice. "Just give me the keys."

"Okay," I reply, my voice cracking a little as I drop them into his hand. He checks us into a room and holds my hand until we get to the door. He unlocks it with a swipe of a card, then gestures for me to enter. I walk in and take in the room. It's spacious, with a king bed, a couch, and a TV. It's a nice room, not a cheap one. I'd know, since my mother only stays in the best of the best whenever we go on family holidays.

"Come here," he says, sitting on the bed and pulling off his shirt. I stare at his impressive chest, wanting to moan out load. Wow, is all I can say. I didn't think men like this existed out of books and movies, but here he is, in all his muscled perfection, standing right before me.

And for tonight—he's all mine.

"Faye," he says. "I said to come here. You will have your fill of me, don't you worry about that."

I do as instructed, distracted by his body, and go and sit next to him.

"You sure you want this?" he asks, running his finger along my jawline. Goose bumps appear on my skin just from that touch.

Was I sure? Fuck yes, I was sure. I didn't want to think, I just wanted to lose myself in him.

"I'm sure," I tell him, shifting on the bed. He nods once, a thoughtful look on his handsome face, then he taps his hands on his lap. Before I know what I'm doing, I sit on his lap, straddling him. When he kisses me, I don't stop him. He feels too good, smells too good, and I want to forget.

More than that, I want a taste of this man.

We both stand, and he strips off my clothes slowly, taking his time.

"Your body is fuckin' amazing, you know that?" he whispers as he stares at me completely naked.

"I'm glad you approve," I reply with a smirk. The way he's staring at me right now . . . I don't think I've ever felt so beautiful in my life.

My eyes follow his hands as he undresses himself. His body is impressive, all hard angles and ripples. My mouth waters.

Naked, he turns and leans down to pull a condom out of his wallet. The dragon's face tattooed on his back is staring right at me, its body coiled tightly behind it. It's beautiful, intricate, and deadly.

Just like the man standing before me.

He faces me once more, throwing the condom packet down on the bed. My gaze drops.

He's huge. I've only ever been with Eric, but I notice that Dex is *a lot* bigger in width and length. He flashes me a grin when he sees me staring. Too turned on to care that I was caught ogling him, I lick my lips instead. His eyes darken. Leaning over me, he gently pushes me back on the bed. He kisses my lips with no preamble, his tongue exploring my mouth. He knows what he's doing, just how to turn me on. I moan into his mouth as his finger slides into me. He makes a sound deep in his throat, a growling sound.

It's seriously hot.

His lips leave my mouth. Ignoring my groan of protest, he trails openmouthed kisses down my neck, my collarbone, the curve of my breast. Teasing me, he licks everywhere except my nipple.

"Dex," I groan, my tone pleading.

I raise my head and narrow my eyes on him when I hear his dark chuckle, but his eyes aren't on mine. His head is lowered as he licks the side of my breast, then drags his tongue up to my nipple.

Just a little more.

When he places his mouth over my nipple and sucks, my back arches from its own accord. It felt so good. I tangle my fingers in his hair and tug gently, encouraging him. More, I wanted more. He moves his head, paying attention to my other breast, while I lie back and enjoy every sensation. Plumping my breasts together, he licks one last time before he lets go, and his fingers wander downward to my pussy again. Stroking me there gently, he brings my wetness to my clit and rubs his thumb. If I were standing, I would have fallen to my knees.

"So wet," he murmurs, sounding thrilled about the fact.

Removing his hand, he grabs the condom off the bed and tears the packet open with a flash of his white teeth. I watch as he slides it on over his rock-hard length, anticipation building.

I'm more than ready for him as he slides himself into me with one smooth thrust. His patience clearly over, he thrusts deeply, a curse leaving his lips. Pumping his hips to get farther inside me, each stroke so deep, so perfect. His pelvis slides across my clit with each movement, making me cry out each time. His body shows me just how much I've been missing out on, his skilled moves giving me more pleasure than I've ever experienced before. His lips find mine, not gentle this time but rough and frantic. He sucks and nibbles on my lower lip, and I wrap my hands around the back of his neck and lift my hips up to meet each passionate thrust. I was on the edge; I could feel it. I think Dex could too, because he reaches down and plays with my clit, pushing me over.

So. Fucking. Good.

I come once, twice, before he finishes. He kisses me on the forehead once before he pulls out. I sit up and frown when I notice the look on his face. He looks angry.

"What is it?" I ask, my voice hoarse and unsure.

He clears his throat. "Nothing." He stands up and heads out of the room. I get dressed quickly, wondering what the hell I just did. I've never done anything like this in my life. I need to get home—right now. Dex comes back into the room, condom taken care of, and lies back on the bed with his arms stretched behind his head. Not a care in the world.

I reach down to grab my clothes.

"What are you doing?" he asks, looking over at me in amusement.

"Getting dressed."

He sits up and pulls me back onto the bed, lightly kissing my jaw. "Not done with you yet, babe; that was just a warm-up."

His mouth finds mine, and I lose all rational thought.

<hr />

"I'll take you home. My friend Tracker will bring your car to you," he says the next morning, not looking at me.

"Okay," I say, awkwardly waiting while he dresses. I fiddle with the hem of my romper, looking around the room distractedly. I got up before him and took a shower, waiting to leave. He wasn't making this awkward at all, but I am. He is obviously familiar with this situation, while I am officially doing my first walk of shame. Last night had me feeling off-kilter. Did I imagine the connection between us? Last night wasn't fucking. It was meant to be, but it didn't feel like it. I don't know what to think. Dex is acting like it was nothing, so I must be imagining things. I only have Eric to compare him to. Maybe Eric and I just didn't have any passion. Is that what it was? Passion? I don't regret anything though, not even a little bit. Last night is something I will never forget.

"Faye," he says, drawing my eyes to him.

"Yeah?"

"Are you okay?" he asks, standing before me, now fully dressed.

I force myself to hold eye contact. "Yeah, I've just never done anything like this before," I admit, looking away shyly.

He lifts my face up with his hand on my chin.

"What do you mean, you've never done anything like this before?" he asks, tilting his head and looking confused.

"I mean, a one-night stand," I say, shrugging my shoulders.

"I hope you're not expecting a ring, or some shit?" he says, looking amused.

"You asshole," I snap, standing up and walking myself to the door. A ring? He'd probably give me a plastic ring from one of those vending machines and tell me to be happy with it.

Dex follows behind me. "I'm just playing around, no need to get angry."

I turn to look at him. "I see age hasn't made you any funnier."

He laughs. "Oh, please, I used to have you in hysterics."

I laugh at the reminder. Okay, so he always did have a good sense of humor.

"How old are you now?" he asks, lighting a cigarette as we step outside.

"Twenty-three."

"Fuck, you're a baby still," he says, puffing out smoke and shaking his head.

"Old enough for you to fuck," I say dryly, examining my manicure.

Dex laughs, a deep musical sound. He always did have a great laugh, the bastard.

"You have a dirty mouth on you, babe."

"You'd know," I mutter to myself.

More laughter.

I stare at him as he laughs, his whole face transforming. My chest tightens a little, because this is probably the last time I will see him.

"Hey, we both got what we wanted," he says, putting out the cigarette with his shoe.

"How so?" I ask him, stepping closer to his bike.

"You got revenge on my brother; isn't that what you wanted? A taste of wild?"

I hate that I blush. How does he know about Eric and me?

I did get what I wanted, but it wasn't revenge.

It was just him.

What I'd always wanted but never thought was in my grasp.

"And what did you get, Dex?" I ask, tilting my head to the side. He could have any woman he wanted. I know that, and he sure as hell knows that. He's good-looking, and when I look at him, I think of sex. He's built for it. He also has a dangerous air about him, like you know there's a side to him you never want to see. You just trust yourself with him and hope that you're whole when he leaves you. He's an addicting kind of man. One that I should turn from and never look back, but don't want to. I have to wonder what he's been up to all these years.

He grins wolfishly. "I got to fuck a fairy."

I grit my teeth. When I was younger, Dex used to call me fairy, because that's the meaning of Faye.

It used to drive me crazy.

Apparently it still does.

"How did you know about Eric?" I ask.

He shrugs. "My ma mentioned something."

His mother was such a gossip.

He smirks as if he knows exactly what I'm thinking.

"Where have you been all these years?" I blurt. "Why don't you ever come by and see your family?"

He looks away for a moment, then turns back to me. "Let's just say that my mom didn't approve of my lifestyle choices. She turned her back on me and told me not to come home anymore."

I open my mouth to ask him what he meant by that when he continues.

"We've been on talking terms for a while now, but it's mainly the odd phone call here and there. Better than nothing, I suppose."

How did I not know this?

"Eric never mentioned anything about that," I say. "He just said you left the city."

Dex shrugs. "Eric and I don't get along. He's family, but we've never really seen eye to eye. We're like water and oil."

I nod slowly. Eric hardly even mentioned Dex, and when I

brought him up, he'd act indifferent and change the subject. I thought he was just upset that Dex had moved away, but apparently I was wrong.

"What now?" I ask, a little shyly. What was the protocol for a situation like this? It was different for me—this was more than a one-night stand. It was with someone I care about, someone I've always cared about. I'll always have a soft spot for Dex. Always. And tonight just intensified it.

"Hop on," he says, giving me a gentle look. "Let's get you home."

≈

Dex kisses me on the forehead, his soft lips lingering for a moment.

Or did I imagine that?

"Be good," he whispers, his eyes softening. He tucks a strand of my hair behind my ear and smiles, a little sadly. "See you around, my fairy."

"'Bye, Dex," I say, forcing a smile.

He pulls me in for one last kiss, just a simple touch of our lips, before he rides away.

I watch his bike disappear before I walk into my house, coming to a standstill when I see Eric sitting with my mother having a coffee. I blink once slowly, then shake my head.

There goes my good mood.

"What are you doing here?" I demand. "I have nothing to say to you, so please leave."

With that, I walk to my room, turning my back on the two of them.

"Faye! Where have you been? Don't talk to your boyfriend like that. I raised you better," my mother admonishes. I ignore her like I usually do. Eric walks into my room like he has a million times before, but never under these circumstances. He closes the door behind him, then turns and exhales deeply, as if gathering courage to face me. He's going to need it. I sit on my bed and stare up at him, wanting to get this over with. My face is impassive, not giving away anything. I show no emotion. I don't want him to have any part of me anymore, even my anger.

He will get nothing from me. He made it so the second he betrayed my trust and made a mockery of everything we had together. The worst part is that his betrayal hurts worse than his actions. It didn't gut me inside that he was with another woman—this really was a wake-up call. I was in the relationship with Eric for all the wrong reasons: it was convenient, easy, and it worked. There was no epic love story, no intense passion or romance. I'm not even sure those things exist outside of the romance novels I like to read sometimes. Our relationship was comfortable. If Eric hadn't cheated on me, I would have gone on like that forever. The thought is now a little scary. I would have been married to someone who was more friend than lover, more routine than love of my life. I could just imagine myself buried in my work and not having much of a home life, probably the occasional planned-out nights that we made love. Christ. Maybe I should actually be thanking Eric for turning my world upside down—but not necessarily in a bad way. This whole situation has really woken me up, brought me back to reality. There's a whole world out there if I choose to live in it; safe isn't always good.

"Where were you last night?" he asks, fists clenching and releasing, bringing me back to the here and now.

I almost laugh at his audacity. How dare he question where I was! It's almost funny that he thinks he has that right.

"I came by to talk to you, and you weren't home," he continues, heedless of the fact that his words are making my blood boil.

"What's it to you? I'm not your business anymore, Eric," I reply, pretending to be bored. I even stare down at my cuticles for effect.

"What the fuck, Faye?" he growls, starting to pace the confines of my room.

"I was single the second you cheated on me. I owe you nothing. Now, get out of my room," I say, my voice like steel. His face turns red. His brown hair, much lighter than Dex's, flops over his forehead, and he pushes it away with a flick of his wrist. I used to find that movement charming. Now I just want to punch him in the face. I might have, had I not worked out a lot of my frustrations last night. A slither of guilt appears after that thought—the fact that I'm sitting here still smelling like Dex, after spending the night in his arms. A picture forms in my mind, of Eric fucking Trisha behind my back.

My resolve hardens.

I didn't owe him anything; I shouldn't feel one bit of guilt.

"Where did you go?" he asks, scowling at me.

"How long have you been cheating on me?" I counter, using a light tone.

He pauses. "It just happened, Faye. I'm sorry. You know it's not her that I want, but you've been so busy lately with school and everything—"

"I understand," I say, cutting him off. I've heard about this before. Men trying to lay the blame on the woman so she thinks it was her lacking that caused the man to cheat. Then she takes on some of the blame and gives him another chance, hoping they can work things out together.

"You do?" he asks, looking hopeful.

"Sure I do. You're a pathetic, weak, cheating bastard who can't even own up to his actions. So instead, you try to blame them on me," I reply, narrowing my eyes on him. I'm not a perfect woman. In fact, I probably don't even know what I'm talking about, considering I've only ever had one relationship. But what I do know is that I won't allow a man to cheat on me or disrespect me. Sure, everyone makes mistakes, but Eric isn't even sorry.

He's only sorry he got caught.

There's a huge difference.

"Faye . . ."

"You control your own actions, Eric. You. Not me. And your actions tell me that you don't deserve me. Now, please just leave me alone," I say, feeling tired, upset, and sick of life fucking around with me.

"So, what, one mistake, and you're going to throw away six years?" he says, his jaw clenching. His face takes on a pinched look that I've never noticed before.

How unattractive.

"Yes!" I yell. "Now, get out! Go annoy Trisha!"

He's her problem now, not mine.

"What the fuck ever," he snaps, closing the door behind him as he leaves.

Finally, peace and quiet.

I know our breakup is for the best, but it still hurts. Not once did I ever think Eric would hurt me in this way. He's been my friend since . . . forever.

He should have just broken up with me. Why didn't he?

I shove my face into my pillow and cry.

THREE

O VER the next week, Eric tries to win me back. He calls me, shows up at my house, and corners me at school.

But it doesn't work and won't ever work. There is no point in us getting back together. I wish we could become friends, but I don't really see that happening after what he did. Once I'm done—I'm done.

I tell him over and over again that there is no way in hell I will ever take him back. I told him that I forgave him, but I'd never forget what he did. He needed to move on with his life. He obviously wanted to sleep with other women, and now he could do that without having me in the way. He couldn't have it all—have a good woman on the side but still sleep around and act like a bachelor. I have a feeling he just wants me back for the sake of it, because he's as thrown off-balance with this change as I am. I'm his comfortable place, and he wants that back, even though we clearly weren't working.

After a while he gets the picture and starts to date another girl. To be completely honest, it hurts, but it's for the best. Now I need to concentrate on me. I can't help but feel confused. Unsettled. We had our life planned out, and now I need to make a fresh plan, one without him. The thought of Eric with another woman used to kill me, but now I just feel sorry for whoever she is. I hope he doesn't cheat on her too. Trisha and I haven't spoken. We pretend we don't know each other, which is perfectly fine with me. I'm just waiting for karma to take care of her for me. Whatever happened to the girl code?

"Hey, Faye," Eric calls out, walking toward me. And to think I'd almost made it to the inside of my car. I was in the university parking lot, about to go home after a long day. All I really wanted was a hot bath and my bed. Maybe some food.

"Hey," I say, opening my car door and staring at it longingly.

So close.

"How are you?" he asks, leaning against my fender.

"Fine," I say. "What's up?"

"I heard something about you . . ." He trails off, brows furrowing.

"And?" I ask, wondering where he was going with this.

"I heard that you were seen out with Dex," he says, his lips tightening into a straight line. He heard? Whoa, this city is definitely too small. Someone saw me and Dex where? The bar parking lot? At the motel? Or in front of my house when he dropped me off?

"And?" I repeat, frowning.

"And? What the fuck are you thinking?" he snaps, shaking his head at me. "I didn't even know that you'd seen him or spoke to him. Why didn't you say anything?"

I still. "Well, this is awkward. I had no idea you had a say over who I do and don't see. Oh, that's right. You don't, so mind your own business, Eric."

"Mind my own business? He's my brother and not a good

guy," he warns, his dark eyes pleading with me to listen. "I don't want you to get messed up with him. So tell me what happened when you saw him."

"And you *are* a good guy?" I ask, eyes flaring. "Look, Eric, thanks for keeping an eye on me, but it's unnecessary. Yes, I ran into Dex. I hadn't seen him in years, and you told me he moved away but apparently left out a few details."

He flinches slightly but doesn't back down. He doesn't know that Dex and I slept together, but he's still acting crazy over this. The question is, why?

"What's the big deal?" I ask curiously, trying to act casual. "It's just Dex."

Eric rolls his eyes, not a good look for a man. "He's a fucking criminal, Faye. He's dangerous."

Now it's my turn to roll my eyes. "He's your brother. He's never done anything to hurt us."

Eric grits his teeth. I grin. "You're just jealous of him, aren't you?" I surmise. He definitely has reason to be. Dex is . . . well, Dex.

His eyes narrow, and his jaw is tight. "I heard a motorcycle the day you walked into your house, and I was waiting for you, but it didn't mean anything to me until now. Your car wasn't in the driveway when I left either, so Dex must have dropped you off at home. The question is, Faye, what exactly did you and Dex do together?"

Well, shit.

I expel a long-suffering sigh. "I went out to a bar, alone. Dex was there; we hung out, and he dropped me off."

Eric scoffs, shaking his head. "I'll bet. Have you heard of the Wind Dragons?"

I roll my eyes again. "Of course I have; who hasn't?"

The Wind Dragons Motorcycle Club was a notorious biker gang. I'd heard nothing good about their members, who apparently take drugs and have sex for a living. They live their life a certain way and make no apologies about it. I'd never actually interacted with a member, so I don't know the truth of it all, just what I'd heard from others in passing. People tended to stay away from them, and no one wanted to mess with them, because you'd end up dead. The club stood up for each other and always had each other's backs, kind of a "mess with one mess with them all" thing.

Eric has a smug look on his face. I didn't like it one bit. "Dex is the vice president."

I freeze for a few seconds. "Bullshit."

Then I remember the tattoo on his back.

The deadly dragon.

The bike.

The badassness.

I could see Dex in an MC. He has this predator vibe about him.

He's hot-blooded.

In fact, if I didn't know him, I would probably steer clear of him altogether. He's the ultimate bad boy. But he's also *my* Dex, the boy I grew up around. I will always see that first, before anything else.

"How come you never mentioned this before?" I ask him, staring at him in suspicion. He kept a lot from me about Dex, and I want to know why.

Something crosses his face. Something I don't like. He's not telling me something.

"You always had a thing for him, Faye; don't think I'm so blind to not have noticed it," he snaps, rubbing the back of his neck. "You were always his number one fan."

I roll my eyes for the third time. "I was a kid, Eric. Seriously, let it go."

"I never thought you'd be stupid enough to get mixed up with him and his stupid group of friends," he says. "Just wait until your mother hears about it; she's going to kill you."

That's the complete truth. My mother is narrow-minded and judgmental about anyone who doesn't have a university degree or doesn't fit into her idea of how people should be. She came around about me dating Eric after she realized he was ambitious and was going to be a lawyer. Status, money, and public image matter to her more than anything. Putting it frankly, she has a stick up her butt and judges anyone who's different from her. My father just agrees with whatever she says and never has his own opinion. I will never marry a weak man like my father—I could never have any respect for someone like that.

"I know he was dating that girl. What's her name?" he continues, oblivious to my inner dialogue. "She's quite beautiful."

"Who knows," I reply, caring only that he *was* dating someone, and not is.

"Don't you want to know who your competition is?" he asks, raising an eyebrow. "I've seen some of the women he's been around. They could be on the covers of magazines."

Has Eric always been this much of an asshole, or am I only just noticing?

"No, what I want is this conversation to be over," I grit out, not wanting to think about Dex with a harem of beautiful women I could never compare to. "I thought you never see Dex?"

He shrugs. "Unfortunately, I've run into him a few times."

Another thing he had failed to mention.

"You know what, after one night with you he'll be done. Don't come crying to me when you end up heartbroken," he sneers, turning away from me.

"Well, I survived being heartbroken once; I'm sure I will again," I reply, unable to keep the bite out of my tone.

"I made a mistake," he replies, sighing with what seemed like genuine regret.

"I hope she was worth it," I find myself saying. Why keep talking about it? No snide comments or words of regret and pain are going to change anything. What's done is done.

"She wasn't," he admits, looking down at his hands. "I guess I'd been with you forever, and I just wanted to play around with someone new."

I look down as the truth finally leaves his mouth. "I have to go, okay?"

"Just remember what I said about him," he says, tone full of warning. "You don't know him anymore, Faye. Dex isn't the boy who used to give you chocolate and keep an eye on you. He's an outlaw biker. Remember that."

"Fine; duly noted," I say, sliding into my car. Eric walks off, and I drive my ass home.

This fuss was all for naught, because I knew I wouldn't be seeing Dex again anyway.

FIVE WEEKS LATER

Dr. Reeves walks in, sitting down in his chair. He's a kind man in his fifties and has been my doctor for a few years now. I'm pretty sure he keeps his lollipop jar stocked just for when I have an appointment. He's seen me at my worst, and I'm definitely comfortable around him.

"I need drugs, Doc," I tell him. "And lots of them. You know how much I hate throwing up."

He doesn't smile at my antics like he usually does. "Faye, I'm afraid it's not the flu that's making you nauseous."

I frown. "Okay, well, what's wrong, then? Do I have a different bug? I knew I shouldn't have caught that bus to campus the other day when my car broke down. I could literally see the germs when one of the men on there started coughing."

"You're pregnant, Faye," he says.

Pregnant? I must have misheard him.

I blink slowly, trying to comprehend this new notion. "I'm sorry, I don't think so. Are you sure those results are mine? I saw this show the other night on doctors mixing up patient files."

Now he fights a smile. "This test says you're definitely pregnant."

I look around the room, hoping for someone to jump out and tell me that this is a prank. "I don't understand."

His lip twitches. "When's the last time you had sex? And when was your last period?"

"I have never had sex without a condom," I blurt out, wringing my hands.

"Faye . . ."

"I guess, about six weeks ago," I tell him with reluctance.

With a criminal.

With a man I was never planning on seeing again.

But we used a condom!

I imagine myself having to fill out a form with our details. I wonder if they'll accept "criminal biker" on the line for Dex's employment.

"Condoms aren't a hundred percent foolproof, you know," he reminds me calmly. My mind flashes to a certain episode of *Friends*, and I suddenly feel like yelling out that they should put that on the outside of the box.

"You remember what happened when I went on the pill," I tell him. I tried it for a month, and it didn't agree with me. I put on weight and felt like shit. Dr. Reeves said we could try another one, but I said I would just use condoms. Eric and I always used one, even though he tried to talk his way out of it a few times with the infamous "I promise I'll pull out" line.

Yeah—not a chance in hell.

"I wasn't criticizing you, Faye, but you are pregnant," he says kindly, pulling out some brochures from his drawer.

"I see," I say, staring into empty space.

And I did see.

What I saw was my life flashing before my eyes.

I saw my career and my life plans crashing. Evaporating. Vanishing.

Disappearing.

"You have options," he says, interrupting my dramatic thoughts by sliding the brochures to me. But I don't. I don't have options, and my life is over. My parents will kick me out, my education is going to take a backseat to changing diapers, and the baby's father is an outlaw biker. This kid doesn't stand a chance. I respect a woman's right to choose, but I could never have an abortion. That's just not me. I stand up, the sound of the chair scraping the floor filling the silent room.

"I'm keeping it," I announce, loudly. A declaration. A promise.

Everyone else be damned.

Doc has a talk with me, gives me a book to read, and tells me to get some folic acid and other things. I leave the doctor's in a daze.

A plan starts to form in my head.

First of all, I need to save money.

Then my baby and I are out of here.

~

I'm three months pregnant when my mother figures it out. And that's when everything goes to hell. My parents kick me out. No discussion. No second chance. My mother just tells me to be gone by the end of the day. My father looks sad but doesn't dare go against her wishes.

You've embarrassed us and yourself. If you have an abortion you can come home, otherwise don't bother! What is everyone going to say? I should have known you'd get knocked up. You are such a disappointment, Faye!

They should have never had a child. I'm going to make sure I'm a way better mother than she ever was—I'm going to learn from her mistakes. How predictable of them. I always knew they would cut me out of their lives the moment they found out, and I was right. That doesn't mean that it doesn't hurt though, but I push the pain away, because I didn't have the time to deal with it. I have bigger problems right now.

Luckily I've been saving every cent during the last few months, preparing for this moment. I cashed in some of my gold and sold everything I could, even my Xbox. I don't need all those material things anymore. What I need is a plan for the future and some stability. I glance around my room one last time, taking in every detail. My queen-size bed, covered in plain white cotton sheets, the cream walls and wooden floor-ing. My childhood teddy bears that I didn't have the space to take with me, except my favorite, which I would give to my child. It was a brown bear named Coco and was my cherished childhood toy. I heave a sigh and close the door to my room, closing this chapter of my life. No point dwelling on the past—it's time to move forward.

I pass my mother in the kitchen. She doesn't say anything as she sees me leaving, my bags in my hand. My dad is at work, and I don't know what his reaction would have been if he were to talk to me one last time before I departed. Would he have told me he was sorry? That I could come home if I found my-self stuck? Doubtful. One look from my mother would have cured him of any thoughts of kindness.

I walk to my car, unlock it, and start to load in my belong-ings. Just as I throw the last bag into my car, Eric pulls up in his obnoxious car.

"Where are you going?" he asks as he storms up to me. He frowns when he sees all my stuff in the back of my car.

"I believe your house is that one," I say, pointing next door.

He scowls. "Where are you going, Faye?"

"Taking a little holiday," I say in a tone that lets him know I'm not in the mood for his shit. You'd think that when you broke up with someone the drama and headaches would end, but that would be furthest from the truth. You still get the drama and headaches, without the added benefit of sex.

He grabs my arm, looking a mixture of concerned and confused. "What the hell is going on?"

I lose it, my composure that had been hanging on by a thread shattering.

Months of hiding, stressing, and crying all burst out of me. "I'm pregnant, and I have nowhere to go, so I'm leaving town, and I'm not coming back. Now, get the fuck out of my way!"

He stands there, frozen, his mouth open in shock. "You were going to leave town without telling me about *my* baby? How could you do something like that to me?"

Of course he had to somehow make this about him.

I can't help it. I laugh. It's more nervous laughter than anything else. I probably sound psychotic.

Eric and I hadn't had sex in a month when I slept with Dex. There is no way the baby is his.

"Baby isn't yours, Eric, so don't worry about it," I say, pulling out of his hold. "Now, move aside so I can leave."

"The fuck?" he growls, his face going red in anger. "Who did you sleep with?"

Typical male. Of course that would be all he cares about.

"Too many to count," I reply, opening the door. I still and turn to him. "I guess I'll see you around."

Or not.

"You don't have to leave," he says, still looking confused and hurt.

The pain radiating from him makes me hurt too.

Why is he in pain? He was the one who ended us, not the other way around. Did he finally realize what he'd lost? Well, it was too late.

"There's nothing left for me here anymore, Eric," I say softly, letting him look into my eyes and see the truth.

We are over. There's no going back now.

"Faye . . ." he whispers, his voice cracking. He sees it. He knows it. It's done.

I smile sadly. "I guess it just wasn't meant to be."

He runs his hand through his hair. "We can say it's mine. I don't want to lose you."

My eyes flare in surprise—I didn't see this one coming. I actually consider it for a moment, but then I see him with that other woman. And I couldn't do that to Dex.

It would all be pretend.

And I don't want to live a lie. "Eric, thanks for the offer, but that isn't going to work. Take care of yourself."

I get in my car and start the engine, his eyes on me the entire time.

As I pull out of my driveway, making sure not to hit his car, I leave him standing there looking helpless.

Looking just how I feel.

 **FOUR**

THE drive back is uneventful. Dex is quiet, playing head-banging music the whole way, giving me a migraine. As much as I didn't want to admit it, I liked that he was still the same in that aspect. He'd always listened to heavy metal.

"Still like shit music, I see," I comment, smirking at him.

"This is Five Finger Death Punch," he replies, sounding offended. "Still only listen to commercial crap, then? You always had the worst taste in music. I remember when you went through a Hanson phase."

I make a Hmmph noise but don't reply. Hanson is a great band, and nothing he says will make me change my mind. The song changes to some alternative, hipster music I've never heard before, so I put in my earphones and stare out the window, into the darkness of the night. I lower the volume so he can't hear "You & I" by One Direction playing; I can only imagine the crap he would give me. I finally fall asleep but instantly wake when Dex touches my arm, his warm fingers sending a spark through my body. He pulls the earphones from my ears and speaks, eyes locked with mine.

"I'm stopping to get gas; do you want anything?" he asks. One of his hands is on top of the steering wheel, and I stare at the tattoos covering his knuckles. On one hand WDMC is spelled out, a letter on each finger.

Wind Dragons Motorcycle Club.

"Faye," he snaps, when I don't answer.

I blink and look at his face. "No, thanks, I'm fine."

"I'll get you some water," he says, sliding out of the car. God, he's so bossy.

And hot—but that's another story. The two don't cancel each other out.

A few minutes pass, when I see Rake walking up to the car. He comes to stand right at my window and taps on it. I blink slowly a few times before rolling the window down.

"Hey," he says, smiling as he lights up a cigarette.

"Um, hi," I reply, staring at him. My lips quirk as I look at him, his smile contagious.

"Can't wait to get home," he grumbles around his smoke. "Got a warm woman waiting in my bed, and I could use some stress release."

"Yeah, sorry about that," I say, shrugging sheepishly, pretending I didn't hear the last part of his comment. Like I cared that he was dying to get home so he could have sex—total overshare.

He chuckles. "Was worth it, seeing Sin get all worked up."

"Sin?" I ask, arching an eyebrow. Is that what Dex goes by nowadays? "Do you know what he's planning on doing with me?"

He smirks. "Don't worry, you're safe with us, and Sin isn't going to bite. Truth is, I haven't seen him this crazy over a woman in . . . well, in fuckin' ever."

My eyes widen. "What do you mean by that?"

He can't mean what I think he does. Dex has had to be with a lot of women, and trust me, he isn't crazy over me, he's just crazy angry that he had to come out and find me, knowing I was pregnant with his child but never told him.

Rake looks over the car, then takes a step backward. I turn my head to see Dex get back into the car, a bottle of water and a chocolate bar in his hands.

"Thanks," I say as he hands them to me.

"Rake, don't fucking smoke around her," Dex growls. "She's fuckin' pregnant. I told you this, brother."

Rake throws the cigarette to the ground, stomping on it. "Fuck, I'm sorry. I forgot."

He looks to me. "You should have said something, Faye."

I don't know what to say to that, so I just shrug. He wasn't that close to me, so I wasn't breathing in the smoke.

"See you at the clubhouse, Sin," Rake says, tapping his hand on the top of the car before walking off.

"Sin?"

"Drink the water, Faye" is all he says in reply. He starts the car and drives back onto the main road, following behind Rake in my car. I take a sip of water to get him off my back, then turn my body toward him.

I have so many questions right now.

Which one to ask? I start with something simple enough.

"Why do they call you Sin?"

Is it because women want to sin when they look at him?

Hell, I could go for some sinning right now.

Because he sins regularly? Because I don't doubt that.

"They just do," he replies shortly, trying to deter my questions.

"Where are you taking me?" I ask, scrubbing a hand down my face and giving up on the name thing. If he didn't want to talk, I wasn't going to push him. Not just yet anyway.

He sighs heavily, like he's sick of me already. I grit my teeth. He probably should have thought about this before he made me go with him. "You're going to stay with me. I heard that your piece-of-shit parents kicked you out, so you're with me until you can get back on your feet. I'll take care of you."

That is kind of nice.

"You should have known from the beginning that I would have taken care of you, Faye, with or without my baby inside you," he continues. "I'm fuckin' pissed you didn't turn to me, when it has everything to do with me."

"Yeah, I got that," I murmur. "But try to see it from my point of view."

He runs a hand over his face. "I am; trust me. That's what's keeping me calm right now. Also the fact that you're going to be under my roof, where I can keep an eye on you."

As much as I don't like being told what to do, Dex looking after me is going to save me a lot of stress—having a stable place to stay during this pregnancy is a blessing. However, I do have other concerns.

"Where exactly do you stay?" I ask hesitantly, wanting to know what to expect. "With a group of bikers?" I ask slowly, not wanting to offend him. But at the same time, I'm not living with a houseful of bikers. Surely he doesn't expect me to.

"Who told you that?" he asks, frowning slightly.

"Eric," I tell him. "He said a few things after someone told him that we were seen together."

"Of course that little bastard did." He sighs, looking straight ahead at the road. I stare at his handsome profile, waiting for him to elaborate, but he doesn't.

"Dex . . . I appreciate you want to keep an eye on me and the baby, but I really don't feel comfortable staying with you and your friends," I tell him, shifting in my seat. "I don't know what to expect. You're kind of throwing me in the deep end right now."

"Was Rake horrible to you?" he asks, his voice hardening.

"No, of course not. . . ."

"Good, and neither will anyone else be," he says. "No one will hurt you. Do you think I would ever let that happen? Because if you do, then you don't know me at all anymore."

"I'm not going to win, am I?" I mutter, pushing my hair off my face.

Dex laughs at that. "You're a fast learner, babe."

Listening to his laugh lightens my mood a little.

I bite my lip, staying silent for about ten minutes before I can't hold it in anymore. "Do you guys kill people? Or do illegal shit? Is it true you have groupies?"

Dex sighs again, this one long-suffering. "Are you going to be a pain in my ass the whole time you're living with me?"

I lift my shoulder in a shrug. "Probably."

"At least you're honest," he grumbles. "I'll tell you what; try and reserve judgment until you meet everyone. Make up your own mind about us."

"I guess I could do that," I reply, bobbing my head. "I don't mean to sound judgmental or anything, it's just that this is a stressful, vulnerable time for me, and I guess I just want some peace."

"You will be looked after; don't worry about that, okay? There is no reason for you to stress. I have no experience with pregnant women, but I do have experience with you—the rest we can learn together."

His experience of me consists of being childhood friends and one night of amazing sex. I don't think either of those things are going to help him deal with a pregnant me. Well, maybe the latter. That would probably cheer me up, right now, even.

"Either way, you're staying with us, so you better make the most of it," he adds, always having to say the last word.

"Is Eric going to come by?" I ask, wondering what's going to happen if he tries to see me. I didn't want to see him, or deal with his reaction when he found out I was going to be living with Dex. I know they aren't close or anything, but how does this biker thing work?

He turns to me then, giving me an odd look. "Do you want him to?"

"Not really," I reply honestly. "I can't deal with his drama right now."

"Good, because he won't be coming around," he says, glancing over at me. "Are you going to eat your chocolate?"

I glance down at the Snickers bar. "Why, do you want it?"

"If you're not going to," he says, eyeing the chocolate. His tongue peeps out over his bottom lip, and I imagine myself drawing that tongue into my mouth and sucking.

"Halves?" I offer, clearing my throat.

Just like when we were younger.

"Sure," he replies with a twitch of his lips. I break the bar in half and hand him the smaller half.

He notices and laughs. "The nice thing to do would be to give me the bigger half. I always did that for you."

"And why's that?" I ask, taking a bite.

"I'm twice as big as you," he says, amusement lacing his tone.

That was kind of him. "I'm pregnant. When it comes to food, from now on I always win."

His deep chuckle makes me smile. "You always win anyway, Faye."

"What does that mean?" I ask, chewing and swallowing another delicious bite.

"You have something about you . . ." He trails off, shaking his head. "You always tend to get your way somehow."

"I think that's just my stubborn personality," I reply, taking a bite of the chocolate.

"Exactly, you have a strong will. Strong spirit," he says, peeking at me before staring back at the road. "You're going to be a good mother, you know that, right?"

I stay silent, lost in my thoughts. It's nice that he thinks that about me. Really nice. Pretty much the opposite of what my mother has always tried to drill into me. I did think I was going to be a good mother—because I was going to make sure I was, I was going to try my hardest.

His hand finds my thigh, drifting up from my knee and lingering there. My breath hitches at the contact, at his casual affection. I slowly pinch myself, on the underside of my other thigh, to make sure this isn't a dream.

"Ouch," I mutter. Okay definitely *not* a dream. That freaking hurt.

"What's wrong?" he asks, cutting his eyes to me, his hand squeezing my thigh.

"Nothing," I reply quickly, turning my head to look out the window.

"I know you think I've changed . . ." he starts. I sit up straighter, interested in what he has to say. "You were just a kid back then. . . ."

"But?"

He glances at me. "I have changed. But for you . . . I'll always be that same person. Does that make sense? You have no need to be scared or wary around me, babe."

I exhale deeply, appreciating his words of comfort. "Thanks, Dex."

"No need to thank me, Faye, it's just how it is. I don't want you to be scared of me, of what you may see when you're in the clubhouse. Just know that I would never hurt you, and I'd kill anyone who tried."

I swallow hard at his proclamation.

"How's law school?" he asks casually, as his fingers start to rub my thigh. Like he didn't mention anything about killing.

I bite my lip, finding myself getting turned on by the simple action. "It's good, actually."

"Heard you were at the top of your class. . . ."

"Who told you that?" I ask. Has he been checking up on me? Why do I like the thought of that? I need to calm myself down.

"Eric," he replies in a toneless voice. "You always were an overachiever."

My lip twitches at that. "I believe the word is *ambitious*."

He laughs. "I always knew you'd do well."

"Oh" is all I can think of to say. "Well, thank you for your vote of confidence."

Although now I'm not sure that "doing well" applies to me. I look down at my stomach and exhale. I have a lot of work ahead of me if I want to be a great mother and have a career, but it is doable, and I always did like a challenge.

An hour or so later the car stops. "What are we doing here? Is this it?" I ask Dex as we wait in front of a gate. A man dressed in black leather runs out and opens the gate for us, then Dex parks the car as I take in the location of my new home. Several motorcycles are parked nearby, and I check them out before I stare ahead at the building. It looks more like a warehouse than a house. It's massive, and quite imposing. Silently I get out of the car and wait for Dex to do the same, trying to stop myself from feeling so nervous. I can feel his eyes on me, burning a hole in the back of my head, but I don't turn around. Instead, I wait for him to lead the way and then follow behind. I can hear music, loud music. The kind Dex listens to. It's about eleven at night, and all I want to do is sleep, but it doesn't look like I'm going to be able to get that chance. Dex looks at me, and I don't miss the grimace as he hears the noise.

"Should have brought you in during the day," he utters

under his breath, then takes my hand in his and walks me in through the door.

Eyes wide, I freeze and take in the scene in front of me. I step closer to Dex, almost hiding behind him.

About ten men, varying in age and appearance, are sitting around drinking and smoking. Most of them are laughing. There are a couple of women about as well, scantily clad. Some are dancing for the men, some are making out with them, and others are—

As soon as I see a couple having sex out in the open, the woman riding a man and wearing nothing but a miniskirt around her hips, I turn around and walk back to the car.

This is what he wants to bring my child into?

Was he serious? I couldn't let my baby grow up around this. Dex told me not to judge, but how could I not? It wasn't just me I had to think of right now. I'd never seen anything like this before, and sure, I guess I'd led a sheltered life up until now. But he wants me to stay here? What does he expect of me? Does he want a woman who acts like that? Because if he does, he is going to be extremely disappointed. I grit my teeth and dig my fingernails into my palm, anger at my situation taking over my senses.

Fuck. Him.

No really, fuck him. He's selfish. He should have just let me be. If he really wanted to help, he could have sent some money for the baby or made sure I had a place to stay; he didn't need to bring me to this.

I hear Dex yelling, and the music turns off. I lean against the car, silently fuming. I hear loud voices arguing until it finally quiets down. Dex storms out, looking frustrated by the set of his mouth, and comes right up to me.

"It's not always like that," he says, avoiding my eyes. He stares at the now silent building, and crosses his arms over his chest.

I stare up at him, unimpressed. "You can't expect me to live here."

"Half those people don't live here; they just come by for a good time," he says in a low tone. "It's just a party tonight, Faye."

"I don't want to live in a place people come to for a 'good time,'" I reply, hands on my hips.

He says nothing.

"Dex," I say, crossing my arms over my chest—copying his stance and lifting my chin up in defiance. He studies me, his blue eyes narrowing slightly, but says nothing. I shift on my feet, his silence making me squirm. His mouth is set in a tight, thin line, and I know he's far from happy with me. It's hard not to feel intimidated in his presence, but I refuse to back down. I force myself to look him in the eye and continue.

"Don't make me stay here, Dex," I say softly, my gaze darting to the front door in apprehension. "This isn't me, you know this isn't me. I said I wouldn't judge, but even I didn't expect something like this. I'm sure this place is a good time for everyone, but I have a baby to think about now. I just want somewhere safe and quiet. How you live your life is your business, but surely you can see why this is really awkward for me. I've never even watched porn before, and I just got a front-row seat for public sex."

He pulls out a cigarette, glances at me, shakes his head, and then slides it back in the pack. He expels a deep sigh as he returns the pack to his jeans pocket. He then studies me, a thoughtful expression on his handsome face. "Need to stop smoking."

I stay silent, waiting for him to say something about what we were going to do.

"Do you trust me?" he finally asks quietly, his gaze unwavering.

"What?" I whisper.

That's all he has to say after my big speech?

"Faye. Do you trust me? Yes or no? And be honest with me," he demands.

I stare into his clear blue eyes. "Yes, I trust you."

And I did.

His expression softens at my admission, his eyes hooded.

"Come on, then, let's get you to bed," he says, tilting his head toward the door. "I know you must be tired. Growing a person inside of you will do that to you, or so I've heard."

I still don't move.

"You let me in; you're carrying my child. What choice do you have?" he asks, raising an eyebrow at me. "You have no other option, Faye."

He doesn't look smug as he says it. Just like he's stating a fact.

And I hate that he's right. Where else am I going to go?

I have nowhere, and no one left to turn to.

I lost everything in one night. Over one mistake.

I put my hand to my stomach. A mistake I would never regret.

"Get inside, Faye," he says, turning around without looking back.

My eyes dart from his car back to him. Rake isn't even here yet with my car.

Do I really have a choice?

"Fuck," I mutter under my breath, gritting my teeth.

Then I follow the dragon into his lair.

FIVE

T HE place is cleared out when I reenter, but I can still hear
muffled laughter, so I know they've just moved their party
elsewhere in the clubhouse. I appreciate it. The whole place is
huge inside, and such a bachelor pad. There is no color in sight,
everything in blacks, browns, and whites. I follow behind Dex,
taking in every detail. I sigh when I come across a wall full of
mug shots—how charming. Dex turns and flashes me a boyish grin when he hears my sigh, as if he knows exactly what I'm
thinking. What exactly have I gotten myself into? We pass some
sort of game room, a spacious kitchen, and an even larger living
room, until we turn down a hallway. We pass a few doors before
we come to a stop. Dex opens the door in front of us and turns
on the light, gesturing for me to enter before him. I step into the
room and look around.

"Get settled. I'll get your stuff from both the cars," he says,
shutting the door before he leaves. The room is spacious, with a
king-size bed, a dresser, and a desk. The rest of it is bare. Utili-
tarian, even. I open one of the doors, which leads to a decent-
size bathroom. When I see the claw-foot tub, my mouth turns
up into a smile. My day just got a little better—it really is the
small things in life.

Dex returns a few minutes later, carrying my bags. He puts them on the bed, turning to me with a contemplative look on his face.

"You hungry?" he asks, his eyes roaming to my stomach. "I can get you something to eat."

"No, I'm okay," I tell him. I still have food in my bag if I do get hungry. He steps closer to me, his fingers lifting my chin up.

"Not the best situation," he says, smirking.

"You think?" I all but growl.

"You can study some of your classes online, can't you?" he asks, scanning my features. "I know school has always been important to you."

"Yeah, I can. That's what I was going to do. I really want to finish my degree, baby or not," I tell him. It's the truth. The degree is for me. It's what I've always wanted. I know a baby changes things, and it might take me longer to do it, but I will reach my goals in the end.

"You do whatever work you can online; you hang out here for a bit, okay?" he says, his eyes softening. "It won't be so bad, you'll see."

"What am I meant to do here?" I ask him, rubbing my arm with the palm of my hand. "I want to do something. I'm not used to being idle."

"You'll find your place. Some of the old ladies are nice women," he says, smiling.

"Some?"

That means some of them are bitches.

"You picked up on that, huh?" he comments, chuckling.

"I'm a lawyer, what do you think?" I say dryly, causing him to laugh harder.

"Not yet, you aren't," he points out.

"Whatever," I sigh. Law student, lawyer—the outcome is still the same.

"I don't think they'll accept 'whatever' in court," he says.

I roll my eyes at him. "Funny."

"What kind of lawyer are you going to be?" he asks, eyes still dancing with amusement.

"I want to work for the DA," I say, raising an eyebrow at him. I don't really know what area of law I'm going to choose yet; I just say it to annoy him. "I want to put all the bad guys behind bars."

"Is that so?" he says, grinning like a damn fool.

"What the hell is so amusing?" I snap, narrowing my eyes on him. I just told him I wanted to put people like his criminal friends in jail; how is that in any way funny?

"Club could use a good lawyer," he says, rubbing his chin thoughtfully. "Someone we could trust."

"Oh, hell no!" I say, lifting my finger and poking him in the chest. "Not happening, buddy."

"Did you just poke me?" he asks, trying to keep a straight face but failing. His lip twitches as he tries to contain himself, but he looks on the verge of laughter again.

"Yes, what's it to you?" I ask belligerently, tilting my chin up.

"How would you like it if I poked you?" he asks, smirking.

"You already did, you asshole! That's how I got pregnant!" I yell in his face.

This time, the laughter doesn't subside. He falls onto the bed, clutching his stomach like a damn kid.

I rub my forehead. "You're seriously weird."

He flashes me a lopsided grin.

I unpack a few of my things, including my teddy bear Coco, which I put on his bed right in the center. Then I stare at Dex and dare him to say something about it.

His eyes widen. "Is that . . . Coco?"

My jaw drops. "You remember her name? That's a little weird."

"How the hell could I forget? You made me have a fuckin' tea party with her when I was ten, and I was traumatized!"

I flashback to that memory. I was five and made him sit in my outdoor playhouse to have tea with me and Coco. Every time he tried to leave I'd cry.

"Good times," I murmur, grinning.

His mouth twitches. "Can't believe you still have that bear. Holy fuck. It's probably diseased or something after all these years."

"Coco is in perfect health." I sniff.

He apparently finds this hilarious, judging by the cackle that escapes him. Is he laughing at me or with me? I think it's the former.

The door suddenly opens to reveal two scary-looking men. Both are wearing leather vests telling me they are part of the MC.

"What the fuck?" Dex snaps at their entrance.

"You all good in here?" one man asks. "I heard a noise sounding suspiciously like laughter."

He looks to be in his late thirties, with brown hair and eyes. He has a beard that, I'm not going to lie, he pulls off nicely. He's sexy in a dangerous, rough way.

His eyes find me and narrow slightly. "This her?"

I glance at Dex in amusement. "Been talking about me, have you?"

A muscle ticks in Dex's jaw. "Had to explain you, didn't I?"

I look back to the bearded man, who doesn't look impressed. "The way he was going on about you, I thought you'd have bigger tits or something."

My mouth drops open.

"Arrow," Dex snaps. "Don't fuckin' start."

"You didn't just say that," I reply, crossing my arms over my chest.

How fucking rude.

Yes, they were smallish, but they were nice. Perky and symmetrical!

"I did. Just wondering what all the fuss is about, is all," he replies in an annoyed tone. "Learn your place around here, and fast, little girl."

Okay, what a jerk.

"Arrow," Dex warns. "Faye is under my protection. No one so much as breathes in her direction, you got it? And you can pass that on. I know you fuckers like to gossip."

At least he was standing up for me. Arrow scowls but doesn't say anything.

Kill them with kindness.

"Nice to meet you, Arrow," I lie, ignoring his look of surprise. I then turn to the next guy. He has dark hair and eyes, a scar across his neck. It looks like someone sliced him with a knife.

"Irish," he says with a slight accent.

"Nice to meet you, Irish," I say, nodding my head at him. They both look at me like I'm crazy, and I probably am. But there's no harm in using good manners.

"Why do they call you Arrow?" I find myself asking. "Do you have an arrow tattoo?" I search what I can see of his body for any signs of it.

Silence, then laughter.

"What the hell is so funny?" I ask, looking between them in confusion.

Arrow leans against the door and stares at Dex.

"What?" Dex replies, no trace of laughter on his face.

Arrow shrugs, and then looks at me in a new light. "Can't remember the last time I heard you laugh like that, Sin."

Dex scowls, eyes darting to me, then back to Arrow. "Is there anything else?"

"No, we just wanted to meet your baby mama," Irish says, looking completely amused.

I wiggle my fingers at them. "I believe that would be me."

"Oh, darlin'," Irish says, "you are *way* too good for him."

"Is that a fuckin' moldy teddy bear on your bed, Sin?" Arrow asks, raising an eyebrow and looking amused as hell. "Holy shit. I need to take a picture of this, 'cuz no one else will believe it."

"You can use my cell," I offer, smirking.

"Get the fuck out, you two," Dex growls, sending a glare in their direction. They leave, and I can hear their laughter echoing down the hall.

I turn to Dex. "Do I have to call you Sin now?" That's going to take some time getting used to.

"If you want to," he says, lying back on the bed. His T-shirt rides up a little, showing off his toned stomach. It should be illegal to look this good. He finds me staring but doesn't say anything about it, so I continue to let my gaze linger.

"I think it would be weird calling you anything other than Dex," I admit quietly.

"Call me Dex, then," he says softly. "I think I'd like that better than you calling me Sin."

I nod. "Okay, good."

"Few things you need to hear. Your actions reflect on me while you're here. Respect the other guys; respect me in front of the other guys. You can get mouthy when we're in private; I kind of like that," he says with a wink.

"So you want me . . . to not be me in public?" I gape, gritting my teeth. Was this going to be like how it was at home for me? My mother not liking anything that came out of my mouth, me always having to watch what I say?

"No. Not at all—"

"If I'm going to have to walk on thin ice with my words, I may as well be back home."

His eyes widen. "It's nothing like that, Faye. I don't want you to stop being who you are. It's just a respect thing. You need to show respect to get respect, do you get me?"

He doesn't want me to stop being me; he just wants me to behave in front of his club members? I guess I could do that. I doubted I'd be talking to them much anyway.

"Fine, I'll try to keep the browbeating to a minimum. In public anyway," I joke. "Anything else I should know?"

"You're lucky I know what that mouth can do. It's worth putting up with your shit," he says, amusement dancing in his eyes.

I narrow my eyes on him. "You better not say stuff like that in front of the others!"

"Why not? Sex isn't some secret thing around here. You'll

learn that quickly, don't worry," he tells me with a quirk of his lips.

"No one is going to—"

"Nothing will happen here that you don't want," he says, the tension in the room reaching an all-time high. "Yes, the men enjoy women, and regularly, but all the women are consenting. We're not monsters, Faye."

"I didn't mean to imply that you are . . . It's just, well, I don't know how things work here," I try to explain.

"You'll learn. Everyone here is open, no judgment, Faye. We have each other's backs."

I purse my lips. "As long as the women know their place."

He laughs at that, like I said something hilarious.

"There is nothing funny about this situation, Dexter Black!" I snap.

"Why are you full-naming me, Faye? Those are fighting words," he says, grinning at me.

I lean back onto my elbows and shake my head at him. "Trust me, if I wanted to fight, you would know it."

He reaches his hands out, his index finger trailing down my cheek. "I have your back, okay? You never have to worry about being safe while you're here."

I swallow. "Okay."

"Everyone will come around with you—don't worry about that," he says, nodding his head.

I wasn't worried until he just mentioned it.

"So . . ." I start, shifting my position. "Where are you sleeping?" I ask, taking in the one and only bed and blinking quickly.

"This bed is massive," he says, lip curving.

"It is," I agree, waiting for him to continue.

"Plenty of room."

"Uh-huh," I murmur, waiting for him to come out and say it. "I can see that."

"So, I'm sleeping here with my baby mama," he says, grinning at me.

"You did not just call me that," I say, crossing my arms over my chest and scowling. "Surely there's somewhere else you can sleep."

Sleeping next to him, wrapped in his arms sounded appealing.

Too appealing.

I didn't think getting even more attached to this man was a good idea.

"I did just call you that. Listen here, woman, this is how things are going to go. I'm going to sleep here every night, but don't worry, I'll be keeping my hands to myself. Like I've said a million times, you are safe from everyone here—including me. Now, go take a shower," he says, covering his face with his arm.

I ignore the feeling of disappointment at the "keeping his hands to himself" part, but it's probably for the best. It *is* for the best. This situation is complicated enough as it is. Besides, who needs hot sex with the sexiest man you've ever laid eyes on and had a crush on ever since you can remember?

Me, that's who.

Not that I'd ever admit it out loud, but I think being pregnant has made me even hornier than usual. Or was it just because I was around Dex? Maybe it was just after I had a taste of him and realized how mind-blowing sex could actually be.

Either way, it sucked to have it once and then be taken away so soon, but I needed to remember that I'm only here because of a broken condom and Dex's supersperm.

I decide to let the future me worry about everything and jump into the shower. I dress in my pink cupcake pajama pants and a white tank top. I consider putting a bra on, but I can't sleep in one; it's too uncomfortable. Besides, my boobs are small, like Arrow kindly pointed out, and nothing Dex hasn't seen before. When I walk out, trying not to cover my chest with my hands, Dex is still on the bed, watching a movie.

"Finally," he grumbles, glancing down at my chest.

He clears his throat.

"My eyes are up here," I say, looking down. Seriously, nothing much going on there, I don't know why he's staring at them like that—like they look like Salma Hayek's breasts.

Now, those are spectacular boobs.

"Fuck," he curses, then heads into the bathroom, slamming the door behind him. *Finally?* That was me trying to be quick. I wouldn't say I was high maintenance, but I'm definitely not low maintenance. Wait, what just happened? Shaking my head, I push my thoughts aside.

Feeling thirsty, I stare at the door, wondering if I should head out or not. My thirst winning, I slip out the door and head to the kitchen. Opening the fridge, I pull out a bottle of water and smell it first, just to make sure it isn't vodka or something.

"May I ask why you're smelling the water?" comes a highly amused voice from behind me. I turn and come face-to-face with a very attractive man. Very.

"Well, hello there," I say, checking him out. Shoulder-length blond hair. Wearing nothing but a pair of low-slung track pants. Amazing body covered in tattoos.

"Nice pj's," he says, staring at my pants and then lingering on my chest.

Props to him for actually noticing the pants first.

"Thanks, I love cupcakes," I say. "And food in general."

"So do I," he says through a chuckle.

I blink slowly, taking him in from head to toe.

"You guys *should* make a calendar," I blurt out, causing the man to grin at me. "Who are you?" I ask, cringing when I realize it came out sounding rather rude.

"I'm Tracker; who are you?" he answers, apparently not offended.

"Oh, good, you aren't going to kill me or something," I say to myself.

"What?" he asks, making a choked sound.

I shrug sheepishly. "I've been warned. I'm supposed to be on my best behavior, but I don't exactly know the rules around here. I already know I'm going to have a problem with them though. Am I allowed to ask questions and stuff? Because I'm curious by nature."

Tracker blinks slowly a few times, then laughs. "Fuck, you're cute. No, there will be no killing for asking innocent questions."

"And for non-innocent questions?" I pry.

He grins, revealing straight white teeth. "Can't make any promises."

"Faye!" Dex calls out.

"That would be me," I say, giving him the small wave.

"You're the baby mama?" he says, eyebrows reaching his hairline. His gaze drops to my stomach.

"Oh, for fuck's sake," I snap, narrowing my eyes. "Is that going to be my name now?"

Dex walks out, a scowl etched on his handsome face. "Why the hell did you leave the room?"

"I was thirsty!" I tell him, waving the bottle of water at him.

"You were thirsty?"

"I'm pregnant, remember? You were there, I believe. Yes, thirsty," I say. I turn to Tracker. "You were just going to tell me about those tattoos of yours?"

"I was?" he replies, sounding amused as hell.

Dex turns to Tracker, and if looks could kill. . . .

"Good luck with that one," Tracker says to him, his body shaking from laughter. Dex, looking considerably less happy, if that's possible, takes my arm and pulls me back to the room. He locks the door behind us. He stares at me, as if thinking about what to say. Then he shakes his head.

"Don't walk around at night by yourself."

"Am I a prisoner?" I ask him, my tone ice-cold.

"No, of course not, but this place is filled with men. You're beautiful. You do the math."

"O-oh," I stutter. God, he can be sweet when he wants to be.

"And don't fuckin' walk around like that with no bra on. Jesus Christ, Faye!" he growls.

"Fine!" I snap.

"I'll give you one of my T-shirts; you can wear that over your top," he says, staring daggers at me.

I roll my eyes. "I thought you said this place was all free love. I'm sure they've seen a pair of B-cup breasts before. It's not like it's cold in here or anything! You can't even see my nipples!"

His eyes were back on said nipples. "Are we fighting over your fuckin' nipples right now?"

"And if we are?" I ask, lifting my chin stubbornly.

"Maybe I'll pull your little top down and suck one into my mouth. All this talk of your nipples has me wanting a little taste. . . ."

My mouth goes dry. Before I can think of a comeback, he says one word.

"Sleep."

"Okay," I say, sliding into bed and getting comfortable. He joins me but stays on his side of the bed. I try and dispel thoughts of him doing as he said, pulling my top down and licking and sucking on my breasts.

Just as I'm about to fall asleep, dreaming of him, I hear him say, "I know you think I'm going to be a shit father, but I'm going to try my best. Good night, Faye."

I fall asleep with a small smile on my lips.

SIX

I WALK out into the kitchen the next morning, rubbing my eyes. I stop in my tracks as I see a man standing over the stove. Naked.

He has an extremely white ass and is frying something in the pan.

"There goes my appetite," I mutter to myself. Arrow turns around, completely unabashed.

"Mornin'," he says, checking out my pajamas. I stare at his huge penis in horror but am unable to move my eyes away. Suddenly, it gets hard, pointing right at me. Like an arrow.

Lightbulb moment.

"Seriously?" I say, covering my eyes with my hand.

"Bit late for that," he says, chuckling. "I saw you looking."

"And I saw you saw me looking," I reply, pouring myself some juice and averting my gaze.

"I think I had the wrong idea about you. . . ." he says, turning back to the stove.

"How so?"

He shrugs. "Thought you were some tramp trying to trap Dex."

"And how do you know I'm not?" I ask him.

"Good sense of character," he says. "I'm never wrong."

"Bold claim," I say as he turns around. My eyes straight-away lower. I can't even help it.

I point at it when he takes a step in my direction. "Don't bring that thing near me!"

He laughs. "It won't bite you; don't worry."

"You're weird," I announce.

He shakes his head. "Do you just say the first thing that pops up into your fuckin' head?"

I think it over. "Pretty much. Is that going to be a problem?"

"Probably."

"I'm sure we will make it work. I don't want to ask you to change your life because of me, but maybe we could work out a warning schedule so we don't have a repeat of this," I suggest, pointing between myself and his nude form.

"Why?" he replies. "I'm not shy, are you?"

Was I shy? I didn't think I was. "No, I guess not. Is this the norm around here?"

"You know," he says, studying me, "I can't remember the last time I heard Dex laugh like he was with you last night. You make him happy, and you're carrying Wind Dragon blood in your stomach, so I'm going to forgive you for being so mouthy."

"Ummmm . . . thanks. I think."

"You take care of one of ours, and we take care of you. That's how it goes," he continues, like I never spoke.

I stand up and walk over to the stove, where he was frying a burnt omelet. "Speaking of taking care of others, do you want me to cook something non-burnt for you?"

"Like what?" he asks, looking interested.

I search the fridge and take out more eggs and some bacon. "Bacon and scrambled eggs? Or maybe French toast?"

I wasn't much of a cook, but breakfast food I could do.

"Really? You'd do that? I don't think I've ever had a woman I haven't fucked cook for me before."

Charming, real charming.

"Sure," I reply, getting busy.

I'd just finished the meal when Dex walks in, sighing when he sees Arrow's bare state.

"Fuckin' hell, Arrow," Dex barks, turning to me and checking my expression. I take this time to check him out myself. Black track pants on his narrow hips and no shirt. I could really get used to the view.

"I'm traumatized, but I'll live," I reply. "At least I know why you all call him Arrow. That thing points at its next victim!"

Arrow spins to me; his eyes wide with surprise. "I'm actually glad you're here, this place was getting boring."

"Arrow!" Dex growls, clearly losing his patience. "That boner better not be for my woman."

Arrow laughs.

Dex stares him down.

I purse my lips.

"I'm gone," Arrow finally replies, taking his plate of food and leaving.

"They don't have to wear clothes on my account," I tell him, wiggling my eyebrows. But then the smile drops from my face, and I run to our bathroom just in time.

I hate morning sickness.

In my haste I didn't lock the door behind me, and Dex

comes in to rub a hand up and down my back. How embarrassing. I think I could have gone through my life without a man seeing me throw up.

"Faye," he says, sounding worried and a little horrified.

"I'm okay," I manage to say, bracing myself.

"What do you need? Tell me," he implores, stroking my hair.

"Can you get me some water and maybe make me some toast with peanut butter?" I ask him, really just wanting a moment's privacy.

"Yep," he says, quickly leaving to do the task. I clean myself up and brush my teeth before he calls out that my breakfast is ready. I see a plate on the bed with two slices of toast and a bottle of water.

"Thanks," I tell him with a small smile, sitting down and taking a bite.

"Do you get sick every day?" he asks, frowning.

I lift my shoulder in a shrug. "Sometimes."

"And you've been going through it alone these last few months?"

"Well, yeah. No one can really help me," I say, chewing and swallowing. "It's just something pregnant women go through."

"Still, I wish I had been there for you," he says.

"I'm sorry I didn't tell you," I tell him, looking down at my plate. Maybe I would have told him one day. I don't really know, to be honest.

"Why didn't you?" he asks, the atmosphere in the room turning tense.

I consider it. "Eric told me you were the VP for a motorcycle club, and I realized I didn't know you at all. We had a one-night stand; that was it. Even though we knew each other growing up—our age gap never really let us *know* each other. I guess I was telling myself I could do this on my own. . . ."

"I went to Mom's to visit, and I heard him telling her you were pregnant. I knew it was mine," he says, rubbing the back of his neck. "Then I came to find you."

"How did you find me?" I ask.

"Tracker didn't get his name for nothing," he says, lips curving into a megawatt smile.

We sit in comfortable silence for a few moments, watching each other. "What are we doing here?"

"You're going to study and relax, and I'm going to take care of you," he says, piercing blue eyes never leaving me.

Take care of me, how exactly?

Because I could use some taking care of right now.

"I can get a job, you know," I tell him. "You don't have to pay for everything."

"You aren't working," he replies simply. "You don't need to."

"I can't not do anything."

"You will be studying and growing a child inside of you. From scratch. How is that not doing anything?" he replies, smirking.

He had a point, but still, it didn't feel right.

"What's going on in that head of yours?" he asks, raising an eyebrow at me in question.

"Oh, you know. The usual things," I reply. "So how did you find yourself in an MC?"

"Sometimes you need to make your own family" is all he says.

It's all he needs to say, because I get it.

"Maybe I could do that," I say, lifting the second piece of

toast to my mouth. I don't have my parents anymore. I don't have Eric—who has been in my life a very long time. I have some cousins and family across the country, but that's about it. It would be nice to have people in my life I can rely on. People who can be there for me, and vice versa.

I wouldn't take that for granted.

"You already are, babe," Dex replies in a gentle tone. "You aren't getting rid of me so easily."

"Who would have thought we'd be here right now?" I say, lip quirking.

"Not me, that's for sure," Dex says. "But I don't regret it. Any of it."

Well, that's nice.

Really nice.

"Thanks for making me come here, Dex. It's a lot better than what I would be doing right now, living in a shitty motel and working my ass off to make ends meet," I admit, letting the expression on my face show him that I was indeed grateful. I might not understand the appeal of an MC lifestyle, but I knew I had it better here than I would on my own.

I felt safe.

I didn't have to work, although I was going to find something to do to earn my keep. I could continue my studies, giving me—and my baby—a more promising future, which benefited the baby.

I appreciated it more than I could express.

"You're welcome, babe. You know you're stubborn as shit though, yeah?" he says, shaking his head at me, something like admiration shining in his eyes.

I gape. "I'm stubborn? You're a brute!"

He grins. "I gotta head out. Will you be all right hanging out here?"

"Who will be here?" I ask, not really wanting him to leave.

"People come and go, babe; there's always someone around. No one will hurt you; don't worry about that, okay?" he says gently. "Just mind your business and try to stay out of trouble. I'll bring you lunch on my way back."

"Okay," I reply. This is my life now, and I have to get used to it.

No hiding behind Dex.

I could do this.

Dex showers and dresses in jeans, a black top, and a leather jacket. Unable to keep my eyes off him, I realize that I like him.

Maybe even more than like him.

I didn't know if that was good or bad, but I guess I was going to find out.

 **SEVEN**

"YOU must be Faye," a gorgeous redhead says to me the next morning. Dressed in figure-hugging jeans and a white tank top, she looks a hell of a lot better than I do in the morning.

"That would be me," I say, smiling at her.

"Jessica," she says. "You want to help cook breakfast?"

Not really, but I couldn't exactly say that. "Sure. Where's Dex?"

"Sin? He went out with the guys. Club business," she says, shrugging like it's irrelevant. I woke up alone this morning, and I didn't like it. I had a shower and awkwardly walked out of the room, not knowing exactly what I was going to find or what I was meant to do. "He told me to get you fed and keep an eye on you. I'm Trace's old lady."

Trace? I haven't met a Trace yet. I tell her as much.

"He'll be around this evening," she says. I smile and help her fry bacon and eggs until the smell begins to be too much. I then spend the next twenty minutes throwing up. I clean myself up and head back out into the kitchen. Several women sit there, chatting and eating. A few of them smile at me, and a few of them don't. I ignore the ones giving me evil looks and sit next to Jessica.

"How are you feeling?" she asks knowingly.

"A bit better now," I say, serving myself some toast.

I've taken a few bites when one of the women starts talking to me. "So you're the one, then. . . ."

"What?" I ask, putting down my piece of bread and staring at the blonde.

"The one who got pregnant on purpose to *try* and keep Sin," she says, sneering at me.

Wait, what?

"Right, because that was my dream in life," I say sarcastically. "Screw graduating and becoming a lawyer. My real dream was to get pregnant at the tender age of twenty-three and get kicked out of my house with nowhere to go. You're really smart, you know that?" I tell her, turning away from her red face when I'm done. Yeah—I've read a biker book or two in my day. I know how this all works. They are like a pack of wolves. They sense weakness. I need to show them that I'm not a pushover.

The women are silent for a second before they burst into laughter.

"She told you, Allie," one guffaws, earning more laughter from the rest of them.

"Whatever, bitch," she taunts. "Sin will come back to me, he always does."

"I'm sure it's for your charming personality," I add, keeping my tone even.

"He'll still be fucking me whether you're pregnant or not," she adds with an evil smile.

"Are you the club whore?" I ask with a smirk.

"You f—"

"Allie, stop," Jessica snaps, slamming her plate down.

Allie shoots me a look but doesn't comment further.

I try not to let her comments get to me. Dex can be with whomever he wants. It's not like we're dating or anything. We had sex, and I got knocked up. Not exactly the best grounds for starting a relationship. The most I can hope for is mutual respect and friendship.

Who the hell am I trying to kid here? I want him.

The women stare at me with a new light. It may even be respect I see in their eyes.

"Do you want help cleaning up?" I ask Jessica, ignoring a fuming Allie.

Jessica grins. "We cooked; they can clean."

That sounds good to me.

"I have to get to work," she says. "Do you have Sin's number?"

I shake my head, a little embarrassed that I don't.

She walks to the kitchen, digs in a drawer, and pulls out a pen and paper. Scribbling down his number, she hands it to me. "Call him if you need anything."

"Where do you work?" I ask curiously.

"I own a beauty shop. You should come by sometime. I'd love to get my hands on your auburn locks," she says, staring at my hair. "Maybe we could go a little darker even."

"Maybe after the baby is born," I reply. "I read that you aren't supposed to color hair when you're pregnant."

"You aren't touching her hair, Jess," Dex says as he walks in. His eyes find mine and roam over me, softening fractionally. "Hey."

"Hey," I reply, unable to tear away my gaze.

"Fine," Jess says, grumbling, not even bothering to put up a fight.

"Hey, Sin," Allie purrs, sliding up next to him.

"Hey, sugar," he replies, turning his head to look at her for a second before returning to me. "Come on, time to meet Prez."

How come I didn't get a "Hey, sugar"? I'm the baby mama!

I fume silently. If Dex is going to parade women in front of me, I don't know how I can stay here. We never spoke about us being together, but I did only just get here. I guess I had kind of hoped . . . but he didn't really promise me anything. I now feel like a first-class idiot, making something out of nothing. Maybe he just wants me here because of the baby. Not because he feels anything for me besides obligation.

Rake walks into the kitchen with Irish and an older man I haven't met before. Dex takes me by the arm and pulls me into our room.

"You all right?" he asks when the door is closed.

"I'm fine. I woke up alone, cooked, threw up, and got stared at all morning."

He stares at me. "You were sick again?"

"Yeah, but I'm fine," I tell him, shrugging off his concern. "What am I meant to do all day while you're out playing criminal?"

He ignores my comment and gestures to his desktop. "I bought you a new laptop. Enroll for your online classes and buy your textbooks." He pulls out a credit card and hands it to me. "For expenses."

"What's the limit on this?" I'm unable to stop myself from asking.

His lip twitches. "Ten grand."

I sigh heavily. "I guess that will do."

I really didn't want to use it, but I would keep it for emergencies.

Now he laughs at me.

"Don't laugh! Since I apparently got pregnant on purpose to keep you, because you know, you're such a catch. At least you come with a credit card," I joke.

I watch as the smile drops from his face. "What did you say?"

I blink furiously a few times. "I don't remember."

"Who said that about you, Faye?" he demands, his playful demeanor gone.

"No one," I mutter. "Forget I said anything."

"Tell me," he demands.

"No."

"Now."

I smirk. "Someone in the house you've slept with."

I watch his face go blank. Jeez, how many women has it been? I snap, "I'm sure you'll be able to figure it out. I suggest a chart or a spreadsheet."

"Fuck, you're a pain in the ass. How did Eric handle you?" he says on a sigh.

"He didn't," I say, smirking once more.

"I'll bet he didn't," he growls, his gaze lowering to my lips.

"How many men have you slept with?" he asks, taking a step closer to me, invading my personal space.

"What a rude question," I muse.

"How many, Faye?"

I count all my ten fingers. "Well, that was just this year. . . ."

"Faye . . ."

"Two, including you. How many women have you slept with?" I ask, wiggling my eyebrows at him. "Do you need a calculator?"

"Eric is a boy. I said men," he replies, tucking my hair behind my ear.

"I guess only you, then," I whisper, caught up in his gaze.

He smiles, showing his straight white teeth. "I like that." It doesn't escape my attention that he ignored my question, but I don't push. I know I won't like the answer.

"Of course you would," I mutter to myself.

"It means that you're mine now," he whispers, then looks away. I think I hear him mutter the word *soon*.

"Dex, you know I have my own money, right? I didn't just skip town. I have enough that will get me by until the baby is born and I can get a job."

His lips tighten. "You don't think I can provide for you and our kid?"

My brows furrow. "No, I'm sure you could, I just don't think that you should have to."

I put up my hand. "No, wait; once the baby's born, then sure, spend all you want. But it doesn't feel right for me just living here and not contributing in some kind of way."

"None of the women who stay here pay any money. They cook and clean and fuck. You don't have to do any of those, although with me the latter would be appreciated. I want you and the baby healthy. Why should you work when you don't have to? I have a fuckload of money anyway, Faye, what else am I going to do with it?"

I suck in a breath. "I'll take your card for emergencies, but I won't use it. I'll use my own money. We can work out the rest later, okay? You're already letting me live here for nothing; at least let me cover my own expenses."

"Fuck, you're stubborn."

"I think I'm more proud than stubborn," I point out.

"I think you're both," he replies, his voice softening. "Use the card, Faye. It's for you. Okay?"

"Hmmm. We'll see."

His mouth twitches. "We will. Come on, we gotta go meet the boss," he says, taking my hand in his. He leads me down the hall and knocks on a door.

"Come in!" a rough voice yells. We walk into an office. Well, I think it's an office. It has a huge table and a cabinet in it, and another door. A man who looks to be in his forties, with salt-and-pepper hair and a beard, sits at a table. He looks fit, no beer belly for this man. He looks up at me and scowls.

"What did I do?" I ask, unable to help myself. He has a grumpy face but kind eyes.

Dex squeezes my hand, as in *Shut up, Faye.*

"Jim this is Faye. Faye, this is Jim, our president. You will show him respect," he says, warning in his tone. I stare at the man's leather vest with the word *president* written on there.

"Hi," I say carefully, not knowing what he wanted to see me about.

He leans back in his huge black chair and studies me. "Do you know why you're here?"

I swallow. The man is intense. "Because Dex has supersperm and now feels sorry for me?"

"Because Sin is a good man, and you're carrying his baby. I hope you're a good woman. Sin says we can trust you, and as my vice president, I trust him."

I nod at the club president. "Thanks for letting me stay here."

"I trust you know your place here?" Jim asks, staring me down.

I nod sagely. "Yes, sir. I won't even tell anyone about the orgies you guys have."

Jim turns a weary look to Dex, who sighs. "I'll handle her, don't worry."

"You damn well better," Jim says, having a silent conversation with Dex with his eyes.

Dex nods back at him. "Understood."

Jim looks back at me. "Help out when you can and keep your mouth shut about anything you hear or see."

I nod, internally fuming at being treated like a lesser human being. Fucking bikers.

"Can I ask you a question?" I ask Jim, pasting a smile on my face. "How come everyone has a nickname but you go by Jim? Can I give you a name suggestion?"

A few come to mind.

He shakes his head at me, but I don't miss the amused look that flashes across his features. "Good-bye, Faye."

Dex grabs me and leads me out. I grin. "I like him."

Dex just puts his head in his hands.

 EIGHT

SPEND the rest of the day enrolling in online classes, ordering textbooks, and making plans. In the late afternoon, I walk past Jim's office when I hear some male voices.

"Call up Greg," a voice said. Jim.

"You sure we need a lawyer for this? They have no fuckin' proof."

That was Arrow.

No proof about what? What did they do this time? Curious, I lean my ear against the door, not wanting to miss a thing.

"Better safe than sorry," Jim murmurs. "Greg's a fuckin' shark. They can't touch us; like you said, no proof. However, with him there they might get scared and back off a little. Let them know we aren't easy targets for their shit."

"We didn't even kill the fucker," Irish replies. "Just maimed him a little."

Laughter.

I gasp.

Suddenly, the door opens and I fall forward and into the arms of Arrow. He keeps me vertical, and then he, Jim, Tracker, and Irish surround me with narrowed gazes.

They were all here?

Fuckity fuck.

"Just walking by," I say, trying to act chirpy.

"By leaning on the door? You eavesdropping, girl?" Jim asks.

I shake my head adamantly. "No, no, no eavesdropping here. Just a good old case of at the wrong place at the wrong time."

They share glances.

"You can't kill me. I'm pregnant with a baby Wind Dragon," I decide to point out.

More shared glances.

"Everyone, give me some cash," Jim demands, pulling out his own wallet and grabbing a five-dollar bill.

The rest of the men do the same, looking to their president for instruction.

"Hand her the money," Jim demands, to my utter confusion.

Arrow steps forward, takes my hand in his and opens it. He slides a twenty-dollar bill between my fingers. One by one, the rest follow. How is this a punishment? Giving me money? I could really use some right about now too.

"Faye, you're now the club lawyer. We paid you for your services. You're bound by client-attorney confidentiality."

Jim looks smug.

I don't know what to feel.

Clutching the money in my palm, I open my mouth and close it, like a fish out of water.

"I'm still a student."

"Then Greg will take you under his wing until you can take over for him," Jim replies. "In the meantime, we can use you whenever we need law advice."

I lift my finger up to protest.

"Shut it. It's that or we shut you up another way," Jim growls.

I shut it.

Arrow walks over to me and wraps an arm around my chest. "I'm glad you're here. I have a shitload of legal advice I need. Let's start when I was eighteen and . . ."

This shit could only happen to me.

As Arrow escorts me out of the room, I call over my shoulder to Jim, "Does this job pay? Or am I working for free?"

~

When dinnertime comes around, I head out in search of food.

"Hello," I say to Mary, one of the girls I'd met this morning.

"Hey, Faye," she replies, smiling sweetly. "Dinner is almost ready."

"Where is everyone?" I ask her. I haven't seen Dex since he brought me lunch at around one o'clock.

"The women are around somewhere; I don't know about the men," she replies, shrugging slightly. "How are you feeling?"

"I'm okay," I say, gently tapping my stomach. "Does everyone live here?" I ask, gesturing to the clubhouse.

"Everyone has a room here, but they don't all live here. They crash here whenever they feel like it," she replies, stirring the pasta she made.

"What about you?" I ask, taking a seat.

"I don't live here; I just come by most days. I'm kind of seeing Arrow," she explains. I want to ask what "kind of" seeing means, but I don't.

"Arrow, huh," I murmur, grinning. The poor, poor woman. Arrow was a pain in the ass.

She nods and blushes slightly. "How are you liking it here?"

I suck in a breath. "Getting used to everything, you know?"

She smiles kindly. "Well, I'm always here if you want to talk, okay? I'll give you my number. Call me anytime."

"I'd like that," I reply, my expression softening at her kindness.

"Is it too nosy of me to ask what's going on with you and Sin?" she asks, winking at me.

My lips kick up at the corners. "When I know, I'll let you know."

She laughs at that.

We're talking about our favorite books when Jessica, Allie, and another girl named Jayla walk into the kitchen.

"Hey, girls," Jessica calls out as she sees us. Allie rolls her eyes, and Jayla says nothing. Mary gives me a knowing smile. She is really beautiful, with dark hair and clear green eyes. She reminds me of a pinup girl, with curves in all the right places and the contrast of her dark hair on her pale skin. Arrow is a lucky man. My phone vibrates—another message from Eric. I really need to change my number.

The men pour in, and I find myself wedged between Dex and Rake.

Not the worst place to be.

"You okay?" Dex asks, his eyes softening when they land on me.

I nod. "I'm fine."

"You smell good," Rake says, leaning in closer, invading my personal space.

I smell him in return. "You smell like leather, cigarettes, and sex."

His lips curve slowly. "I had a busy day."

"I can see that," I reply through laughter, taking a bite of my pasta. Mary is a good cook too. Arrow needs to marry her, pronto.

"How was your day, Dex?" I ask him, speaking softly so not everyone can hear.

He gently nudges me with his shoulder. "Busy."

"What did you do?" I ask, knowing I was pushing it a little.

"Worked," he replies, taking a bite of his food.

"Where do you work?" I ask.

He puts his fork down. "I'm a bike mechanic."

I lean in closer to him. "Is that what you tell people?" I mock-whisper.

Rake laughs, wrapping his arm around my waist and pulling me into him. Dex's lips tighten as he glares at Rake's hand. His jaw clenches, and his eyes narrow to slits. I stare at him, watching us, waiting for him to say something, but he doesn't. So he doesn't care if another man touches me?

"How was your second day in the clubhouse?" Rake asks around a mouth of food.

All eyes are suddenly on me.

"It was . . . interesting."

Rake's phone beeps and he looks down at it, and his expression softens. "Anna messaged me."

"Who is Anna?" I ask him.

He smiles. "My baby sister. I'm hoping that she'll move back here soon. I miss her like fuckin' crazy, and I hate not knowing if she's safe or not."

Arrow speaks. "I thought you had a guy keeping an eye on her."

Rake nods. "I do, but it's not the same, you know." He looks over at me. "She's a fuckin' beauty, my sister. You should see her."

He finds a pic and shows it to me.

Anna was tilting her head to the side and smiling in the picture. With the same blond hair and green eyes as Rake, the girl was indeed a beauty. Rake shows the picture to Arrow, who studies the picture a little too closely. Rake snatches it back from him and narrows his eyes. Arrow shrugs, shifts on his seat, then returns to his meal.

"She's gorgeous, Rake," I tell him honestly. It's obvious to see how much he adores his sister, and I love that he isn't shy about it. He's clearly very proud of her.

Minutes later, Arrow is done and is the first to leave the table.

Rake rubs his thigh against mine, and I see Dex staring daggers at me.

What did I do?

"Are you going to eat that?" Rake asks when I sit there without touching my food.

Dex scowls. "You gonna take food from a pregnant woman?"

I try and hide my grin.

Rake shrugs. "She's not eating it, she's just looking at it."

Dex slaps the back of Rake's head, then looks at me like everything that happens in life is my fault.

I grit my teeth and smile at Rake, telling him I was done eating, then pick up my glass and take a sip while Rake finishes the food. Why does Dex want me here when he doesn't want me? I can't seem to do anything right without annoying the man.

"You need to eat more," Dex demands, staring me down.

"I ate plenty," I reply, keeping my tone light. He wanted a fight, but for once, I wasn't going to give it to him. I'd fight him on my own time, not his.

"You ate a quarter of what I ate."

"So you want me to eat the same amount as you? You're like three times my size. Are you one of those weird creepy men who likes feeding women to make them fat? I read about it the other day. Feeders. It's an actual thing."

Rake laughs beside me and mutters something under his breath that I was going to pretend I didn't hear.

Dex looks at me and shakes his head, but I don't miss the twitch of his mouth. "Just want you and the baby healthy."

"We are," I reply, my expression daring him to question me further.

He nods, amusement flashing in his eyes, and wisely keeps his mouth shut.

I narrow my eyes, sitting back in my chair and taking him in.

His son or daughter is probably going to come out dressed in leather. I glance up in time to see Allie smirk at me. Smug bitch. Did she notice that Dex wasn't telling Rake to stop touching me? Am I overthinking this? It wasn't like he was fondling me; just a casual touch. Still, Dex should be the one touching me, not Rake. Even though he's hot, he isn't who I want. I ignore Allie and everyone else, including Rake and his roaming hands, then rinse and put my bowl and fork in the dishwasher. After that I grab some juice and head back to my room.

"Where are you going?" Dex calls out.

Where was I going? Where the hell *could* I go?

"To my prison cell, where else would I be going?" I reply in a dry tone. I don't wait around for his reply.

Trying not to feel sorry for myself, I watch my favorite movie on my laptop. Mario Casas always makes me feel better.

When Dex hasn't returned to the room two hours later, I feel the loneliest I've felt in my life. I even consider messaging Eric back. How desperate am I? Another moment of weakness—I seem to be having a lot of those lately. I take a long shower to keep myself busy and dress in the oversize shirt I sleep in. It belonged to Eric, but that's not why it's my favorite. It's soft, falls just to my knees, and is my favorite shade of blue. I stick my head out the door and look around. I know everyone must be in the game room. It's a vast space with a pool table, darts, and huge comfy couches. I walk toward the noise, coming to a standstill when I see Dex. He's in the corner of the living room, Allie pressed tightly against him. She leans in to kiss him, and I look away.

He's not mine.

I need to remind myself that. He's not my boyfriend. He's not my anything, other than my child's father. I run my hands along my stomach. I ignore the hurt that I'm feeling, and walk toward the kitchen. I'm getting some warm milk and then going to bed. Today needs to be over already. On my way to the fridge I bump face-first into a hard chest. A *very* hard chest.

"Sorry," I mumble into someone's shirt.

A deep chuckle. "Well, if it isn't the club's new lady lawyer. I definitely like these pajamas better."

"Tracker!" I gasp, looking up into his handsome face.

"How are you doing, beautiful?" he asks, dark eyes gazing into mine.

"I've been better," I say honestly, forcing a smile. "I'm going to get some milk and go to bed."

"Where's Sin?" he asks, eyes narrowing.

I shrug nonchalantly. "With the guys, I guess." Or sucking face with that hag.

Tracker scowls, then walks in front of me to the fridge. He pulls out the milk, tips some into a saucepan, and puts it on the stove. He's warming milk for me? I stare at him, covered in tattoos, dressed from head to toe in black, warming milk. A giggle escapes me.

"What's so amusing?" he asks, turning to look at me.

I shrug, grinning. "Big, bad biker heating up milk for me. Thanks, Tracker."

He smiles and returns to the task at hand, pouring the heated milk into a mug and giving it to me. "You want to watch a movie with me?"

"I'd love to," I whisper, eager for company. He leads me down the hall, past my room, farther into the back of the compound. Opening one of the doors, he leads me inside and sits me down on the bed.

"You sure you want to spend your night with me?" I ask him.

"What else would I be doing?" he asks as he puts the TV on.

"Engaging in hot public sex? A threesome? I don't know."

He laughs. "No offense, but you've been here for what? A couple of nights? I'm not saying that doesn't happen here, because it does, but that's not the only thing we're about."

"I don't mean to be judgmental, but . . . I don't know. I don't think I could get used to seeing that."

"Sin told everyone to be on their best behavior, so don't worry," he says, coming to sit down next to me. "You aren't going to walk in on anything too crazy."

I sip my milk. "Want some?"

He laughs at me, looking amused.

I frown. "Does that mean you don't want any milk?"

He takes it from me and takes a sip. When he leans forward and brushes his lips against mine, I don't stop him. I don't really have a reason to. Dex is out there with a woman that he has a past with, making it clear that he doesn't want me. Tracker sucks on my bottom lip as he pulls away. He tilts his head to the side, watching me. The kiss was more sweet than sexual; he didn't even use his tongue. It was a nice kiss, but it was nothing like Dex's kisses.

Great. Am I going to be like this for the rest of my life? Comparing every man to him, and none of them matching up to him even though he's not even mine?

I needed to get over him, I needed to see him as a co-parent to our child and that's it.

Even the thought of it hurt.

"Lie back and get some rest," he says, turning his attention back to the TV. I do as I'm told, staring at the huge screen.

"Thanks, Tracker," I tell him. "It sucks being alone here, where I don't know anyone."

He sighs and strokes my hair. "You aren't alone here, Faye.

Don't forget that. Besides, I think Dex is going to get a wake-up call concerning you real fuckin' soon, and if he doesn't, I'll be here, okay?"

I didn't know exactly what he was talking about, but I smile sleepily and lay my head down, falling into a deep sleep a few minutes later.

 **NINE**

WAKE up in the middle of the night to yelling. Rubbing my eyes, I sit up, confused. Then I remember watching TV with Tracker. I put my phone light on and see Tracker fast asleep on his stomach. I really appreciate him looking after me, keeping me company when I was feeling like shit. I hear a loud crash and quickly touch Tracker on the shoulder.

"Tracker, something's going on," I say, shaking him lightly. He wakes with a start, rolling me under him.

"Faye?" he says, sounding confused. Another crash. He lifts his head up and then looks back down at me. "Stay here."

I nod as he gets off the bed, grabs a gun from one of his drawers, and exits the room. A gun? More yelling and something else breaking. What the hell is going on here? I hear Tracker's voice, shouting, and I heard my name being said. I stand up, turn on the light, then move into the corner of the room as I hear pounding steps. Then, the door opens with a bang. Dex stands there, fists clenched and expression set in anger. Tracker stands behind him, shooting Dex an unhappy look.

What on earth?

"What happened?" I ask, seeing Dex's bruised knuckles.

"Get in my fuckin' room right now, Faye," he growls, his

tone laced with fury. I look at Tracker, which makes Dex even angrier.

"Don't look to him, he isn't going to save you. Now!" he yells, taking a step toward me.

"Sin—" Tracker starts.

"Shut the fuck up, brother," Dex snaps at him, his eyes set solely on me. I walk out of the room, walking past and ignoring the two of them. I see smashed glass as I detour to the kitchen, everything broken and lying on the floor. What in the hell? I hurry to the room and get into bed. I'm too tired to deal with this drama right now. I check the time on my phone: 3:00 a.m. Dex storms back into the room, angry tension radiating from his body. I ignore him as he turns on the light and paces, until he stops right in front of me.

"I came back to the room, expecting to find you asleep. You weren't here. What the fuck, Faye?"

"Sorry, I fell asleep in Tracker's room," I say, yawning.

"You're a selfish bitch, you know that? I thought maybe you left, tried to run again . . ."

"Fuck you! I'm not selfish! You're selfish! I don't know any-one here, and you left me alone all night, feeling miserable. You just got back to the room at three a.m.? What did you expect me to do all night? Sit here and stare at the wall?" I yell back at him. I'm not taking his shit.

"So what? You decided to get into Tracker's bed? You want a place here as one of the club whores?"

I stand up, take a step to him, and slap him right across the face. "Fuck. You!"

When the tears start to fall, I can't contain them. They pour. His eyes soften a little, as he examines my features.

"Don't cry," he says hoarsely, a demand and a plea. I stare at his face as a red handprint starts to appear on his cheek. I don't feel any satisfaction over it.

"Tracker comforted me when I needed it. When you weren't there to do it. I know we aren't together, or anything like that, but you brought me here. I didn't want to be here, but here I am. It's your job to look after me," I tell him, my voice cracking at the end.

He nods, rubbing the back of his neck. "You're right. I'll try harder, but you aren't sleeping in any bed but mine. Don't try and put me against my brothers, Faye."

How the hell do I have the power to do that? I wouldn't do that even if I did.

"Look, if you want to go sleep elsewhere, with whomever, then do it," I tell him, acting like I don't care. "It's obviously not any of my business."

Silence.

I close my eyes and attempt sleep when he says, "I was drinking with the guys. I wasn't fuckin' someone else."

I see a flash of him and Allie in my mind, her rubbing herself against him.

"I'm going to sleep, Dex. Good night."

"'Night," he whispers.

He heads for a shower, and I fall back asleep.

The next morning, I wake up cocooned in Dex's arms. I slowly get out of bed, untangling myself from him, and head into the kitchen. I find a broom and start to sweep up all the glass. It isn't really fair for one of the other women to have to do it.

When everything is cleaned up I make myself two slices of toast with butter and jam, then I head into the bathroom to have a shower. Dex wakes up as I'm sitting on the bed in my towel, rubbing my lotion into my skin.

"So that's why you smell like cherry," he says, his voice thick with sleep. His face is turned toward me, half buried into the pillow.

"Morning," I say quietly.

"I fucked up last night," he admits, nibbling on his bottom lip. "I'm sorry, babe."

"Why did you smash all that shit?" I ask.

"I came into the room, and you weren't here," is all he says.

"Yeah, and?"

He hides his face into the pillow. "I lost my temper," he says, words muffled.

"Yeah, I got that."

He sits up, the sheet falling and showing off his muscled chest and abs. Fuck—those abs. Perfectly sculpted and ripped. Yum.

"You like what you see?" he asks, his voice a low rumble.

"You know I do," I reply, pointing to my stomach. He laughs and slides closer to me, resting his head on my lap. When he kisses my stomach, my breath hitches.

"I think it's a boy," he announces, his eyes alight with pride.

"Why do you think that?" I ask him.

He shrugs. "Someone once told me that when a woman is pregnant with a girl, her beauty fades slightly. That sure as hell isn't happening to you. You're even more beautiful—if that's possible."

Wow. Did he just say that?

"So what does a boy do, then?" I ask, clearing my throat.

"A boy takes your energy," he says.

"Definitely a boy, then," I mutter, rolling my eyes. "We should call him Sirius."

He makes a face. "Why would we do that?"

"Your last name is Black!"

"And?"

"And? Sirius Black! From *Harry Potter*!" I say, getting excited.

He pauses. "Yeah. We're not doing that."

"Fine." I pout.

"Did you fuck him?" he suddenly asks.

"Did you fuck her?" I counter, gripping my towel so it doesn't drop.

"Who?" he asks, frowning.

"Allie."

"You know I didn't," he replies in a gentle tone. "I wouldn't, Faye."

"I didn't, and I wouldn't either."

"Good," he replies, getting out of bed. "Saves me from kicking my brother's ass."

Good? I seriously don't get this guy.

"What's the deal with the two of you anyway?" I ask, trying to act casual.

Dex shrugs. "No deal, we used to fuck, is all."

I don't know what to say to that.

"I have a past, babe," he says. "I'm sorry it's here in our faces, but it is what it is."

It was right in my face at least.

"I know you have a past," I grumble.

His eyes soften. "You have nothing to worry about, Faye, trust me. I'd never go with Allie or any other woman, all right? With you right here? I'm not that much of a dick. We're tied together for life now, and I want ours to be a good relationship. Our kid deserves that."

He heads into the bathroom while I think on his words.

By the time he comes back out, I'm dressed and ready to take on the day.

"I'm going to work, I'll be home by about five," he says, dropping his towel to the floor. I stare at his naked tattooed back, at his perfect ass, as he bends to his drawer to get out his clothes.

"Umm, Dex . . ."

"Yes?"

"I think we need to establish some boundaries," I say hesitantly, my gaze on the dragon tattoo on his back.

"How so?" he asks, his voice sounding amused.

"You're standing here. Naked," I say, enunciating each word.

"I know," he says, pulling on a pair of jeans with no underwear. Does he always go commando?

Concentrate, Faye!

"Well I don't know, doesn't it seem weird to you? We aren't together and . . ." I trail off.

"Do you need to label it?" he asks, lifting his arms to slide on a skintight white T-shirt.

Did I need to label it? I realize that yes, I do.

"Yes, I think I do," I blurt out.

He faces me. "Friends who are going to raise a baby together?"

Friends?

"Is that what you want?" I ask in a soft voice.

"I think that's all I can offer right now, babe," he says, looking regretful for a moment before his expression goes hard. Does he want something more between us? Is it because of Eric?

"Right, okay," I reply, trying to hide my disappointment. I should be happy, because things could be a lot worse. We're getting along okay, and I'm somewhere safe. I know some parents who don't like each other at all; at least we won't be like that.

"Will you be okay here? I'll send one of the prospects with some lunch for you," he says. He walks toward me, leans down, and kisses me on my forehead. "Bear with me, babe, please."

What does he mean, bear with him? Before I can ask he walks out of the room.

TEN

"WHAT about all our shit?" I hear Arrow ask. "We don't want the fuckin' cops to seize it. We don't need that shit."

I walked into the living room to hear a conversation I know I wasn't meant to. I'm about to open my mouth and alert my presence when they continue.

"I've put my main assets in my old lady's name," Jim says.

I decide to put in my two cents. "It doesn't work like that actually."

Arrow and Jim turn to me.

"What're you talking about?" Arrow asks, scowling. "And how long you been standing there?"

"Not long," I say innocently. "Putting assets in someone's name doesn't protect them, you know."

"Explain," Jim demands.

Charming man.

"If the courts think that you did it to avoid the assets being confiscated, then they can still be seized."

Arrow points to the couch. "Sit down. I have some questions for you."

Trying to stifle my grin, I sit down and cross my hands over my lap.

Finally I can be of use.

"It's called a cut, not a vest," the prospect says, laughing at me. His name is Vinnie, and he is my age. Too young to be living this life, if you ask me, but no one did, so I keep my big-ass mouth shut.

"A cut, then," I say, rolling my eyes at him. The Wind Dragons' cuts are awesome. The back has Wind Dragons on top, the badass dragon picture in the middle, and their location under it.

"No, you can't get your own cut," he says, shaking his head at me. "Why don't you ask Sin?" His tone tells me Sin is going to tell me to go right to hell.

I nod sagely. "I think I will."

I finish eating the pasta he brought me for lunch, thanking him once more. "Do you have to leave right now?" I ask him, pouting my lip out a little bit.

I'm bored.

So damn bored.

He runs a hand over his shaved head. "Sorry, Faye, I gotta get back to something."

I perk up. "What is it?"

He pats me on the head. "Learn not to ask; trust me on that."

"I'm a law student. I'm naturally inquisitive." Okay, it's more than that. I'm nosy and like to know everything.

"Curb that inquisition," he suggests, giving me a salute and then walking out. I puff out a breath, stand up, and walk into the game room. After playing a game of pool with myself, I take my pregnancy vitamins, then grab my e-reader and walk out back. Today is a good day, because I didn't throw up. Maybe it's the end of my morning sickness. Once I'm comfortable on one of the outdoor chairs, I pull out my phone and send Dex a text.

> Me: I need ice cream.
> Dex: And?
> Me: And get me some.

I reread the message, and realizing how rude it sounds, I send another one.

> Me: Please.
> Dex: Get Vinnie to get you some.
> Me: Vinnie left. I'm all alone, and the baby wants bubble
> gum flavored ice cream.

No reply. I sigh, trying to forget about my craving and concentrate on the rock-star book in front of me. I've finished half the book when I hear some laughter coming from inside the house.

"She'll come here eventually," a voice says. Allie.

"It's not our business," I hear Jessica say.

"I don't want to miss out on the drama," Allie snickers. When I walk into the kitchen all conversation comes to a halt.

"Hey, Jess," I say, ignoring Allie completely.

"Hey, how are you feeling today?" she asks, giving me a genuine smile.

"Good. Just bored," I say, slumping into the chair. A bulky man walks into the kitchen and gives Jessica a deep kiss. When he finally looks away, his eyes find me. Giving me a chin lift in greeting, I smile in return and watch as he drags Jess out of the room without a word, leaving me with Allie. Ignoring her, I stand up, grab my keys and my handbag, and walk to my car. I'm so over just sitting here doing nothing. Deciding to head to the store to pick up some ice cream and food, I'm about to slide into the driver seat when I hear the rumble of a motorcycle. I turn to see Dex straddling his beast of a bike, looking sexy and completely badass. He pulls off his helmet, dark hair blowing in the wind, and pins me with his gaze. I look away from him and get into my car and close the door. I count down, five, four, three, two, one, before he's standing in front of my window.

"Where are you going?" he asks, opening my car door and glaring at me.

"To the store," I say.

"Why? I went and got you some stuff," he says, smiling at me.

"You did?" I ask, eyebrows rising.

He smirks. "Can't let my baby mama go hungry, can I? Come on."

He holds his hand out to me, and I take it. A car pulls up, and I see Vinnie driving it. When it's parked, Dex goes to the trunk and pulls out four plastic bags filled with goodies. Curious, I follow him back into the kitchen.

"Two tubs of bubble gum ice cream," he says, placing it on the table. "And more junk food. Also a bag full of fruit, veggies, yogurt, and salad."

My eyes start to water as I grab one of the tubs of ice cream in my hand.

"Jesus, you really wanted that ice cream didn't you?" he says, eyes wide.

I nod as he goes and gets me a spoon from the drawer. "Thanks," I tell him around a mouthful of ice cream.

His face softens, and the look he gives me is so gentle that I don't know what to do with it or how to process it. "You're welcome. Anything you want, me or one of the prospects will take you to get, okay?"

"Why can't I go get it myself?" I ask.

"You can . . ." he says, trailing off.

"But?"

"But I'd rather someone be there with you. We have enemies, Faye. I don't want anything to happen to you or the baby."

"Enemies? Explain."

"Misunderstanding. Issues with a rival MC. There was a bar brawl a few weeks back. Two members of their MC were shot, and they think we're behind it. We weren't, although one of our members was present. Until that shit gets sorted we're being safe."

"Fine, but I need freedom, or I'm going to turn into a bitch," I tell him.

He laughs. Bastard. Well, I tried to warn him.

"When's your next doctor's appointment?"

"Next week," I reply.

"All right, I'll be going with you to any and all appointments," he announces. "I want to be a part of this every step of the way."

"Okay," I say, around another spoonful of the most delicious ice cream I've ever tasted. Dex goes to the drawer and gets his own spoon, digging it into my tub.

"Let's see what all the fuss is about," he says, opening his mouth and having a taste.

"Not bad at all," he says to himself, sitting down and pulling the tub closer to him.

"You just double-dipped!" I growl, snatching the tub back.

"You did it," he says, grinning wolfishly.

"Yeah, but it's mine, so the rule is different for me," I explain.

"Babe, we've fucked," he says, leaning back in the chair and shrugging his broad shoulders.

"I remember, I was there," I reply, wondering where the hell he's going with this.

"So that's more intimate than double-dipping some ice cream, don't you think? I've had my mouth on every inch of you."

I put my spoon down, swallowing, and try to ignore the images of him doing just that. "Yeah, you fuck everyone though," I reply, trying to play it off, meanwhile I'm replaying our night together in my mind. Yeah, I could really go for seconds.

He studies me. "Says who?"

"Says me."

We all know he's been around the block and back, I don't think there's any point in denying it.

"Babe," he says, shaking his head.

"What?"

I lick my spoon.

He watches me do it.

"You're nothing like those women. They didn't mean shit," he says, his eyes darkening as my tongue peeps out to lick my bottom lip.

"Should I feel special?" I ask, batting my eyelashes. "I don't know how having one night of sex with you makes me any different than any other woman you've had."

His lip twitches. I think he likes my attitude. "You're sitting here with me right now, aren't you? You're here, and I'm taking care of you."

"Why, have you knocked up other women and not brought them to the clubhouse to take care of them?"

His lips tighten at that.

I shrug, backtracking a little. "So we had hot, filthy sex. I'm sure you have that all the time."

"I haven't fucked in a while, so don't remind me," he says in a low tone. Oops, I think I've pissed him off a little bit.

I stand up and put both tubs in the freezer. "I think your *a while* and my *a while* are a little different."

He doesn't say anything to that, so I turn around and pin him with a speculative look. "You're the last person I slept with," I say, waiting for him to talk.

He doesn't.

"And you?" I ask, my voice deceptively innocent.

He pauses, wincing slightly. "You really want to do this?"

I cringe. "That bad, huh?"

"I haven't slept with anyone since I found out you were carrying my baby," he says finally, his eyes never leaving me.

I bite my bottom lip, my eyes narrowing slightly. "That was the other day."

Did he want a medal for going without sex for a couple of days? Because he wasn't going to get one.

He nods slowly. "It was. I'm not going to lie."

"Okay," I say slowly, looking away from his steady gaze. The last thing in the world I want is to picture him having sex with another woman. Which he was doing up until a couple of days ago. With who? With Allie? The thought makes me scowl.

He was fucking Allie or whoever while I've been panicking, working, and preparing for our baby. While I've been sick?

Whose fault is that? He didn't even know about the baby.

"Don't overthink things, Faye," Dex says softly, interrupting my thoughts. "Okay?"

I nod my head, biting my bottom lip.

"I'm taking you out tonight, so be dressed by six," he says, standing up to leave the room.

"Where are you going now?" I ask him, hating the neediness in my tone.

"Out," he says. "Look, I get that you're having my kid, but I don't explain myself to any woman, all right?"

Ouch.

Is that what I was expecting him to do? I look at him, standing there. Dressed in tight jeans, a white V-neck and his cut, he looks intimidating. Unattainable. Breathtaking. I suddenly feel angry. This isn't me. Sitting here, being so out of control. Letting a man, who just said he doesn't even have to explain himself to me, control my life. I let my parents have control of me my entire life; now that I'm free of their hold, I don't need another. Even if it comes in the form of a sexy-as-sin, badass biker.

"Why don't I just leave, then, and get out of your way?" I snap, walking out the door before he can. I ignore his presence behind me as I grab my bag and my school folder and walk to my car. Was it always going to be this way? Me having to explain my every move and him having to explain nothing? A relationship was give and take, share and receive. It didn't work otherwise. I wanted Dex to see me as his equal, his partner. I imagined Dex and me in the future, having a conversation.

Me: Where are you going, Dex?

Dex: None of your damn business, woman, get back in the kitchen where you belong.

Me: Okay, dear. See you at dinner.

I cringe. Yeah—that wasn't happening. I'd rather be without Dex and be my own woman than with him and having to change. Did he really expect that though? He may complain and try to get his way with me, but he does put up with everything I have to dish out. He's never once said that if I acted a certain way, I'd lose him or his protection and care.

"Where the fuck do you think you're going?" he growls, taking me by the arm and pulling me from my thoughts.

"I'm going to study at the library," I tell him through clenched teeth. "I don't like explaining myself to you either. Who are you to me? Some asshole who had me once and knocked me up. You don't own me, Dex, any more than I own you."

"Faye—"

"Which would be a big fat not-at-all."

His jaw tightens. "You and I both know that isn't the truth."

I throw my hands up. "Why have conversations at all, Dex? I'm *just* a woman, right? Who am I to question you in important matters, such as what you might be doing today?"

He licks his bottom lip. "I think that's enough, Faye."

My lips purse. "Well, if you think that's enough, then it must be enough," I say with enough sarcasm for a class of high school students.

Dex cups my face. "You can't even remember why you're angry at me, can you?"

My fingers dig into my palm, his words inciting my fury to another level.

"Of course I know what I'm angry about, you arrogant—"

"Please," he says, lip twitching. "Do tell me."

I swallow. "I'm angry because I just realized another reason we're never going to work out."

With that, I turn around and storm to my car. I hear him barking for Vinnie, probably to babysit me.

Poor Vinnie.

I drive off, through the gate—which was luckily open—and away from the confines of a man I want but can never have.

# ELEVEN

WALK out of the library and come face-to-face with Vinnie.
The poor guy must have been waiting out front for the last few hours.

"Sorry, Vin," I say when I see him looking bored out of his mind, standing next to his bike.

He doesn't even try to smile at me. Instead, he sucks on a lollipop and says, "Where to next?"

"Want to ride with me? We can get your bike on the way back."

He shakes his head, looking put out at my question. Okkaaaayyy, then.

"Let's go get some gelato," I decide. Vinnie looks less than thrilled at my decision but doesn't complain. He must really want to get patched in.

When we arrive at my favorite gelato place, my phone beeps with a message.

Dex: Ice cream again? Really?

I huff. This is his way of letting me know he knows exactly where I am and what I'm doing. Controlling asshole. He can't even give me an inch, can he?

Me: Hoping to get Vinnie to lick it off me.

Immature, I know. But I'm moody and hormonal. Hormonal—now, there's a good excuse if I'd ever heard one.

I grin at the thought as Vinnie sits on the stool opposite me, enjoying his chocolate ice cream.

"It's good, isn't it?" I say with a wink.

He rolls his eyes. "Fine, it's good."

"Want to go and see a movie next?" I ask him, enjoying the freedom and the company.

He stops midlick, moving his mouth away from the ice cream. "You don't wanna go back yet?"

"Do I have to?" I whine.

"Yes, you do," he says, chuckling at me. "It's not so bad there, is it?"

I shrug. "It's not bad there, no. But I feel like I have nothing to do but sit there like an incubator while everyone goes on living their lives."

He laughs, loudly. "An incubator?"

"Come on, Vin. I can't even go get ice cream without it turning into a spectacle."

That comment stops the humor on his face. "He just wants you safe. The clubhouse isn't that bad. Just tell him what you want and he'll get it for you. Trust me, he won't say no to you."

"Yeah, but he can't control me like that," I say quietly, looking away.

"Do you know how many women would love to be where you are right now?" he says, flashing me an amused look.

I huff. "Not liking where this is going, Vinnie."

He grins. "Women flock to Dex, Faye. I've never seen him pay any of them any attention, not like the way he is with you. That has to count for something, right?"

I shrug my shoulders. "I know I sound like a brat, complaining about this when he's been good to me. I guess I want more from him, something I'm not sure he can give me."

A warm hand cups my jaw, lifting my head up. "You're a strong girl, you know that?"

My cheeks heat. "I don't think I've had the opportunity to prove that yet."

"You will," he says, standing up. "Now, let's go. Last thing I need is Sin getting pissed off at me."

I wince when I think of the message I sent Dex without considering the impact of my actions. I hope he doesn't take it out on Vinnie.

"Race you there?" I call out, grinning.

He looks down at my tummy. "Maybe in a few months."

I giggle. "Deal."

Dex isn't home when I get there. I grab all my snacks and head straight for my room, not planning on sharing any of my goodies. When I walk past the living room I see Arrow sitting there with a woman on his lap. A woman who isn't Mary. He looks up when he sees me, my hands full of chocolates, candy, and baked goods and grins.

"Need some help with those, little girl?" he calls out to me, a dry chuckle escaping his cheating lips.

I step into the room, the packets crinkling in my hands. "I think I have it under control, thanks. So where's Mary? You know, your drop-dead gorgeous, stunning, non-slutty girlfriend?"

Shit. I probably shouldn't have said that, but he was cheating on someone I considered a friend. I couldn't just leave and do nothing, could I? I would want someone to stand up for me. Like Trisha should have instead of sleeping with Eric. She should have told me my boyfriend was scum, not joined him in the betrayal. I didn't want to do that to Mary.

His eyes narrow. "I don't know where she is, but I think it's time you went to your room to eat that week's worth of snacks."

One of the bags of chips almost falls out of my hands, and I juggle to keep it from dropping to the floor.

"I can't even take you seriously when you stand there like that, looking like you just robbed Willy Wonka," he mutters, shaking his head.

I ignore his comment, which would usually have me smiling, and stare at the woman on his lap. "Arrow, come on. Don't do something you'll regret."

His face turns mean, and I get kind of scared. I step away as the woman on his lap throws me a haughty look.

"So . . . when's the last time you had an STD check?" I ask her in a mock casual tone. Arrow growls, and I wince, taking another step backward. "Well, I'll just be going now . . ."

"Looks like it's you who needs to use protection," she sneers, staring at my stomach. At least she knows I'm pregnant, not just fat. "Do you even know who the father is?"

Annoyed, I look to Arrow.

An idea forms.

As if knowing what I'm thinking, he shakes his head, the gleam in his eyes letting me know that he's not pleased with me.

I ignore his warning and point at him.

"Arrow is the father," I say, pretending to start crying. "You broke my heart, Arrow! You cheating bastard! You better be there for little Sirius when he's born or I'm taking your ass to court and getting every cent from you!" I turn to the woman, who is staring at me with wide eyes. "I recommend you getting a health check, because he sleeps with everyone and never wraps his dick. He gave me something when I was with him!"

Then I run to my room, unable to stop laughing.

I'm halfway through a packet of Oreos when Dex walks in, looking extremely unhappy.

"Babe," he says on a sigh, rubbing a hand down his face, looking tired.

"What?" I ask, shoving another cookie in my mouth.

"You couldn't make things easy on me, could you?" he says dryly, lying down on the bed next to me.

"I like Mary," I say, assuming he's talking about the Arrow incident.

"What does this have to do with Mary?" he asks, sitting up. Oh, shit, I guess Arrow didn't snitch on me after all. Does that mean he's going to extract revenge on his own? I feel a little scared; I'd rather Dex just tell me off.

"I saw Arrow with someone who isn't Mary," I say in a quiet voice. Dex goes stiff next to me, then pulls me closer to him. "I like Mary, and I didn't like seeing it. She deserves better than that, but I like Arrow too, so I'm feeling a little at odds with myself right now."

"That's not our business, okay?" he says in a firm tone.

One I don't like.

"If someone knew things about me, things that would hurt me, but looked in my face every day and pretended to be my friend, I'd feel hurt. And pissed off. And betrayed," I tell him.

Silence.

"It's not you hurting Mary. It's their business, and you shouldn't judge them. Has anyone here ever judged you?" he says.

I think on it. "I guess not."

"We have a 'don't ask, don't tell' policy here, babe," he says, leaning back once more. "And that goes for you too. Just mind your own business, and everything will be fine."

I gulp, wondering what Arrow was going to do to me.

"Okay, you're right; it's none of my business. If it was me though—I'd want someone to tell me."

"Is this about Eric?" he asks in a gruff voice.

I scoot closer to him and look him in the eye. "I guess so. I was with him forever, you know? I realize now it's just what we were used to. I just wish he'd broken up with me before sleeping around."

"He doesn't deserve you, Faye. He never did," he says, steel lacing his tone.

"He's been calling nonstop," I say, tracing the tattoos on his knuckles.

"I'll get you a new phone tomorrow," he says instantly.

"Okay. Are we still going out somewhere tonight?" I ask, fighting a yawn.

"Are you tired? We could just order in," he replies, playing with a lock of my hair.

"Sounds good," I say, smiling.

"You know, when I first heard you were pregnant I was a little pissed off—"

"A little?" I reply in a dry tone. "Understatement of the year."

"Okay, I was fuckin' angry, but come on. It was you, and you never told me."

"What do you mean, it was me?" I ask, frowning.

"I was angry you didn't tell me, but I wasn't angry you were having my baby," he says, clearing his throat. "If it was anyone else . . . but it was you."

Our gazes collide. "You didn't even know me though, I mean, you didn't know the kind of person I'd turned out to be. I could be a bitchy psycho."

"And you can be," he replies, lips curving at the corners.

I slap his shoulder and watch as he chuckles deeply. "I've known you forever, Faye. You've always meant something to me, first as a punk kid, then as a friend . . . now it's more. You were always special, you know? Oh, and you're fucking hot, with a talented mouth."

I pinch him.

"Speaking of talented mouths . . ." I whisper, glancing up at him through my lashes.

"What am I going to do with you, Faye?" he says, leaning forward and kissing me on my nose.

"I could think of a few things," I say dryly, raising an eyebrow suggestively.

He pulls back, his expression going blank. "There are some things I need to sort out before we even think of going there."

"What things?" I ask. I move closer, close enough that I can smell a hint of his cologne.

"Nothing, babe, nothing," he says, brushing it off and rolling away from me.

I groan in frustration.

What the hell is he hiding?

When I wake up in the middle of the night, Dex isn't in bed. Feeling thirsty and a little curious, I tiptoe into the kitchen to get some milk, then look around for him. I hear voices outside, so I move the blinds to the side to take a peek. I can't hear, but I can see Dex's lips move as he talks to a man I've never seen before. His hand is around the guy's neck, squeezing.

I gulp.

Would Dex kill him?

What did the man do?

Finally he shoves the man to the floor and then points to the gate. Next, Dex turns to Arrow, says something to him, and then punches him in the stomach.

What the fuck?

Why did he do that?

I get back to bed before they notice me.

An hour later, Dex slides into the sheets and pulls me into his arms, hugging me. He even kisses the top of my head.

I feel safe with him, but there's a side to him I obviously don't know.

One question lingers.

Which Dex is the real Dex?

# TWELVE

THE next day, after a morning of studying, I exit my room and walk straight into Mary.

"Oh, sorry, honey," she says in her sweet voice, her arm going to my waist.

"Sorry," I mumble, giving her a small smile. She is looking beautiful today in high-waisted shorts and a tank top with a picture of a pinup girl on it. She's so hot! How could Arrow cheat on her . . . with that skank!

"I was just coming to get you, actually," she says. "You've been cooped up in your room all morning; do you want something to eat?"

Could she get any nicer?

"Sounds good," I say. "How have you been?"

"Good, busy with work," she says as we walk side by side into the kitchen. I look down at what I'm wearing: track pants and a cami with a chocolate stain on it. I look like shit, compared to her.

"Where do you work, again?" I ask her, sitting at the table.

"I'm a vet," she says, opening the fridge and pulling out a large container.

"Wow," I say, impressed. "Beauty and brains."

Except for dating Arrow.

She laughs. "You're sweet. Here, Sin told me to make this for you and make sure you eat it."

She puts the container in front of me, a healthy-looking spinach and chicken salad. "Thanks."

"I've never seen him care for someone so much," she says, staring at the salad.

I smile but decide to ignore that comment. "Where's Arrow?"

She loses her smile. "Club business. Listen, he told me about what happened yesterday."

My jaw drops open. "He did?"

She laughs at my expression. "Yes, he did. We aren't exclusive, he and I. But thanks for standing up for me all the same."

"I don't get this club," I admit.

"You don't have to, honey. Love the man, love the club; that's just how it goes. Dex was pissed at Arrow for letting you see what you did."

I choke on a piece of lettuce. "Love?"

Is that why Dex hit Arrow? Because he had to deal with my reaction to seeing Arrow cheat?

"Oh, I've seen how the two of you look at each other," she says, flashing me a knowing look.

"Do you need glasses?" I ask her, keeping a straight face.

She giggles. "Oh, come on, anyone can see it. He's crazy over you."

I purse my lips together, then change the subject. "So do you sleep with other men?"

Her eyes widen.

I cringe. "Don't answer that. I'm sorry, that was really rude."

She grins. "No, I don't sleep with anyone else. Arrow is the only man I want."

I bite the inside of my cheek. "So do you want him to be with only you?"

She smiles, sadly this time. "In an ideal world, I'd love nothing more than for Arrow to only want me. But he's not like that, and I'd rather have him in my life like this than not have him at all."

"You'd rather share him than be without him," I muse, thinking that I'd stab Dex with a fork if he tried to have this little situation with me.

"I know how it must look," she says. "But I love him. I don't want to change him, so I have to take him as he is."

Arrow is such an asshole. He has a good woman standing right in front of him, and look what he's doing. I'm about to say so when Tracker, Irish, and Allie walk in.

"Hey, you," I say to Tracker, giving him a warm smile.

He walks straight to me, leaning down and kissing me on the head. "I'm hungry, cook me some food."

I gasp. "You have hands, use them."

"He was using them pretty creatively just before," Allie purrs. What? Does she just sleep with anyone?

"Get the fuck out, Allie," Tracker growls.

I stand, looking at Mary and only Mary. "Thanks for the food."

Heading back to my room, Tracker stops me in the hallway. "What's wrong?"

I sigh and turn to face him. "I guess I thought you were my only friend in this place, and now you're fucking the enemy. I don't know. I guess I'm just hormonal."

Yes! Saving me once again.

"Faye—"

"She hates me, and now you've given her another thing to throw in my face. Oh, she fucked Dex and now she fucked you—the other person I'm close with here. Am I the only one not getting any action in this fucking house?"

"Faye—"

"I know, I know—I'm acting stupid. Still, I wish you would fuck around with anyone else except her. I don't like her, if you haven't noticed. And she can't be that good in bed for everyone to put up with her personality, or lack thereof," I continue. "What, does she have beer-flavored nipples? A golden snatch? What is it?"

"Faye—"

"And you kissed me!" I blurt out. "I guess that wouldn't mean anything to you though, considering the way everyone around here is so free with their . . ."

"The fuck," comes a heated growl. I turn and look into angry blue eyes.

Shit. Fuck. Shit.

"Umm . . ." I mumble, visibly cringing.

I'd really done it this time.

Shit.

Yeah, I have nothing.

"You kissed her?" Dex growls at Tracker, who stares him straight in the eye and nods once, sealing his fate.

Dex grits his teeth.

His hands curl to fists.

I think I see steam coming out of his ears.

I stay silent, not knowing what to say to make the situation better. I didn't want Dex being angry with Tracker over something so small as a kiss, and one that didn't mean anything at that. I'd really fucked up.

"Outside," Dex snarls, then walks off without even a glance in my direction.

Tracker turns to me, eyes piercing into mine. "Sorry, Faye, but you're his. You know it, and I know it. And *he* definitely fuckin' knows it."

With that, he walks off, leaving me standing there looking like an idiot with my mouth hanging open. I go to follow them, but I hear Dex call out, "Arrow, keep Faye in the room. Don't let her out of your sight."

Shit, he couldn't call anyone else?

"Hello, little girl," Arrow says as he walks up to me, grinning. He points to my room door. I shake my head, put my hands on my hips, and stand my ground.

"Room. Now, Faye," he says casually, no heat in his tone.

Why is he not worried?

He should be there, telling them to stop acting like cavemen. Maybe a speech about bros before hoes? I don't know, anything to get them to stop fighting over a stupid kiss.

"Aren't you going to stop them?" I ask him, my voice raising. In answer, he herds me into the bedroom with his hands on my shoulder blades.

"Now, about the other day," he starts, pretending as if there weren't two men out there doing God knows what to each other. And all because of me and my big mouth.

You messed up this time, Faye.

I laugh nervously. "Yeah, sorry about that."

What was Arrow going to do to me for *that* little scenario?

"What are you sorry about?" he asks, smirking. "By the way, don't bother trying a career in acting. You were laying the theatrics on a little thick, don't you think?"

I frown. "My pregnancy stunt didn't cock-block you?"

He laughs now, holding his stomach. "Fuck no, as if these bitches care. They'll ride my cock no matter who it belongs to."

Lovely.

"How charming," I sniff. "You really know how to pick them."

He grins. "It's the truth."

"I just really like Mary, okay. Don't worry, Dex gave me a warning to mind my own business from here on out."

His face softens lightly. "Yeah, Mary is a good girl."

I roll my eyes. "A good girl? She's a catch! She's fucking hot and sweet and someone needs to wife her like now."

His lips curve. "Now, don't be saying things you can't take back."

I blink. He blinks. Then we both laugh.

When our laughter subsides, Arrow looks at me intently. "Need to ask you something."

"Go ahead," I say.

"You realize Sin is going to take over the club someday. . . ."

"As president?" I ask. I'd never really thought about that before. What does that mean for me and our child?

"Yeah. Being the old lady of a president isn't just for anyone," he says, playing with his beard. "You need to learn when to keep that mouth of yours shut."

I open my mouth and then snap it closed.

"Good, you're learning," he comments, looking amused. "We like you, so we let you get away with shit, but not all bikers are like that, you know. You can't go running your mouth in front of others."

"I've already been told this. And Sin doesn't even want me," I say, unable to keep the bitterness out of my tone.

Arrow grins. "He fuckin' wants you; trust me on that, little girl. Otherwise he wouldn't be out there right now, beating the shit out of one of his best friends and brothers just because he tasted your sweet lips."

"No, he doesn't want me, he just doesn't want me being with anyone else." I huff, staring at the door. Before Arrow can grab me, I run to the door and through the house. When he doesn't come after me I realize he let me go, and I have to wonder why. I see all the bikers and women standing around Dex and Tracker, who are both beating the shit out of each other. Tracker has blood streaming down his face, while Dex just has a cut lip. Dex lifts back his arm to hit Tracker once more.

I can't take it.

"Stop it!" I yell at the top of my lungs. "I'm sorry! Please, just stop!"

Dex doesn't even turn my way; instead, he calls out one word. "Irish!"

Irish walks to me, lifts me in his arms, and carries me away as I squirm and scream. "Why aren't you stopping them?" I yell, pushing myself away from his body. He carries me like a bride instead of over his shoulder, obviously being careful about my stomach, but I don't have time to dwell on how sweet that is. As we enter my room, Arrow is still sitting there, looking bored.

"Why the fuck did you let her out?" Irish growls unhappily. "You're gonna get your ass kicked after Tracker."

Arrow shrugs. "She doesn't think Sin wants her; thought it'd do her good to see him fighting over her." That's where he was wrong.

He wasn't fighting over me, Faye Connor.

He was fighting over his possession.

The difference in those two things is astronomical.

"I suck at life," I mutter under my breath. I mean, I don't really know Dex, do I? I don't understand the reason he does things or how he will react. I never should have kissed Tracker, and I sure as hell shouldn't have opened my mouth about it. I didn't want to cause trouble in the club for Dex. He warned me before that my actions reflect on him, and now I'm starting to understand that a little more. His wanting to fight Tracker though, it seems like he's punishing Tracker for touching what he considers "his." Whether he actually wants me is trivial. I'm still his because he brought me here and I'm carrying his child. How I feel about it doesn't matter. My feelings are inconsequential, or at least it feels that way right now.

I'd always wanted Dex. I remember thinking how gorgeous he was, how he had a certain spark that I was drawn to.

He *is* gorgeous.

But it's more than that.

"What did Tracker do anyway?" Arrow asks, leaning on his elbow.

"Nothing," I lie, not wanting them to know what went on. I'm sure Dex wouldn't want them to know either, so I'm keeping my mouth shut from here on out.

"Bullshit."

"Hey, I was told I'm not allowed to mention anything I see going on in this club," I say, grinning impishly at the two men. "And I'm a woman who keeps her word."

They both laugh.

"You're a million times better than Renee," Irish adds.

Arrow punches him in the arm.

"Who's Renee?" I ask, trying to sound casual, but the curiosity in my tone can't be hidden.

"No one," Arrow says, giving Irish a look I can clearly see means *Shut up*.

I throw my hands up. "No one tells me shit around here!"

"Would you rather be back home?" Arrow asks, raising an eyebrow. I picture myself back home, my parents breathing down my neck every two seconds.

Faye, did you study?

Faye, I don't think you should wear that. Cover up more.

Faye, you already have a boyfriend at your age? The whole town is talking about you.

"No, I wouldn't," I reply with total honestly. "But this place is boring."

Irish huffs. "Only 'cuz Sin is keeping you locked up here like a fuckin' princess. If you were allowed out to play, you'd have a good time."

Interesting.

"Oh, and if you weren't knocked up," Arrow adds gruffly, eyeing my belly like it's contagious.

I run my hands over my stomach. "This is true."

The door slams open and Dex stands there, adrenaline and fury radiating from him. The air gets sucked from the room as we stare at each other.

"Out," he growls to Arrow and Irish. Arrow flashes me a sympathetic look before he leaves. One I don't appreciate.

Dex starts to pace, and I sit and wait for him to explode. I can feel it coming.

Feel it pulsing throughout the room.

"My kid in you, and you're kissing another man?" he yells, punching the door twice. I flinch with each hit, then stare at the crack in the door.

"It was just a kiss! And I saw you with that skank in the hallway!" I yell, losing my temper.

"So what? It was going to be another revenge fuck? You seem to like those, don't you," he sneers, shaking his head in disbelief.

"Don't twist my words! It was one kiss, and he's a nice guy," I tell him, looking away. "I was feeling alone, and I know it shouldn't have happened."

He laughs but without humor. "None of these guys are nice guys, Faye. They're just being that way to you because they know you're under my protection. They don't have a fuckin' choice. It's me who has your back, who's looking after you and trying to make you happy, but it's them you sing praises about? *They're* nice guys? But not me, is that it?"

I open my mouth to reply, but he cuts me off.

"Tracker, the man you think is a 'nice guy,' killed someone last week," he says in a tone I've never heard from him before. "And do you know why he did it? Because I gave him the order to."

My eyes flare as I take in this information. Instead of feeling scared, all I can feel is anger.

"And you want to bring my kid up in all this?" I yell, standing up. "What the fuck do you want from me, Dex?"

His face goes blank. "I don't want anything from you, Faye, except my kid. Now I'm going to go fuck someone, while you stay here and think about what a bitch you are."

My face falls as he slams the door shut.

He wouldn't, would he?

I grit my teeth.

Fuck him!

I'm so done.

 THIRTEEN

H E doesn't come back to the room that night.

I stay up all night, overthinking everything, and wondering what he was doing. Should I have gone after him? I thought that letting him cool down would be the best option; I just hope I was right. I felt so confused. I wanted Dex, but was it always going to be this way? I didn't think I could handle it.

I make myself get out of bed early to have breakfast, and write Dex a note.

After I'm showered and dressed, I'm about to leave the clubhouse when I see the girls. Jess, Mary, Allie, and a couple I've never met before. A beautiful woman who looks to be in her forties stares at me, and I have a feeling that this is Jim's wife. The queen bee of Wind Dragons. She walks over to me, and I muster up a smile.

"You've been causing quite a commotion around here, I see," she says giving me a once-over. She has very light hair, and very dark eyes, the contrast quite attractive.

"Faye," I say by way of introduction, offering her my hand.

"Cindy," she says, shaking my hand with a tight grip. "Don't hurt him."

"Nice to meet you," I tell her, thinking I'm pretty sure it's the other way around, but whatever. I nod and smile, saying hello to the other girls, then getting the hell out of there.

I don't belong here.

I smile when I see the gate open and no one else around. As I drive off in my little car, I feel something.

Regret.

I ignore the shit out of it.

When I turn and see a bike riding next to me I curse. It's Vinnie—the poor guy must have been told to babysit me once again. I try to lose him, to no avail. Sighing, I turn into the mall parking lot. I get out and wave at him before walking into a store that sells baby items. I look over the little baby clothes, so tiny and cute. Buying a few unisex outfits with my own money, I leave the store and head into another one. I buy some clothes I can wear as I get bigger—loose tops and stretchy dresses and pants. My phone starts to ring.

Dex.

I hit IGNORE and continue on my shopping expedition. After my phone rings for the fifth time, I put it on silent. There is nothing I want to say to him right now. When I walk past the movie theater, I decide to go in and watch a movie. Anything to take my mind off the fact that at some point today, I'm going to have to return to the compound. Whether I want to or not. Dex will bring me back if Vinnie doesn't. Choosing a vampire movie, I get some popcorn and water and choose a seat in the middle of the theater. Halfway through the movie, someone sits next to me. I don't need to turn to know who it is. His cologne is a dead giveaway, along with the way my body responds by merely being in his presence. He doesn't say anything, and I don't feel his gaze on me. He just sits there in silence, watching the second half of the movie. I try to concentrate on the screen in front of me, but my mind is now solely on Dexter Black. What is going to come out of that mouth of his now? Did he sleep with someone last night? Allie? Do I have the right to be upset? Probably not. He made me no promises, and I'm beginning to give up hope that he ever will.

What seems like hours later, the credits run and the lights turn back on. I peek at him, to find him staring back at me with a gentle look on his handsome face. Running a hand along the stubble on his jaw, he flashes me an apologetic smile.

But he isn't going to charm his way out of this one so easily.

"What are you doing here?" I ask, breaking the silence. Everyone else stands to leave the cinema, shuffling around us.

"You were gone when I woke up" is all he says.

I grit my teeth. "I'm allowed to go wherever I want, Dex."

"Faye—"

"And maybe if you actually slept in our bed you would have known when I left it," I add.

"Look, Faye," he says, glancing back at the screen. "There's some shit going on right now with another MC. I just want to make sure you're safe, that's all. Even if you're fuckin' pissed at me, I need you to stay put, all right? I can't always be chasing you; I got a lot of shit on my plate right now."

"I get that. I do. But you don't need to be an asshole," I reply in a voice devoid of emotion.

"Babe, everyone knows you're mine. You're mine to take care of. I brought you here," he says, cupping my chin in his hand. "You're carrying my kid. Tracker should have known better than to touch you."

"So you don't want me, but no one else can have me either?" I ask, our eyes connected.

His swim with indecision.

Mine swim with hope.

"Wanting you isn't the issue, trust me on that," he finally says, giving me a sad smile.

"Then what is it?" I dare to ask.

I squeeze my eyes shut as his lips touch my forehead. He murmurs, "You know what you want, and you won't accept any less. Truth?"

I nod my head.

He pulls back and his eyes cloud over. "When I come to you, I need to know that I can give you everything you deserve. I need to be ready for you, and I'm going to be. Soon."

"It didn't stop you from having me before," I point out.

He grins crookedly. "That was one night. This is a little more permanent."

"How permanent?" I ask, drawing each word out.

Now he smiles. "Ball-and-chain permanent."

Wait, what?

Ball and chain? Marriage? Commitment? Do my ears deceive me?

"Wh-what? What does that mean for us, Dex?" I bravely ask, my gaze boring into his.

His eyes soften. "Do you think you could be an old lady, live this lifestyle with me? I know I'm not always easy to be around, but fuck, Faye, for you, I'll try to be who you need me to be. I'm going to give everything to our kid, everything; do you understand? I'm not going to be one of those fathers who ignores their kid, or leaves you to do everything for him. I'm going to be there every step of the way, taking care of the two of you."

My eyes flare. "I think this is the first time you're talking about the future with me."

He flashes me a sheepish look. "I might not talk about it, but that doesn't mean I don't think about it or make plans for it."

I tilt my head to the side. "What plans? What do you think about?"

He swallows before he answers. "I put you on my life-insurance policy, so if anything happens to me, you will both be taken care of, stuff like that. My brothers will always look out for you, so I don't have to worry. I've given you my family. It might not be much to you, but it's everything to me. It's one of the few things I have to give."

"I appreciate everything you've done for me," I say. "I really do, Dex, but I need some freedom too, you know? I'm my own woman, and I didn't escape one jail to be sent to another."

He nods. "I get that."

"I think I could make a good old lady," I reply, shrugging casually.

He grins. "I think so too."

"Really?"

"The best."

I curl my arm around his and rested my head on his shoulder. For the first time, I felt not just safe, but content.

"Do you want him?" he asks, eyes darkening.

"Who?" I ask, eyebrows furrowing. I was still in "ball and chain" fantasyland.

"Tracker—do you want him? This is the first and only time I will ask you this, Faye, so answer carefully."

I lick my bottom lip before I answer. "No, I don't want him in that way, but I care about him as a friend."

He nods, seemingly satisfied with my answer, and stands, offering me his hand, pulling me up when I place it in his. "Let's get you home."

"I can't believe you didn't tell me any of what you were thinking until now. I've decided I'm still pissed at you," I tell him as he picks up my shopping bags from the seat next to me.

"I wouldn't expect any less," he replies, sounding amused as hell. "What did you buy?"

"Baby stuff."

"I hope you used the card I gave you."

"As a matter of fact, I did not," I reply.

He makes a noise deep in his throat. "It's my kid too, you know. If he or she needs anything, I will provide it."

"What? Did we travel to the past and someone forgot to tell me?"

"Stubborn. I'm buying everything else, and don't even think of arguing. Choose your battles, Faye."

"You do the same," I warn him. But I'll let him win this round.

"Where did you go last night?" I ask him as he walks to his car. "Where's your bike?"

"You're pregnant; no bike for you. And I went out, but I didn't fuck anyone," he says bluntly, opening the car door with a press of a button. "I wouldn't do that to you. I was pissed when I said it, but I know I shouldn't have. I wouldn't have done it, Faye. Even angry as hell I wouldn't have done something to jeopardize my future with you."

"Where did you go, then?" I ask when we're seated.

"Babe," he says, lip twitching.

"Don't you 'babe' me, you jerk," I growl, narrowing my eyes on him.

"You know, I don't think anyone's ever spoken to me this way," he muses, not sounding like it's a bad thing.

"Well, you better get used to it," I add, flashing him a fake smile. "And you're going to have to learn to answer my questions. I'm sick of being ignored and evaded."

"I'll try," he says reluctantly, reaching out and rubbing his thumbs along my knuckles.

"You do that," I reply. "Try hard. Really hard."

"You were always a feisty one, even as a kid," he says, lifting my hand to his lips and pressing a kiss there. My pulse races. He continues talking like he didn't just almost make me swoon. "Even your crazy mom couldn't break your spirit."

I think about defending my mom but then don't bother. What he says is true. "I used to follow you around."

He huffs. "I remember. You tried to make me eat a cupcake you'd made. It was all squashed, and I'm pretty sure you'd dropped it on the floor!"

My shoulders shake with my laughter. "What do you mean, tried? You ate that damn cupcake and loved it!"

He scoffs. "What was I supposed to say? No? You with your huge hazel eyes and auburn ringlets, I don't think anyone could say no to you."

"Big, bad biker afraid of some puppy dog eyes?"

"Yours," I think I hear him mutter under his breath.

Whoa.

"Then you started dating Eric . . ." he says, looking straight ahead at the road. He drums his fingers on the steering wheel in beat with a made-up rhythm.

"Yeah, and that ended well. How did you know I was pissed at him when we slept together?" I ask him, remembering the comment he made about wanting a taste of wild.

"My mom has started calling me" is all he says. His mom is a gossip. I'd always known that. "She said Eric was upset."

I scoff. "I'll bet. Eric and I were just together because it was convenient. I guess he just realized it before me, since he started screwing around."

"And I'm sure he'll regret it when he realizes what a great woman he lost," he says simply. "But it's too late for him. You never should have been with him anyway."

"Does he know?" I ask, wringing my hands.

"Yeah, I told him. I also told him to leave you the hell alone. I got you the new phone too; it has my number programmed. And all the brothers' too. Just in case."

"God, you're bossy."

"You love it," he replies. "I probably should warn you."

"What?" I ask warily, my head snapping to him.

"Brothers are having a party tonight," he says, looking at me with a grin.

"How is that different from every other night?" I ask, thinking about how they all hang out, drink, and hook up every night.

"Doesn't matter; you and I are staying in the room. I bought a few things for us to check out," he says.

"Like what?" I ask, getting excited.

"Be patient."

"I don't want to be patient. I want to know," I grumble.

"Too bad." He smirks.

"Fine. Oh, and one more thing, Dex," I say.

"What's that?" he asks.

"Talk to me again like you did last night, and I'm gone," I whisper, then turn my head to look at him.

He nods once, slowly. His eyes harden at my threat, but he manages to hide his anger. "I lose my temper sometimes, but I'll always make it up to you."

"Is that your apology?" I ask. It might need a little work. I tell him so.

He grins and says, "I guess it was."

I sigh. "We need to communicate better. I don't want to be one of those couples always fighting in front of their kids."

"We won't be. And kids? You already planning for more?" he teases.

I purse my lips. "You know what I mean."

"No, I don't; please enlighten me."

"I'm hungry," I say.

"I'll accept that change of subject," he replies, flashing me a wolfish grin.

"Good. Now, take me home and feed me," I demand, smiling.

He laughs and, for once, does as he's told.

FOURTEEN

W HEN Dex and I walk back into the clubhouse, there are people everywhere. He wasn't joking about the party. The place is filled with new faces—bikers I haven't seen before, who Dex explains are Wind Dragons from other chapters. He stops to greet a tall, burly-looking man.

"Long time no see," the man says, slapping Dex on the shoulder.

"I know; how you been?" Dex asks him.

"All good," the man replies, staring at a woman who walks by.

Dex laughs. "You enjoy yourself, you hear?"

"This city has so many beautiful fuckin' women it's not even funny. You not sticking around?" the man asks, looking down at me as if finally noticing me. "Maybe we could share this fine little thing."

He licks his lips and eyes me from head to toe, his gaze lingering on my hips and breasts.

I manage to stop myself from cringing, or from replying with a sarcastic or rude comment. Instead, my expression remains impassive as if this man isn't looking at me like he wants to eat me. I should start playing poker, because I really liked this new control I had over what I showed on my face.

Dex stiffens, slowly pulling me closer to him. "No can do, bro, she's mine, and there's no way in hell I'm going to be sharing."

The man doesn't look pleased. "When you come my way, I let you have any bitch you want."

My poker face was being tested to my newly found limits. *Any bitch he wants?*

Dex nods slowly, his eyes flashing with warning. "This one's different. No disrespect, but no one touches her but me. Any other woman would be a different story."

"Your possessiveness intrigues me even more," the man replies, licking his lips once again.

Dex's fingers tighten on my waist. "This is a party. It would be a shame if it had to turn into something else, don't you think?"

That was a threat, plain and clear, and the man knows it.

I was pregnant and he still wanted me? I put my hands on my stomach, and he follows the motion.

"I see," he murmurs, nodding stiffly in acceptance. "Luckily this place is swarming with beautiful, eager women."

"I'm sure they'll show you a good time," Dex replies, nodding his head, then moving me forward to leave.

I keep my mouth shut, knowing this is not the time to speak, but I'll admit it was hard. They did just have a conversation in front of me, about me, or rather about "sharing" me. The feminist in me is dying to kick up a fuss, but I know it won't change anything, other than get Dex into another fight.

I look around and notice that the place *is* swarming with beautiful women, and I don't miss the looks they shoot Dex. My fist clenches as I see one in particular, staring at him as though she's already had him. When Dex steers me away from her, I assume she has.

"Who is that?" I ask, my eyes narrowed to slits.

"No one," he instantly replies, not looking at me.

"Who is she, Dex?" I ask again. "Why is she staring at you and why are you avoiding her?"

"She's no one," he repeats.

I'll bet.

Before we can walk down the hall that leads to our room, a stunning redhead stops in front of Dex and puts her hand on his chest.

Oh, hell no!

I move to take a step forward, but Dex pulls me to his side, hand in mine.

"Sin, long time no see," she purrs.

Dex pushes her hand off, which I appreciate. "Not interested."

"That's not what you said last time," she replies, sinking her teeth into her lower lip. She has wide green eyes and hardly any clothes on. I can't even lie—she's a knockout. If I swung that way. . . .

"It's what I'm saying now. Now, get the fuck out of my way," he says in a voice so cold, even I cringe.

"You've never turned me down before," she says, now frowning and finally looking to me. "Sin . . ."

"He said no. Have some fucking self-respect," I say before she can start begging.

She opens her mouth to say something when Dex pulls my hand and walks around her, leaving her standing there with her mouth hanging open. He locks the door behind us as we enter the room and puts all the shopping bags on the bed.

"Well, that was interesting," I say slowly. "An old friend of yours?"

"Babe" is all he says.

Like that's an answer!

"An ex?" I pry, trying to get some information.

"Just someone I've fucked," he says, looking up at the ceiling. "Is this the part where you get angry and jealous and ignore me for the rest of the night?"

I smirk. "I can't say I'm happy I have to keep seeing women you've been with, but I wouldn't go that far. You handled her well enough that I don't need to get angry."

I don't address the jealousy part, because, well, I *was* jealous. Nothing I couldn't handle though.

"And who was that man?" I ask when he doesn't say any more on the subject.

Dex grins. "Good thing he backed down, or we would have had a huge fuckin' problem. And you stayed quiet; good girl."

"I'm learning," I say dryly. "At least with the men. Although I'm not going to lie, it was extremely hard not to say anything."

He laughs at me. "You did well. Although if he kept staring at you like that, I was going to take him out just for the sake of it."

I roll my eyes, secretly feeling pleased. "He was a little pervy, wasn't he?"

"A little? He was fuckin' drooling."

I grin. "He was, wasn't he?"

He grunts. "Maybe I should take you through the back entrance next time there's a party going on here."

I smile at that, shaking my head. "I don't think that's necessary. So what did you want to show me?" I ask, sliding my shoes off and sitting on the bed.

"Oh, right," he says, opening a drawer and pulling out four books.

"Books?" I ask, my eyebrows reaching my hairline.

He sits down next to me on the bed and spreads them out. Two are baby-name books, one is a book about pregnancy, and the other is about labor. My throat starts to burn at the thoughtful gesture and the proof that he's serious about this. "This is really nice of you."

He shrugs it off. "I want to be prepared. Soon we can move into my house, and the baby will have his own room we can fix up."

"Your house?" I ask, feeling confused.

He winces. "I have a house, babe. It's getting renovated right now. It will be ready in a month. I don't expect you to stay here forever, especially not with the little one."

I blink. "You have a house, and you haven't mentioned it before? Isn't that a little weird?"

He looks down. "What's the point? Not like we can live there now anyway."

I guess, but still.

"How long have you owned it for?" I find myself asking.

"A couple of years."

The atmosphere in the room changes slightly as I question him, so I decide to change the subject by opening one of the baby books and browsing it. "I like this name."

"What is it?" he asks, sounding relieved that my questioning is over. Interesting.

I point to the name and show it to him.

"Gertrude?" he asks, snatching the book from me. "Nice try, Faye."

I giggle. "Fine, what names do you like? Since you've now said no to Sirius and Gertrude, which were both excellent ideas, I might add."

"Maybe we should make a list," he surmises.

"I'll find out the sex at the appointment on Thursday," I tell him, lying back on the bed.

"Really?" he asks. "I think it's going to be a boy."

"Think you're that lucky, do you?" I smirk.

"Well, if I have a girl who looks as gorgeous as you, I'm going to be screwed."

I blush, looking away from his intense gaze.

"Can I?" he asks, touching the hem of my top.

"Yeah," I whisper as he lifts up my top and runs his hands over my rounded belly. When he places a kiss right below my belly button, I stop breathing.

"I'm gonna see you soon, little one," he murmurs to my stomach, placing one more kiss before pulling my top back down. I look away so he doesn't see the tears gathering in my eyes.

He clears this throat. "I got us *Supernatural* to watch."

I love *Supernatural*. "How did you know?"

He shakes his head in amusement. "Your phone background."

A practically naked Jensen Ackles. Right, that would do it. "Of course."

He puts the DVD on and turns the volume up high to block out the music from the other side of the house.

"So tell me the deal with the redhead, and the other woman you were avoiding tonight," I find the courage to ask.

He shrugs and licks his bottom lip. "They're around at parties, or at the clubhouse when we want women."

I really don't think that's an answer. "No emotional connection?"

"You always this nosy?" he asks, sighing.

"Yes," I reply honestly.

"I thought so," he replies, his tone of voice letting me know that he's amused rather than annoyed. Eric used to always get annoyed with me when I asked questions, which now makes sense, because he had a whole lot to hide. Dex, on the other hand, is rather patient with me, which I appreciate. "And to answer your question, it sounds bad, but no, there aren't any emotional connections with them, or with any other women. It was just sex. They knew it, and I knew it."

I like the fact that he used past tense. I really do.

"Good," I reply, trying not to sound happy and failing. I wince when I realize I'm acting like a jealous girlfriend would, or a wife, when in reality, I was neither of those. Yet, at least.

His deep chuckle fills the room. "Come here, babe."

I slide over to him and rest my head on his chest. His fingers gently comb through my hair, and he kisses the top of my head. "Do you care that you're missing the party?"

"No, not at all. That's been my life for years; I'm ready to move on to something else now, something better. A new chapter. That's not to say we can't go out and have some fun though," he replies after a moment.

Feeling bold, my arm reaches out and over his hard abs. I risk a glance at him to see him watching me, amusement glistening in his eyes.

"That was a pretty smooth move there, Faye," he teases, and I hide my face in his shirt.

"It's not my fault. You're hot," I grumble, breathing him in.

"I thought I was a jerk," he replies, stroking my hair once more.

"You're a hot jerk."

His chest shakes under my head. "You're making my pillow shake!"

"Your pillow is my chest," he decides to point out.

"Exactly," I huff, lifting my head up and staring at him. God, his face is so close to mine. If I leaned a little closer, my lips would be on his.

"Don't look at me like that," he growls, hand cupping my jaw.

"Like what?" I ask breathlessly.

"Like you want me more than anything else in the world," he says, his eyes on my lips.

"Right now I do," I say, slightly leaning forward until our lips touch.

Hell, I always did, whether I was angry with him or not.

We stare at each other for a few tense seconds.

"Fuck it," he says, capturing my lips with his. He licks at my mouth until I open for him, then he delves inside—tasting me.

Owning me.

The kiss is possessive, filled with raging want and need. All rational thought disappears, and there is no one else in the world besides the two of us.

I want Dex, and he wants me.

It's simple. Basic.

And the only thing that matters.

He sucks on my bottom lip, then moves his tongue inside my mouth, tasting me. Moaning, I run my tongue along his, loving the taste of him. He then pulls away to trail openmouthed kisses down my jawline and my neck. Rolling me over onto my back he lifts up my top over my bra, kissing my stomach. Pushing up the cups of my bra, he licks around my breasts, teasing me. My breasts are so sensitive, and I'm thankful that he's gentle with them, licking and sucking and taking his own cool time. After a few more moments' torture he finally pays attention to my nipples, his tongue darting around and over them. He pulls back to tug down my shorts, ogling my red boyshorts in appreciation for a second before he wrenches them down as well. He spreads my legs and kisses around my inner thighs, nibbling and scraping his teeth along them before his mouth finds my center.

Pure heaven.

"Dex," I moan as his tongue hits the spot. My hands tangle in my hair as my head tilts back against the pillow. His tongue is magic and is giving me just what I need, swirling around my clit, then darting lower and inside me. A curse leaves my lips, and my thighs quiver as he inserts a finger and sucks down on my clit at the same time, pushing me over the edge.

I scream his name as I'm lost in the throes of pleasure, wave after wave breaking over me. He doesn't remove his mouth, prolonging my release. It's not long before I'm begging him to stop, feeling too sensitive. He gives me one last lick before he pulls back, staring at me with a possessive look on his handsome face, a devilish gleam in his heavy-lidded blue eyes. He continues to watch as I try to regain my breath. I reach for him but he shakes his head slightly.

"What's wrong?" I ask, sitting up.

"Nothing, babe. It was just for you," he says, lying back down next to me. *It was just for me?*

"What about you?" I ask him, staring down at the hardness straining against his jeans.

"Shh," he says, pulling me into his arms.

"Dex . . ."

"Babe, I just wanted to take care of you; I don't expect anything in return," he says in a deep rumble.

I lie there feeling confused. And a little rejected. Did he just reject me?

"Did you just reject me?" I ask, voicing my concern.

He sighs heavily. "No, sweetheart, I did not reject you. We will talk more about this tomorrow, okay? Let's just enjoy tonight."

I don't understand, but I let it go.

I try to dampen my disappointment, but he can explain tomorrow, if that's what he wants.

Feeling sated, I snuggle into him and fall asleep.

FIFTEEN

WAKE up in the middle of the night needing to pee. After finishing my business, I hear something. I look at Dex, who is fast asleep on his stomach, and then eye the door. I quickly get dressed and go to investigate. A woman calls out Sin's name again, and curiosity gets the better of me.

Who is calling out his name?

Was it the redhead, or the other woman who was trying to get his attention at the party?

I open the door and head toward the voices out the front of the clubhouse.

"Sin!" the woman screams. I peer outside through the window.

"Shut the fuck up!" a man growls. The man is Arrow. His back is to me, but it's definitely him. The woman, a curvy blonde, says something to him. Arrow pushes her backward, with a hand to her chest. She staggers and trips over, falling to the floor. Irish, Trace, and Rake are standing by but don't do anything.

They just watch.

What the fuck?

I walk to the entry and slam the door open as I run out. "What the fuck, Arrow!" I yell, bending down to see if the woman is okay.

"Fuck," Arrow says when he lays his eyes on me. "Go inside, Faye. Now!"

I'd never heard that tone from him before, and I didn't fucking appreciate it.

"Fuck you!" the woman yells out. I think she's talking to Arrow, but then I realize she's talking to me.

What the fuck did I do?

"What?" I growl, getting pissed. "You better not be fucking talking to me!"

"You! You fucking bitch!" she squeals, pointing at me.

Okay, so she is talking to me.

Rake walks over to me and pulls me into his hard body. "Darlin', go inside, yeah?" he says, ushering me toward the door.

"Who the hell is that?" I ask Rake, my voice filled with confusion and anger. "And why is she pissed at me?"

"Ahh, babe," he says, giving me a look filled with pity. Pity?

"Don't look at me like that!" I snap, pushing away from him.

"Like what?"

"Like you feel fucking sorry for me! Who is that woman, and why does she hate me?" I ask him. Rake looks behind me, and I know Dex is standing there.

"Come here," he demands, his mouth tight. I walk to him, but only because I want answers.

And I'm going to get them.

"Who is that?" I ask him. He ignores me, lifting me in his arms and carrying me back to the room.

"You can't just stay in bed, can you?" he mutters as he puts me down.

"Dex!"

"It's not what you think," he says, running a hand down his face.

"You don't even know what I'm thinking right now," I snap.

"Don't be angry, Faye, all right? Can you just hear me out before you jump to any conclusions?"

I nod my head, a sharp angry movement.

"This is the reason I couldn't exactly give you any promises . . . just yet," he says, grimacing at his own words.

"Explain," I demand.

"She's my soon-to-be ex-wife," he says, slowly taking a step closer to me.

I stop breathing.

"You have a wife?" I say softly, not quite understanding what the hell was going on right now.

"No, babe, I *had* a wife. We're separated and getting a divorce," he says, studying my expression.

A wife? A fucking wife.

"Oh my god," I say to myself. "I'm a fucking home wrecker! No wonder she hates me! I fucked her husband!"

"You aren't a home wrecker. We were separated *before* you and I hooked up," he explains, his hands making a calm-down gesture.

"You made me a home wrecker, you asshole!" I yell, ignoring him.

My mind races.

"Why did Arrow push her?" I ask. "Is this how you treat your women?"

Now he looks angry. Eyes narrowed, he says, "Have I ever treated you badly?"

"I guess not," I say with a shrug.

His eyes narrow further. "She was under my protection. Now she's not. She's nothing to us now. I told you, we're not all good guys, babe."

But Arrow? He was growing on me. A lot.

"Why was she here?" I ask, my voice smaller.

"She doesn't seem to understand the concept of us breaking up. I can't even get her to move out of my fuckin' house. I've given her a couple of weeks to find a new place," he admits, running his fingers through his messy dark hair.

I gape. "That was your renovation? Your wife?"

"I couldn't exactly tell you that my ex was living there and I was waiting for her to get her ass out of there, could I?"

"Not without sounding like an asshole," I say, staring daggers at him.

"Exactly," he says. "I didn't wanna scare you off before you were even mine."

That shuts me up. For a few seconds anyway.

"I'm not moving into that house," I say, crossing my arms over my chest.

"Fine, I'll buy you a new house," he says, throwing his hands in the air.

"I can't believe this shit," I growl. "You have a wife. A wife. Oh my god, how did I not know this?"

"I'm sorry! I wasn't planning on you and our baby coming into my life. That's not to say I'm not happy you're both here, because I am. But cut me some slack, babe, I'm trying to make things right. I just needed a few weeks, that's all, then she would be out, and we could move on. Start our life together."

"That's why you were trying to put some distance between us? Until everything was sorted out?" I ask, trying to understand.

He nods. "I wanted to do something right for once. I wanted the divorce to be finalized. I wanted us to get to know each other in the meantime. Build a friendship before we build a relationship. Set the groundwork for a relationship that will last. I want this with you, Faye."

I purse my lips together. "So you want points for good intentions?"

"Faye," he says in warning. His patience is waning, but too damn bad for him.

"Why don't you go home to your *wife*?" I say, emphasizing the word.

"Have you not been listening to anything I've said?" he says, starting to pace up and down the room. I wouldn't be surprised if there are going to be holes in the carpet soon.

"I have been listening," I snap. Well, sort of. "I need some time to process this."

"What the fuck does that mean?" he growls, stopping in his tracks.

"It means I'm going to bed, and you're not sleeping here for the rest of the night," I find myself saying. "You should have been honest with me, Dex."

He stands there unmoving. "You know what, fine. I tried to do the right thing with you. I haven't been with anyone else; I haven't even looked at anyone else! I was going to get the hell away from Renee before I got in deep with you, then commit to you. If that's not good enough, then I don't know what else I can do," he says, walking out and closing the door behind him. It doesn't slam, but the sound of it closing still makes me flinch.

I climb back into bed and think over everything. I hate the fact he was married to that woman. Is that his type? I try not to be judgmental and fail. I'm sure there is judgment written all over my face right now. At least they had separated before the night I spent with him. Am I still the "other woman"? I'm way too young for all this shit. I take a deep breath and put my hand on my tummy.

"It's going to be okay, little one," I whisper.

I didn't think being with Dex was going to be easy, but I thought it was going to be worth it.

But how much more of this could I take?

I try my hardest, but sleep doesn't come.

SIXTEEN

ALL conversation stops as I enter the kitchen. Tracker, who is sporting a black eye and a cut lip, stares at me intently. Arrow scowls, and Rake grins. Trace, Irish, and Jim stare at me impassively. I pour myself some juice and take a seat. It's then I realize something.

"Ummm where are the women?" I ask, looking around.

"The women who know their place leave when the men are having a discussion," Jim says, looking less than impressed with me.

I want to say something smart, but instead I keep my mouth shut. Even I know pissing off Jim will not go down well. I bite my lip and sip on my juice.

"Well. I'll just be going then . . ." I say into the awkward silence.

Jim sighs. He looks tired. "Are you okay?" I can't help but ask.

"Give us a moment," he says, and all the men stand up. Tracker is the last to leave, his eyes never leaving me until they have to.

"I'm getting old," he says.

"You're what, in your late thirties?" I ask, staring at his ripped biceps.

His laugh sounds like it's been honed by years of smoking. "Add a decade onto that, little girl."

"Awkward," I mutter. He's old enough to be my dad.

"It's Sin's turn to take the gavel, except he's a little preoccupied right now," he says, raising his eyebrow at me.

"You're not going to kill me, are you?" I ask, laughing a little nervously.

Jim grins. "I can see why he's so taken with you."

"Yeah, because I'm a trophy compared to his ex-wife," I blurt out. My hands cover my mouth as Jim laughs harder.

"You remind me of Cindy at your age," he muses, smiling fondly. "Woman was full of sass."

She still is, from what I'd heard from Jessica.

"Look, Faye, the truth is my health isn't what it used to be," he says, looking unhappy to admit it.

"And you need Sin to be on his game," I surmise.

"Right."

"Is it possible to be a family man and the president of an MC?" I ask him, looking deep into his eyes.

"It's not easy, and it's not always safe, but yes. It is possible. And no man will take better care of his family than Sin."

"That I believe," I reply. "Any idea where he is?"

"He went for a ride," he replies. "We'll be joining him. Be back in two days."

"What's the deal with the wife?" I can't stop myself from asking.

"She cheated on him; they broke up when he found out," he says, casually lighting a cigarette. "They were only married a year."

I hate that he loved someone else enough to marry her. I realize I'd said that out loud when Jim replies, "She's got nothing on you, darlin'. I've seen how he looks at you."

"Like how?" I ask.

"Fishing for compliments, eh? Like he's dying of thirst and you're an ice-cold beer."

I'm pretty sure that's not how the saying goes, but I appreciate the sentiment all the same.

"So," I ask. "What's the deal with the other MC you're having issues with?"

His mouth tightens around his cigarette. "Negotiations with another MC." He pauses. "Women don't get involved with club business, Faye. You seem like a girl who thinks she's the exception to every rule, but not this time."

I hate that he has me pegged.

"You said that in the future I'm going to be the club's lawyer," I blurt out. "I'm not just another woman. I can help, you know. I know that when you spoke to me about helping the club you weren't a hundred percent serious, but now that the idea is out there, I am."

He studies me under a new light. "Then that's different, I guess. But you'd still be on a need-to-know basis."

"So I guess I'll never be getting my own cut, then," I sigh, thinking about my conversation with Vinnie. Jim laughs again, then starts coughing.

"That doesn't sound good."

He glances up and looks at me, his eyes flashing. "It's not going to be long."

"For what?" I ask.

"I have lung cancer, Faye. Everyone knows it, but no one is talking about it. It's like the fuckin' huge-ass elephant in the room. But ignoring it isn't making it go away. I have to make sure the club is set for when my time comes to leave."

My eyes flare. "You're dying?"

A ghost of a smile plays on his lips. "Tactful girl, aren't ya?"

I cringe, rubbing my hands together. "I'm sure you'd prefer that over sympathy."

He nods once, a sharp movement. "Damn right. Don't need no fuckin' pity."

He starts coughing again, louder this time. Chestier.

My brows furrow, wanting to help but not knowing what I could possibly do. "Anything I can get you?"

"A new set of lungs?" he replies, smirking at me.

"How about some water?" I offer instead. He nods, so I pour him a glass of iced water. Placing it in front of him, he takes a sip, then resumes smoking. I want to point out he should probably quit, but instead I stand up.

"I'm going to do some assignments," I tell him. "Hope you feel better, Jimbo."

His rumbly laugh follows me to my room.

≈

I save my work and close my laptop the moment I hear the rumble of motorcycles. Is one of them Dex?

Only one way to find out.

I glance at my phone to check the time: 5:00 p.m. He's been gone for two days, and I've missed him like crazy. Mary's been cooking for me—apparently Dex had called her and told her to look after me. I was a little annoyed, but I thought it was cute too. Even angry, he was still keeping an eye out for me, caring for me. We had a healthy lunch yesterday and chatted for a while before she got called into work to treat an injured dog. Then I cleaned the kitchen, the living areas, my room, and the bathroom. Like spring cleaning. You could now eat off the floor, it was that clean. When I tried to clean up Jim's office, Cindy yelled at me. That woman is scary. So I snuck into Arrow's room and cleaned his instead. It took the longest—the man lives like a pig. The pregnancy book mentioned something about nesting, but I didn't think that was supposed to happen so early. I make my way to the front door and stand there, watching Dex sliding off his bike. Dressed in his cut, he looks amazing. Arrow and Tracker stand next to him, chatting, until they spot me. Arrow nudges Dex, who turns to look at me, then makes his way over in long strides.

"Everything okay?" he asks when he reaches me. I jump onto him, latching my arms around his neck.

"I missed you," I say, catching him off guard with my open-mouthed kiss. His hands grip my ass, holding me up. I hear the others whistling and catcalling, and I smile against his lips as I pull away.

"Weren't we fighting?" he asks, breathless.

I run my hands through his thick head of hair, slightly tugging on the ends. "I thought it over. Yes, you lied, but you also tried to do the right thing. Next time, I want honesty, Dex, do you hear me?"

He nuzzles my neck. "I hear you, Faye, even better, I feel you. Fuck, this feels good."

"I think you're worth the risk, Dexter Black," I whisper into his ear. "I want you."

He curses again and carries me into our room, ignoring the leers from the others. Laying me back on the fresh white sheets, he pulls down my jeans and panties, then sits me up and removes my top and bra. I lie there bare, while he stands before me completely dressed.

I feel a little shy, but the look in his eyes stops me from covering myself.

He likes what he sees—lust claiming his expression. His eyes are dark with need, his teeth sinking into his bottom lip as he rakes his gaze over me.

"This is all mine?" he finally asks in a deep rumble. His voice alone sends shivers up my spine, tingles throughout my body. Yes, this was his. I was his, and I think I'd always been his.

"If you want it," I reply, arching my back a little.

"You know I do," he growls now, pulling off his cut, T-shirt, and then his jeans. In nothing but his boxer shorts, I can see how much he wants me, how turned on he is from here. I can picture what his cock looks like in my head, and there's nothing I want more than to see it again. To taste it. To tame it.

"When you look at me like that," he groans, his heavy-lidded gaze not leaving me as he slides down his boxer shorts.

"I'll be gentle," he says, rubbing his hand on my tummy. He braces himself over me, and I pull him down against my body. I sigh at the skin-on-skin contact, and he catches my mouth in a hungry kiss. He tastes like mint and smells like leather, and I can't get enough of him. Digging my fingers into his back, I move my lips down his neck. He suddenly rolls us over so I'm straddling him, then lifts his head and pays attention to my breasts with his mouth. When I can't take any more, I take him in my hand and guide him into my body. We moan simultaneously as he fills me up, stretching me deliciously. I grind on him in smooth strokes, lifting and lowering my hips. He thrusts his hips up in rhythm, his finger finding my sweet spot and circling.

Slowly.

Heaven on earth.

"Come for me," he growls, his eyes dark.

Two more strokes and my body obeys. Staring straight into his eyes, I let him see what he does to me. The effect he has on me. I mouth his name as the pleasure hits, enjoying the look on his face when he follows me into oblivion. I collapse onto his chest, sighing in contentment. As the haze lifts, I try to hop off him, but he holds me in place.

"You're something else, you know that?" he says when I've caught my breath.

"Want to go again?" I ask, smiling with my eyes closed.

"Death by fairy," he says, causing me to laugh. "First I need to feed my baby mama."

I slap at his chest playfully. "I'd rather you call me fairy than baby mama."

"Baby mama it is," he says, running his finger over my nipple.

"Hey! Hands off; don't be a tease," I say with mock sternness.

He groans. "You stay here, I'll bring you something to eat. Then I'll show you the meaning of the word *tease*."

"Sounds good," I reply, unable to stop myself from smiling.

Dex looks around the room. "Did you clean the room?"

I hear Arrow yelling, asking who has been in his room.

I hide under the covers.

SEVENTEEN

I SIT in the waiting room, nervously tapping my foot. Today we're getting the scan to make sure everything looks good with the baby. We can also find out the sex if we choose to. Dex holds my hands, sitting beside me patiently. I lean into his warmth, laying my head on his shoulder.

"Faye," my doctor calls out, smiling at me warmly.

"Hey, Doc," I say as I walk into the room.

"How have you been?" he asks, pushing a pair of reading glasses on his nose.

"Good, thanks. This is Dex," I say. They shake hands, then we get down to business. The doctor weighs me and makes me pee in a cup. When all looks well, we have a chat, and then he sends me to another room for the sonogram. I lie on my back as a technician applies cold gel to my stomach. Dex stands by my side, supporting me as much as he can. I appreciate his efforts. I stare at the screen, trying to make sense of it but seeing nothing but a blob.

"Everything looks great," the lady says. "Do you want to find out the gender?"

I look at Dex. "Yes, please."

"It looks like you're having . . . a baby girl! Congratulations."

"Fuck," Dex mutters, but smiles while he says it. I squeeze his fingers, emotion consuming me. I'm going to have a little girl. I try to picture what she might look like—dark-haired like her father? Will she have my eyes? Dex leans down and whispers in my ear, "She isn't dating until she's twenty-one."

"Well, with you and the rest of the MC, I don't think she stands a chance," I say. "All the boys will be too scared to even look her way."

"And with good reason," he says, sounding smug.

"I don't know; you're going to be an old man by then," I tease as he wipes the gel off with a paper towel and helps me up. We thank the lady and head home.

Home.

Is it becoming my home?

Staring down at my phone, I walk into the living area and come to a standstill as I survey the room. Dex is sitting in the single recliner, while two club members stand on each side of him, Arrow and Rake on one, Tracker and Irish on the other. My eyes turning to slits, I look at each of their faces in confusion.

"Faye, we have something we'd like to discuss with you," Dex says, gesturing for me to take a seat on the chair in front of him. Way to make me feel small. I take two steps toward them, curious as hell, when it hit me just what this is.

It's a fucking intervention.

What could I possibly need one for? I rack my brain to think of what they could have to say to me and come up empty.

I sit down in the middle, facing my man. He's trying to keep a straight face, but his crinkling eyes are a dead giveaway.

"Is this an intervention?" I ask him, sitting with perfect posture and my chin lifted.

A lip twitch. "I guess you could call it that."

Smiles all around.

"And what is it regarding, exactly?" I ask, putting my lawyer face on.

Dex manages to keep a straight face. "Arrow, would you like to begin?"

I turn to Arrow, my face daring him to say something.

"When you cleaned my room, it felt like an invasion of my privacy," he says, causing the men to all laugh.

I gape. "I was doing you a favor!"

"You picked my lock and snuck into my room to do it!" Irish calls out.

I cringe. "Well, when you put it like that . . ."

I look at Tracker, who is staring down at me like I'm the most adorable thing he's ever seen. "I haven't even made it to your room yet," I say, wondering why he's here.

He grins wolfishly. "I know; I'm here for a different reason, to ask why I've been singled out."

"Discrimination!" Arrow yells out.

I rub my palm down my face. "Fine, I'll tone down the cleaning, but you," I say pointing at Dex, "can't stop me from doing our room."

More laughter at my choice of words.

He puts his hands up. "I didn't complain, I just have these assholes on my back all the time."

"And you," I say, pointing to Tracker, "I'll be visiting your room later today."

Tracker gets a warning glance from Dex that I don't miss. I roll my eyes.

"Am I done here?" I ask, standing up and feeling amused. These big, bad bikers—if only other people could see the side of them that I get to see on a daily basis.

Pussycats, the lot of them.

"Whose idea was this, by the way?" I ask them.

"It was a club decision," Dex replies, smirking. He's wearing a skintight white T-shirt today that looks delicious on him, showcasing his powerful chest and broad shoulders. I lick my lips. His eyes follow the motion.

"You want something, babe?" he asks, voice lowering.

I purposely lower my gaze to the crotch of his black jeans. "I think you know what I want."

"Ew," Arrow says, standing up to leave the room. "This is like watching my sister."

Dex, who still has his eyes on me, stalks forward until he's close enough that I can almost touch him. My breath hitches as his lips touch my ear and say, "Meet me in the room and be naked."

"And if I don't?" I ask, baiting him.

His eyes darken. "Try it and see."

I sink my teeth into my bottom lip. "I'll do it if I feel like it."

Now he chuckles. "You always feel like it."

I lift my hand to run it along the stubble on his jaw. "Hurry."

Then I turn and head into our room.

≈

How do I get into situations like this? I ask myself the next morning as I stand in the kitchen, clutching my juice like it's a lifeline. When I walked in here five minutes ago, a girl was sitting here in her underwear, drinking coffee. She started talking to me and hasn't stopped. I don't even know her name.

"You don't dress like a biker chick," she says, judgment in her tone. I look down at my jeans and vintage T-shirt and frown. I have no idea what to say to this chick.

"I just dress like I always do," I manage to say, clearing my throat. Am I being judged by a club whore? Well, this is a little awkward.

"So, who were you with?" I ask, wondering who I have to kill for making me have this conversation.

"Oh, Rake," she answers, leaning forward conspiratorially. "He's a beast in the sack."

Awesome.

"Where is Rake now?" I ask her, looking toward the hall that leads to his room.

"Oh, he's in bed with Tiffany," she says casually. "I needed coffee."

Rake. Doesn't take a genius to figure out how he got his name.

I stand. "Well, nice meeting you."

"Oh, where are you going?" she asks.

I blink. "To my room."

"Can I come and hang out? I heard you were the vice president's old lady, be cool if we can hang out," she says, standing up and moving toward me.

Okay, enough is enough.

"Rake!" I yell at the top of my lungs. I turn to the girl and raise my finger in the air. "Please excuse me one moment."

I storm up to his room and open the door. My jaw drops open at the scene before me. "I hope you got her to sign a consent form or a contract or some shit," I say, staring at the two of them. "Fifty shades of Rake!"

"What the fuck, Faye," Rake growls, hiding his package with a pillow. He turns his back to me, giving me a look of the dragon tattoo he has on there, the same one that Dex and the rest of the men have. I take a second to admire it, and then lower my gaze to his taut ass. Not a bad set of buns.

"You forgot one girl out here," I say, widening my eyes, hoping he gets the point. "Please come and collect her."

He turns and sighs, like his life is so tough since he has two women here.

"Yes, I know, Rake," I say dryly, "It's hard out there for a pimp."

He chuckles, slapping the girl on her ass and pulling away. "Maybe you should gag the other one too," I suggest hopefully. Before I back out of the room I look around it, scrunching my nose. "Can I clean your room tonight? It's so messy, it's going to drive me crazy now that I've seen it."

"Fine; anything to make you leave right now," he growls at me.

Whoa, touchy.

You'd think he would be in a better mood after doing two women.

"I'll find some storage for your paddles and whatnot," I say as I walk out. "I might have to do a trip to the Container Store."

Rake follows me out, shaking his head in exasperation, and retrieves the other girl.

"You're lucky I like you, Faye," Rake says to me, his arms full of one very chatty woman.

"You're lucky I like you," I reply, sniffing. "After what I've endured this morning."

He smirks. "Prude."

"Man-whore."

"Preggers."

I put my hands on my hips. "And how is that an insult?"

He shrugs. "You're looking a little wide this morning."

I gasp. "Oh no, you didn't!"

He grins boyishly. "I'm just playing, Faye, you look beautiful. Glowing, even."

"Nice save," I mutter.

"Rake," the woman whines. "Take me to bed and tell me how beautiful I am. Why are you complimenting her?"

Rake smirks, looking up at me. "Why indeed?"

I arch my eyebrow. "Probably because I'm not going to let you tie me up and whip me, but she is."

Dex walks into the kitchen and stares at me, the random chick, and a very naked Rake.

"Do I even want to know?" he asks, narrowing his eyes on me.

Rake groans. "No, brother, I don't think you do."

"I thought so," Dex murmurs. "Please take your naked ass out of the kitchen."

I watch wide-eyed as Rake disappears with the girl, then I go and sit on Dex's lap.

"What was that about?" he asks, looking amused. "Can't take you anywhere, babe."

"Rake forgot one of his girls, and I had to sit here talking to her. It's a few minutes of my life I'm never going to get back. So I went to his room and told him to get her. Apparently he didn't like being interrupted. Did you know he was into some kinky shit?"

His jaw clenches. "Just how much of my brother did you see?"

I shrug, nonplussed. "I saw everything. Him, butt naked. Him, apparently into bondage."

Dex sighs. "Faye—"

"Hey, I'm not going to repeat it to anyone other than you, jeez. Have a little faith in me."

He kisses my lips. "I do have faith in you. You wouldn't be here if I didn't."

"So what time are you leaving today? I thought that maybe we could . . ." I trail off, freezing when I feel a peculiar sensation. Putting Dex's hands on my stomach, I whisper, "Can you feel that?"

I know when he does, because his eyes widen with wonder. "Did she just move?" he asks.

"Yes," I nod, feeling her kick again. I'd felt her before, of course, but nothing like this. Before it was just slight butterflies, but now she's kicking the shit out of me. Dex kisses my stomach, and my heart melts.

"She's going to be a soccer player," he says, chuckling.

I roll my eyes. "Is that so?"

He kisses my cheek. "You know I'm riding out today."

"I know," I sulk. He's going away on "club business" and will be gone a few days. I don't like it, but I don't say anything. This is his life, and I knew what it was about before I agreed to be with him. Our relationship is new, and Dex is going to do what he has to do.

"Vinnie and two other prospects are staying behind to keep an eye on you, and Mary and the other women will be here to keep you company," he says, turning my head to look at him.

"I'll be fine," he says, knowing that I'm worried about him. Whatever business they have, it's not the kind one does in an office.

"If you even *look* at another woman—"

He cuts me off. "Don't threaten me, babe. Besides, my hands are so full with you, trust me, the thought of another woman doesn't even cross my mind."

"Fine, but I don't care who offers you hospitality with their women, you say no. There is no 'what happens on the road stays on the road' with us." I let my expression tell him how serious I am about this.

"Have you been watching *Sons of Anarchy* again?" he asks, his body shaking with laughter. Jerk.

"Maybe," I admit, shrugging sheepishly. What? Jax is hot.

"I'm gonna miss you," he admits, pushing my hair behind my ear. "I'll call and message you when I can."

"Yeah, I know," I sigh. "I'll just do my contract-law assignments."

And try not to fall asleep.

"Don't go anywhere without Vinnie, all right, babe?"

I promise him I won't.

"I gotta get ready to head out," he says, standing with me in his arms. Fuck, he's strong.

"What? I don't get good-bye sex?" I ask, pouting.

"Wasn't that what we had an hour ago?"

"No, that was morning sex," I say, nodding sagely.

"Can't leave my woman wanting, can I now?" he says.

He carries me into the room and slams the door behind him, then throws me onto the bed.

"Naked, now," he demands as he undoes his jeans and pulls them down. "This is gonna be hard and quick, babe."

"I like hard," I whisper, making him grin.

"I know you do," he replies, watching me bare my body to him. "Beautiful. I don't think I'll ever get sick of seeing your beautiful body, Faye."

"Good," I reply. "Now, stop staring and fuck me."

He smirks and says, "You don't get to make demands here, babe," but then gets onto the bed and does exactly what I'd asked him to do.

He stops talking, and uses his mouth for something a lot more fun.

And he fucks me, quickly, hard, deliciously.

And thoroughly.

He leaves me sated and smiling.

EIGHTEEN

CALL my parents, but they just hang up on me. I stare at the phone for about twenty minutes, wondering what kind of shit people they are. So I got pregnant? I don't really see that as a reason to cut me out, more like a reason to support me when I'm clearly vulnerable. I try to ignore the hurt, but it's hard. They were far from perfect parents, but surely they had to care about me just a little? I shouldn't be surprised. I wasn't when they kicked me out, but as a mother-to-be I guess I can't understand cutting your child out of your life without so much as a backward glance.

I send Vinnie a text message asking if he could take me to run some errands. He replies instantly, telling me he will be ready in five minutes. I get ready, dressing in a yellow baby-doll dress and putting my hair up in a high ponytail. My hair is long and wavy and can be difficult to handle. Sometimes it needs to be beaten into submission, but it actually looks good today. I want to look nice and feel even better after that call with my parents and Dex's absence.

I'm determined to make today a good one.

My phone beeps with a new message.

Dex: Stick with Vinnie today, babe. Want you safe.

There needs to be an acronym for rolling my eyes. Maybe I could start one? RME?

Faye: RME! We will be fine. Come home safe, don't worry
        about me.
Dex: Not possible.
Dex: WTF is RME?!

I start to giggle.

Faye: Rolling my eyes.
Dex: Babe.
Faye: What?
Dex: Be good.
Faye: I'm always good.
Dex: That's what I'm worried about. Heading out.
Faye: Love you.

I click SEND and then realize what the fuck I just said. It came so naturally I didn't even think. So much for a good day. I spend the next few hours at the library, stressing over how Dex would take that message. He didn't reply. He didn't call. And now I'm freaked right out.

What if I've scared him off? What if he doesn't feel the same?

I'm such an idiot. I told him I loved him for the first time via text message.

Who does that?

High school kids or cowards, maybe. I'm neither, but what I am is pretty damn embarrassed.

Vinnie and I get ice cream together, which is becoming routine for us. Every time he's sent out to watch over me, we end up there, trying a different flavor each time.

"How's the toffee?" I ask him, coveting his ice cream.

"Really good. How's the strawberry?" he asks, taking a bite out of his cone.

"It's okay," I say, still staring at his.

He laughs knowingly. "I'll get you a toffee one if you want."

"Can't I just have a bite of yours?" I ask, eyeing the delicious treat.

He sighs and puts it in front of my mouth, within biting distance. I take a bite of it with my teeth, because it's weird to lick someone else's ice cream. Biting is okay though; well, at least in my book it is.

"Delicious," I murmur, licking my lips.

He grins. "Do you want it?"

"That's okay, I'll get one next time," I say. "So what's new with you?"

"Nothing much. My dad wants to see me," he replies, cringing.

"That bad?" I ask.

He lifts his shoulder in a shrug, and licks at his ice cream. "Let's just say I found out some information recently, and he's the last person I want to be around."

Dex said Vinnie's father was someone famous. I'd asked him who, but he wouldn't tell me. I didn't know if it was a secret or if maybe Vinnie just didn't want people to know. Either way, as much as I wanted to find out, I didn't ask Dex again. I thought about asking Vinnie, but if he wanted to tell me, then he would. Vinnie looks in a shittier mood than he was before, so I decide to change the subject.

"I had a productive morning. I made up an acronym. RME . . . rolling my eyes!"

Vinnie stares. "That already is one; you didn't know that?"

"No," I sulk. "How did you know?"

So much for that. No one has ever said it to me before—just saying.

"You're so fuckin' weird sometimes," he muses, looking back to his ice cream.

"Is that bad?" I ask, my gaze darting to the door as someone enters.

My eyes widen when I see Eric standing there with a girl. His date, maybe? Shit, this is awkward. He sees me, looking surprised, but instantly walks over, taking in my appearance.

"Hey, Eric, how have you been?" I ask. Then, feeling rude, I say, "This is Vinnie. Vinnie, this is Eric."

Eric nods his head at Vinnie, who—looking completely un-impressed—responds with neither word nor gesture.

"I've been okay, trying to call you. Did you get a new num-ber or something?" he asks, the girl with him standing by awk-wardly.

"I did," I reply.

"I've been worried about you, Faye. You could have at least called or messaged me yourself," he says, frowning. "We've known each other for years, and, now what, Dex speaks for you?"

"I have no reason to contact you anymore, Eric," I tell him.

"How quickly you change sides," he says, fists clenching. I sigh. "Is that all?"

"What the fuck are you doing to your life?" He sneers, shaking his head. Vinnie stands up at that comment, so I stand as well. "My brother will only bring you down!"

"Let's get out of here, Vin," I say, giving Eric one last look. "Good-bye, Eric."

Once again, I turn my back on him. This time, with no plans to ever see him again.

≈

I pour another round of tequila shots—not that I'm having any. The women decided to have their own party with just us: Mary, Jess, Allie, Cindy, and several other women I hadn't met yet. They've all been doing shots, laughing and dancing, while I've been sipping on water and watching their antics from the safety of the couch. The prospects are all here, keeping an eye on things, and only letting in people who are meant to be here. The main gate is locked, so no one else can enter. Dex hasn't contacted me since I sent "the message," and I really don't know what to think. I know he's spoken to Vinnie, making sure everything is okay, so he's not indisposed and unable to pick up the phone. Will he be awkward with me now? Maybe I've scared him off. Allie sits next to me, making this day even worse.

"What?" I ask her, wanting to get this over with.

"God, you're a bitch," she says with a smirk, downing a shot.

"What do you want, Allie?" I ask, sounding tired. I relax against the couch, turning my body to face her.

"I wanted to apologize," she says. I do a double take. Surely I heard wrong.

"About what?" I ask warily, suspicion lacing my tone.

"Being a bitch, hitting on Dex when I knew he was yours—"

I cut her off. "At least you're honest."

"After he left Renee he just had casual sex, well, with anyone, really," she says, and I cringe.

Just what any woman wants to hear.

"But after he met you . . . Look, Dex never cheated on his wife when they were together, he knows how to be faithful. He's a good man. I knew what we had was casual, but I'd been hoping for more. My dad used to be in the MC, but he died three years back. That's why they let me stay: I'm family even if I'm no one's old lady. I'll always have a home here because of their loyalty to my father."

That actually explains a lot. I feel bad for thinking she was kept around for other reasons. . . .

Less charitable ones.

"Apology accepted," I say hesitantly. I'm not very good at forgiveness—I tend to just cut people out and move on with my life, but Allie lives here, and I can actually see things from her point of view now. I'd fight for Dex too, so I can't really hold that against her.

"And about Tracker . . ." she says, sighing.

Tracker and I have a sort of strained friendship. Sometimes I catch him staring at me like he wants me but knows he can't have me. I never lead him on, and I shouldn't have been mad at him over Allie. I had no right. I saw it as a betrayal, not one as a lover but as a friend. But I was wrong to feel that way.

The way I saw it, he slept with my enemy, and I didn't like it. However, I realize that it might have given him the wrong idea, and that was my fault. Tracker can sleep with whomever he wants, and it's not my place to have any opinion about it. In truth I should have made that clearer, because I really want things to be back to normal. I miss our easy friendship and banter, but I know we'll get it back in time. I think he just wants someone to love him, and be there for him. Not because of who he is, a Wind Dragon's member, but because he's Tracker—an all-around amazing man with a good heart and a lot to offer a woman. Sure, he's got a dark side, they all do, but he'd treat a woman right, I know that.

"Tracker is a good man," I tell her, smiling. She could be so lucky to have him. Especially considering she isn't the easiest of people to be around.

"I like him a lot," she admits, sighing heavily. "He has this piercing . . . and wow."

Really?

"So what's the problem?" I ask. It's a little awkward that we kind of have the same taste in men. If I wasn't head over heels for Dex . . . Yeah I'm not going to go there.

But even I can see that Tracker is a good catch. He's good-looking, caring, and has a sense of humor. And apparently an interesting piercing.

"Usual shit, he doesn't want a commitment," she says, sounding resigned. "No one here sees me as old-lady material."

I want to suggest that maybe she shouldn't get around all the men, then, because I'm pretty sure they don't want an old lady who has been with all the brothers, but I don't.

"Well, hopefully it works out for you two," I say with sincerity.

She gives me an odd look. "Thanks."

Allie gets up and heads out of the room, just as Vinnie walks in and takes her place. "How you doing, Vinnie?" I ask him. I notice him staring where Allie just exited from.

"Allie? Really?" I ask, surprised.

He throws me a look. "She's pretty, that's all."

Yeah, that pretty much sums her up, I joke to myself.

"So when do you patch in?" I ask him, using some of the biker lingo I've been picking up.

"Couple of months, hopefully," he says, smiling.

"You must be excited," I say, leaning over and rubbing his bald head. "You're a good man; you know that, right?"

He's put up with a lot of shit from me and has also been there when I needed it. He didn't have to do any of that, so I appreciate that he did.

"Why are you rubbing my head?" he asks, blinking slowly.

"For good luck," I reply with a cheeky grin.

He laughs. "You're crazy."

"Crazy and tired," I say, yawning. "I'm going to bed."

"I'll be up all night making sure everything's okay," he says, cracking his neck from side to side, causing me to grimace. Ew.

"Are you sure that's necessary?" I ask, frowning.

"Rather be safe than sorry," he says. "With the rest of the men away, I'm not going to take any chances."

"What about Liam and Trev?" I ask, referring to the other two prospects.

"I've been put in charge, not them. No way am I messing

that up," he says. I guess he must be under a lot of pressure to make sure nothing goes wrong.

I kiss him on the cheek. "Good night, then."

"'Night, Faye," he replies, looking down.

Was he feeling shy that I kissed him on the cheek? Grinning to myself, I head to bed.

# NINETEEN

WAKE up to the sound of a scream and then a gunshot. I sit up and listen, confused as to what I am hearing. Is someone in the clubhouse? What is going on? I rush out of bed and hide in the corner of the dark room, behind the cupboard just as the door is slammed open. The light is turned on, and I can see a young man quickly scanning the room. He's dressed in all black, a gun loosely held in his right hand. I hold in my breath until he leaves, thinking no one is in here. When I think it's safe, I crawl on my hands and knees to the drawer where Dex keeps one of his guns and pull it out with trembling fingers. I take in a few shaky breaths. What the hell am I going to do?

I swallow hard and know that I need to keep my shit together right now.

Panicking isn't going to help.

I grab my cell phone and send Dex a quick message. I also forward it to Tracker and Arrow just in case Dex isn't near his phone. Making sure my phone is on silent I leave it on the bed and walk to the door.

I wish I could say I am one of those badass girls who knows how to use a gun, but I'd be lying.

I have no idea how to use it. Surely it isn't rocket science.

I could see now that it was a mistake on my end, and if I make it through tonight, one I am going to rectify at my first opportunity.

What I did know was that the safety was on, and I needed to turn it off, which I do with a flick of my thumb. Aim and fire, right? How hard could it be? I swallow hard when I think of the baby. What could I do? If I hide I'd never be able to live with myself. I open the door and walk down the hall, trying not to make a noise. I hear the loud bang of a door. I run into the living area, where I see all the women sitting there, looking terrified. Allie has black mascara smeared down her cheeks from crying, and Mary's lips are trembling something fierce. The poor girl is scared out of her mind. All of them are crouched on the floor, in front of the couch, huddled together.

In front of them stand four men. All wearing cuts.

Bikers from an enemy MC, I assume.

Their eyes immediately go to me as I enter the room.

"Looks like we missed one," the leader says, grinning at me with an evil look in his eye.

"Who are you? And what the fuck do you want? Do you take pleasure in scaring innocent women?" I ask, lifting the gun and aiming it at him. I fake my confidence, like I've done many times before.

Don't let them see your weakness.

He laughs. "And she has claws. Put down the gun, princess. I could kill all these bitches before you even shoot one bullet."

"Who says you aren't going to kill them anyway?" I ask.

My mind races with how this is going to play out. How do I save everyone?

The pressure!

The leader smirks. "Guess you're going to just have to wait and see. You're at the mercy of the Wild Men now, princess, so shut up and do as you're told, or we'll have to kill you first."

The Wild Men.

What did these assholes think they were doing?

Cindy stares at me, the only one of the women not crying. Her eyes are trying to tell me something, but I can't read them. How did this happen? This is supposed to be my safe place.

"Wh-what do you want?" I stammer, swallowing hard. I don't take my eyes off the men. The wrong move could cost us our lives.

The leader sneers. "Revenge. An eye for an eye. Wind Dragons killed two of ours. Now the Wild Men will take what's due."

Revenge.

"They really should have left you better guarded. . . . Although, to be fair, we made sure those fuckers thought we were out of state," he says, laughing like a hyena.

Okay, think, Faye, think. Four men, armed with weapons not drawn.

Fuck. Fuck. Fuck.

I need time. I need to stall. "Where are the prospects?" I ask, pulling in a shaky breath.

"Those two dumb fucks are bleeding out outside," he says, smirking. Fucking asshole. Wait, he said two.

A small movement flashes in the corner of my eye.

Vinnie.

Maybe that's what Cindy was trying to tell me. I look to her, and she nods slightly. She gets it. I get it. Now it's up to me to make my move.

"Put the gun down," he commands.

"Faye!" Vinnie hollers, appearing from the other door and shooting the leader in the head. I block out the man, block out the screams as I aim and fire at one of the other bikers. I get him in the chest, and he goes down. My hands shake. I don't have time to consider the fact that I've just killed someone, because it's not over yet. We aren't safe yet. The other two have their guns drawn and start shooting. Vinnie is able to take out one of them, then turns to the other. The final man standing shoots at the women twice more, who are in the process of exiting the room, then turns to me. His gun trained on me, he smiles, letting me know that he's not afraid of death and that he's going to try to take me down with him. Vinnie shoots, and so does the man. He gets taken down but not before a stray bullet flies past me. I duck, crouching in a ball on the floor.

Then, silence.

Please, let everyone be okay.

Too scared to move, my whole body trembling in shock, I stay like that until Vinnie comes and sits next to me. He puts a hand on my shoulder, making me flinch.

"It's over. You really handled yourself, Faye," he says, his voice unsteady.

I lift my head, tears dropping down my cheeks like raindrops. "Who made it?"

That's not what I wanted to ask. What I wanted to ask is: Who did we lose?

His face crumples. "Liam and Trev are dead. I'm sorry, Faye, but she didn't make it—"

Prospects dead. She didn't make it? Who *didn't make it? One of the women died?*

His phone rings, and he walks off to answer it. I stand up and place my palms on the wall, too scared to see the damage these men have caused. Swallowing hard, I wipe my eyes with the back of my hands and wrap my arms around me.

My baby is safe.

Taking a deep, relieved breath, I walk to the table where the girls were all hiding during the gunfire. I see Cindy okay, hugging Jess. I see Allie there, crying, but alive. I look around for Mary.

Where is she?

"Where's Mary?" I ask in a shaky voice. The women all cry harder, except Cindy, who hasn't shed a tear but has devastation written all over her face.

"No," I whisper, my eyes going behind them to the dark-haired woman lying on the couch. Blood drips from her chest. Her eyes are closed. I walk to her, falling to my knees and run my fingers through her hair and kiss the top of her head. Why Mary? She was the sweetest, kindest person I'd ever met. She didn't deserve this. All she did was love Arrow—that's why she was here. She would never harm a soul.

I start to sob inconsolably.

"Faye, Dex is on his way. He wants to talk to you," Vinnie says gently. I shake my head and continue to stare at Mary.

"She needs you right now, man," Vinnie tells him, his eyes going red when he looks at Mary. "She's fine physically, but I don't know," he says into the phone.

He doesn't know if I'm fine emotionally. Well, I'm not.

I sit there with Mary until the men arrive. For the rest of my life, I will never forget the look on Arrow's face. Never. He ran inside and dropped to his knees in front of her. He buried his face in her hair and cried. He cursed, he swore, and he kept asking *why* over and over again.

Why her?

In that moment, I know that Arrow loved Mary. I wonder if he only just figured it out himself. Doesn't matter if he did— now it's too late.

Dex wraps me in his arms, his body trembling, shaking with fear and rage.

And relief.

He takes me to our bed and just holds me. "I was so worried," he whispers. "I'm so fuckin' sorry, sweetheart."

I can see his face in the moonlight, his pained eyes tearing through me. They hurt to look at, so I squeeze my own shut.

I'm just about asleep when he says, "I need to go help the others. I will be back as soon as I can."

Help must mean take care of the dead bodies.

I killed a man today.

I killed someone.

And I lost someone.

I think of Liam and Trev, and I feel sad, but when I think of Mary being gone I feel a pain in my chest.

The good die young; the saying must be true.

Dex joins me back in bed early that morning. He smells like soap, freshly showered. I explore his smooth chest with my hands, then place my right hand against his heart.

I feel it beating.

"I love you too," he whispers to me. "I wanted to say it to you face-to-face."

He kisses my lips once, then we fall asleep wrapped in each other's arms.

# TWENTY

"W HAT'S this?" I ask, peering at the box curiously. Jim smiles at me, his eyes crinkling, and places the box on the table.

"You earned this," he says as I open the lid and pull out what's inside.

It's a cut. One made in my size. On it, it says "Property of Sin."

I should be offended at the proclamation, but I'm not. I know what it means, what it symbolizes. I'm one of them. And they would protect me with their own lives.

"You're the first woman to get one. Ever."

Dex watches me, his eyes full of pride and sadness. I think he's feeling pride over my actions but sad that I was forced to do it. Sad that I was almost killed and that others were. I know he feels guilty too.

"I didn't do anything, really," I mutter. "It was all Vinnie."

Vinnie was patched in the week after the funerals for Mary, Liam, and Trev. Seeing Arrow at Mary's funeral was the worst. I could see that he blamed himself for her death. I wasn't sure how he was going to handle it, or what he was going to do. It was a large burden for a man to carry.

One long soul-searching month has passed.

I didn't leave my room for the first week. I cried more than I've ever cried in my life, and then I got mad at Dex. I had to blame someone, and he was closest to me. He brought me here. He didn't deserve what I threw at him, but he took it and comforted me as much as he could.

"Stop crying, Faye," he'd whispered to me, rubbing my back.

I pulled my head back and narrowed my eyes at him. "We were all in danger! You should have protected us better!"

He pulls me back against his chest, my body shaking with sobs.

"I know," he'd gritted out, then muttered a curse. "Don't you think I know that? I brought you here to protect you, and I fuckin' failed. I'm just happy you were okay, Faye, and how fuckin' selfish is that? Others lost their lives, but I was thanking God that you were okay, because if you weren't, I don't know what I would have done."

"My baby was in danger! You brought us here," I'd cried. "Our baby, we could have lost our baby. We lost Mary. . . ."

"I know," he whispered to me, devastation written all over his tone. "I know, babe, I know. And I'm so fuckin' sorry, I would have never forgiven myself if something happened to you and the baby."

After I calmed down, we spoke. I told him it wasn't his fault, and I shouldn't have blamed him. I was just hurt. I was shaken. I was destroyed at what I had lost and at what I had almost lost.

And I was thankful my baby was safe.

After feeling nothing but anger, I felt something else.

Guilt.

I killed a man. I was a murderer.

Who was I to take someone's life? I wanted to be on the other side of the law, but now I was tainted. I'd killed a man. Even though it was self-defense it isn't something that was so easily forgotten. It left a scar. A scar that I had to carry around, one that I had to learn how to manage. The club protected me from what I did. No one mentioned that I played a part in it, so there were no ramifications on me. They had my back, like I had theirs.

After the guilt, I felt something else.

Something easier.

Acceptance.

It happened. I survived. I was one of the lucky ones.

I had two options in my life. Stay with Dex and live the life, or leave him.

I think Dex knew what I was thinking, so we talked. A lot. About everything. About us as a family. About the future. I didn't want him to leave the club; the club was who he was. I didn't want to change him. But I couldn't have it both ways. This was my life now. I wasn't born into it but was brought here by circumstance. And I'll stay here because of love. He said he would do anything to keep us safe; he would lay his life down. He would leave the club, if that's what I wanted from him. He would give up everything that he holds dear for me. For us— our family.

I fell in love with him even more.

There is no way I could leave him.

A lot has changed since then. Dex and I sold his old house and bought a new one. Renee was pissed, but Dex and I couldn't care less. The clubhouse upped their security. It's now harder to get into than a maximum-security prison is to get out of. There will not be a repeat of what happened that night, not if we can help it. Dex is sorting it out, making sure we will be safe, and I believe him. No matter what it is—we will get through it together.

I touch my rounded belly and smile. "I love my cut." I won't be wearing it out, but I think I'm going to seduce Dex in it tonight.

Wearing the cut and nothing else. Sexy.

Jim lifts his hand and touches my cheek. "Proud to have you in the family."

"Proud to be here, Jimbo," I reply, smiling up at him.

He looks to Dex. "Knocking her up was the best thing you ever did, Sin."

"Don't I know it," he replies, his lips curving into a cocky smile.

I roll my eyes. "When do you guys head out?" They were going on another run, except this time Dex was staying with me. I don't know how he talked his way out of that. I don't even know what they do on these "runs," but I have a feeling it has to do with drugs. Jim doesn't allow any club members to use hard drugs, and I thought it was just good form, until I realized maybe he didn't want them sampling the wares either. I've asked Dex, but he didn't answer, so I let it go. His expression didn't let me know if I was wrong or right about the assumption. I know they make good money. They own several different businesses, from a strip club named Toxic to several bars, clubs, and the auto mechanic shop Dex works in sometimes.

"Leaving tomorrow morning," Jim replies, taking a swig of beer. "Cindy is busy organizing the charity event. Why don't you help her out?"

"Yeah I will," I assure him.

"Good girl. I'm gonna go spend time with her before I have to leave in the morning."

"All right," I say, taking that as my cue to leave his office. I'd learned that his office leads to the room where the men have their secret meetings. Church, they call it. That's why I was yelled at for trying to clean around there. They probably thought I was trying to snoop. The thought makes me smile.

"You want to go out for dinner, babe?" Dex asks as we head to our room. The house will be ready for us to move in to in a few weeks. I'm not in a rush, to be honest, at least until I give birth. I can't imagine being alone in a house when Dex goes out on club business, but I can't imagine living here with a newborn either. I think we will benefit from having our own space; a civilian life, I heard one of the men call it.

I like to think I'm giving my daughter the best of both worlds. A nice house in a good area, but also having good men to look after her for her whole life and an extended family.

Nothing bad will touch her—I will make sure of it.

"Yeah, I'm hungry," I reply, absently rubbing my stomach.

"You're always hungry," he says. "You're supposed to eat to live, not live to eat."

"I'm pregnant, so you shush," I tell him, pushing him against the wall in the hallway and slipping my hand into his shirt. I feel the expanse of his smooth, toned chest, then have ideas other than food.

"Sex, then food, please," I tell him, wiggling my eyebrows.

"Fuck, you're romantic," he says sarcastically, grinning down at me. "That line was one for the ages. Some pure Shakespearean shit."

I slap at this shoulder. "Do not say *Shakespearean* and *shit* in the same sentence—"

He cuts off my rant with a kiss. He starts slow, gentle, igniting a fire within me.

"Bedroom," I demand against his lips. I want him, and I want him right now.

"I want you here," he replies. Here? As in the hallway?

"Dex—"

"I want you here, Faye," he whispers. "I need you right fuckin' now, and I'm not waiting."

He lifts me up against the wall, careful not to press his weight against my stomach. Running his hand up my thigh, he lifts my dress with it, riding it up until my underwear is bared to him. Ripping my black lace panties with one quick movement, he frees himself with one hand, kissing me senseless at the same time. I moan into his mouth, encouraging him. His kisses turn more frantic, more desperate, and mine do the same. He reaches down and plays with my clit, sliding a finger inside to test if I'm ready for him.

I am.

I always am. A hum of approval resounds deep in his throat as he confines me to the wall. He examines my features for a second, leaning his forehead against mine and staring deep into my eyes.

Sliding himself inside me gently, he groans at the contact. "God, I love you," he murmurs against my lips. "So.Fucking. Much."

"Love you too," I manage to get out breathlessly.

"You're mine, babe," he says on a thrust. "All. Mine."

His hands hold my hips up, gripping with each smooth

movement. My heels dig into his ass, urging him on as my climax builds.

Then I feel it. That moment you know you're so close, but you just need . . . a little more. A little push over the edge. Dex feels it too; he always knows exactly what I need—he's so attuned to my body. His mouth finds the spot between my neck and shoulder and bites down gently. He knows that spot is sensitive, one of my favorite places to be kissed. It does the trick, and I feel myself explode, the pleasure consuming.

"That's it," he whispers. "Come for me, Faye."

I close my eyes and let the sensations take over. Nothing exists in this moment besides Dex and pleasure.

"Show me those pretty hazel eyes," he demands. "Show me what's mine."

I open my eyes, meeting his crystal-blue ones. "You're mine too."

"Always, babe," he grits out as his release hits him. He never moves his eyes away from mine, allowing me to see him in the throes of pleasure.

It's a good look on him.

He peppers kisses on my jawline, my cheeks, my forehead, then finally my mouth.

I hear cheering from behind us and look to see Rake standing there. I hide my face in Dex's neck, my cheeks heating with embarrassment. Dammit, Rake will never let me live this down.

"Get the fuck out of here, Rake," Dex growls at him.

Way to ruin our afterglow, Rake.

"Hell no, this is payback," he says, chuckling.

I cringe when I remember walking into his room and an-

noying him and his two houseguests. Sighing, I tap Dex's
shoulder for him to let me down.

"I hope payback is worth the black eye you'll be sporting tomorrow," Dex adds, carefully putting me down on the
ground. I pull my dress down, while Dex does up his jeans.
We both turn to face Rake, my cheeks bright red. Dex, on the
other hand, looks like he wants to kill him, and I know it's on
my behalf. I don't think he really gives a shit whether people
see him having sex, but he knows I'm more private. Dex picks
up my ripped panties off the floor and scrunches them in his
hand, then shoves them into his pocket.

When I see Rake pulling out his phone, my mouth drops
open, anger overriding my embarrassment. "Don't you dare,
Rake! I swear I will kill you!"

He laughs, holding his stomach like this is the funniest moment of his life.

Men!

"I'm just playing. I wouldn't take a picture of you. Well, I
would, if Sin wouldn't kick my ass."

I sigh. "Why are you still standing here?"

He grins lavishly. "Just enjoying the view, Faye. Now I know
what Sin sees in you. That was fuckin' hot."

I cover my face with my hands until Dex pulls them away
and kisses my mouth. "Ignore him."

Dex turns to Rake, an evil grin appearing on his mouth.
"Let's go have a chat."

I puff out a shallow breath. What he really means is, let's go
to the boxing ring and beat the shit out of each other. The ring
is a new addition to the compound, and the men like to get in
there and show off their fighting skills. It's all I've been hearing

about recently. The lot of them have been looking at any excuse to get in there.

"Not the face," I tell Rake, pointing a finger at him.

Dex turns to me. "As if he'd even get a shot in."

"Hey, not all of us have trained with Reid Knox," Rake adds. "You have an advantage."

Dex gives me one last lingering kiss. "I owe you some spooning," he whispers into my ear.

"What?" I ask, laughing.

"I don't want you to feel like every time we have sex I just get up and leave," he tries to explain. "I want to hold you afterward, skin against skin. But it will have to be later this time."

I hide my smile. He doesn't want me to feel like he's using me, like he was just going to fuck and run like he did with the other women. "Baby, it's okay. Go do your thing—we can snuggle tonight."

"I think I'm going to be sick," Rake says. Shit, I forgot the bastard was even there.

I flash him a pointed look, then head to my room for a nap.

TWENTY-ONE

"WHAT about Akira?" I ask, my nose stuck in the baby-names book.

"What else do you have?" he asks, stretching his arms above his head.

"What's wrong with Akira?" I ask, turning the page.

"Nothing," he replies. "It's just not *the* name."

We'd been at it for over an hour. Every name I liked, he didn't. It was starting to get on my last nerve.

"Lilliana, Rose, Chloe . . ." I say, trailing off. Then I see it. The name I want. I glance up at Dex, hoping that he likes it, because I am in love with it.

"What?" he asks.

"I've found the name, but I'm scared to say it, because if you don't like it I don't know how I'll react."

He chuckles. "Tell me."

"Clover," I say, studying him, waiting for his reaction.

"Clover," he says slowly, as if testing the name on his tongue.

I wait for him to speak, holding my breath.

"I love it," he finally says. "How could I not when you love it so much?"

I smile, throw the book down, and wrap my arms around him, squeezing him in happiness. "Are you sure?"

He nods. "It's a beautiful name. Unique. Perfect for our little princess."

"Clover Black," I say, seeing how the names sound together. "It is beautiful. I have good taste."

I lie down beside him.

"Not as beautiful as she's going to be," he replies, pulling me into his side. I rest my cheek against his chest.

"Well, that's a given," I reply, earning me a chuckle.

"Are you ready for your exams?" he asks, absently stroking my hair.

"Yeah, I am. I'm actually excited to sit for them," I say, smiling widely. I'm looking forward to going to campus for my exams. Tomorrow is the first one I have. Family law.

He chuckles. "You're a nerd, babe. It's so fuckin' hot."

I shake my head at him. "You think everything is hot."

"Everything about you, yes," he agrees. "Do you need to study tonight? Or can we do something?"

"I need to study. I want to ace this exam," I tell him carefully. I was ready, but I wanted to go over everything once more for good measure. "Aren't you going into work now?"

"Yeah, in about a half an hour," he replies. Good, I need him out of the house. Tomorrow is his birthday, and I need time to get his surprise ready. Then time to kick his ass for not even telling me it was his birthday. I remembered that it was in June from when we were younger, but I couldn't remember the date. June nineteenth.

A date I would never forget again.

"Okay, well, I'll see you when you're done, then."

He gives me a weird look.

"What?" I ask.

"Nothing," he replies, lip twitching. "Let's stay in bed until I have to leave."

"Sounds good to me," I say, placing a kiss on his chest.

"If you do that, you know I'm going to want to fuck you," he says frankly, running his hand down my arm.

I smirk. "I don't know, Dex, you only have thirty minutes . . ."

His hand palms my ass. "Plenty of time. Let me show you."

I play coy. "What did you have in mind?"

His mouth covers mine, letting me know exactly what he had in mind.

An hour later Dex heads into work while I start to plan like crazy and get everything ready. I want tonight to be perfect, and I want him to be surprised. I cook him his favorite meal, set up the dining table with a tablecloth, candles, and a red rose in the middle. Okay, so the romantic setting is more for me than him, but it looks pretty. I set the wrapped presents on the table.

"Rake, will you text me when he's about to leave the shop?" I ask, organizing the presents so they are displayed nicely.

"Yeah, I got you, babe," he replies, watching me for a second. "You know you're a pain in the ass, but you're the best thing that's ever happened to him."

"Thanks, Rake. Although from what I saw with you and that woman, *you're* the pain in the ass."

I laugh at my own joke.

"Fuck, you must be good in bed," he grumbles.

"Hey, you saw for yourself, remember," I smirk.

He laughs. "You're right, I did, that wall sex was fuckin' hot."

I laugh and step to him, wrapping my arms around his waist and laying my head on his hard chest. After a moment, he returns the hug.

"Don't know how he lifted you against the wall though," he says, pulling back and grinning down at me.

I hit his arm. I can't wait to have this baby, if only so the heavyweight jokes stop.

"I'm taking Dex out tomorrow night for a brothers-only birthday celebration," he tells me, pushing a lock of blond hair off his forehead.

"Fine," I grumble. "You guys better behave though."

"Vinnie will stay with you," he says.

Poor Vinnie. He's always missing out on all the fun, usually because of me. I make a mental note to get him a kick-ass Christmas present this year.

"Why? I thought that shit with the Wild Men was over?" I ask, frowning. After the incident happened, the Wind Dragons met up with the rival MC. I don't know what happened, but Dex came home saying that it was over, at least for now. I didn't know what that meant but assumed some kind of temporary truce had been met. I'd heard him talking to Tracker about how members of the Wild Men MC had gone rogue, and the rest of the club condomned their actions. Apparently the men had been dealt with.

"Better to be safe," he says. "Look what happened last time."

I sigh and look up into his face. "Wild Men is a stupid MC name."

A lip twitch. "It is. I'm going to the shop. I'll message you when he leaves."

"Okay, thanks."

I have a long shower, shaving my legs and other places. I rub in my cherry-blossom lotion, apply makeup, and iron my hair straight. I put on my robe and head to check on the food in the oven. Arrow walks in, looking a little worse for wear. Wrinkled clothes, lipstick on his neck, and . . . I could smell the alcohol from here.

"Hey, Arrow," I say, smiling sadly. Ever since Mary's death, he's not the same person he was.

"Hey, Faye," he says quietly. I walk over to him and kiss him on his cheek, his prickly beard brushing my skin.

"Can I make you something to eat?" I ask him. I wish he would let me look after him, but he doesn't. He drowns his sorrows with alcohol and easy women. I'm not going to judge his methods of coping, but I hope he gets back to himself soon.

I miss my friend.

"Don't worry about me, Faye. I'm gonna have a shower, then get out of here so you can spoil your man for his birthday," he says, walking away.

I sigh and watch him as he leaves. I spend the rest of the afternoon painting my nails and pampering myself. When I get the text from Rake, I set out the food, light the candles, and put on my outfit.

The cut and some black lace panties.

And that's it.

I look in the mirror and smile.

I look good.

My long hair frames my face and has volume on top, giving me a sexy look. My eyes are dark and smoky, my lips a bloodred. The sides of my breasts are visible, but my nipples are covered by the black leather cut. My fair skin stands out even more. I had planned on wearing sexy heels, but I choose comfort instead and go barefoot.

When I hear him enter the door, I walk out to greet him. He stops in his tracks when he sees me standing here.

"Holy fuck," he whispers as his gaze devours me. He walks toward me, eyes on my body. "This is the sexiest thing I've ever seen in my life.

"Stay still. I need a photo of this," he says, taking a picture with his phone. He slides it away, then kisses my mouth. "How did I get so fucking lucky? I'm going to send a thank-you letter to the condom company."

I gape. "You did not just say that."

He grins crookedly. "What's the occasion, beautiful?"

"I have exams for the rest of the week, so I thought we could celebrate your birthday early," I say, rubbing my body against his. "You didn't even tell me it was your birthday."

"Not a big deal, babe. Just another day."

"Not anymore, it isn't," I reply, breathing him in.

"Let me have a quick shower. I have grease on me," he says, kissing me once more before walking into the bathroom. I make myself busy in the kitchen, waiting for him to finish.

He enters the kitchen moments later, wearing nothing but a pair of low-slung jeans. I stare at his body, appreciating the view.

"Take a seat," I say in a husky tone.

He sits down and stares at the table. "No one's ever done anything like this for me before."

I smile. "I'm glad you like it."

"I fuckin' love it. Now, come here," he demands. I walk up to him, laughing as he pulls me onto his lap. "I'm going to make you scream my name a few times before we eat whatever smells so fuckin' good."

He kisses me greedily, cupping my cheeks with his palms. I grip onto his shoulders, giving it back to him, kissing him with an intensity that surprises even me. He picks me up and carries me to the couch, laying me on it and opening the cut to reveal my breasts. He sucks one into his mouth, and then the other, nibbling before pulling away. His eyes on mine, he slides down my panties while I wait in anticipation. Then, his head lowers between my legs and his mouth works its magic. Once I've come, he fucks me, and I love every single second of it.

I love his expressions, the sounds he makes, the dirty way he talks to me.

"So wet, Faye," he whispers. "Such a good girl; do you want me to lick those sweet nipples again?"

I nod, sticking out my chest, offering myself to him.

He licks his lips and makes a deep sound in his throat as he lowers his head and licks once gently, before drawing the nipple into his mouth and sucking. He then does the same to the other. I moan loudly.

He pulls back and grins, still thrusting inside me.

"I love that noise you make, fuck!"

I love the way he takes joy in my pleasure.

And his bossiness and his demands.

I give as good as I get. I match his passion and his intensity.

He was made for me, this man.

I dig my fingers into his dragon tattoo and let the pleasure consume me.

TWENTY-TWO

VINNIE drives me home from my university exam the next day, and for that I'm grateful. I'm feeling extremely drained today and just want to go home and sleep.

"How did you do?" Vinnie asks.

"I think I did well," I reply. "It wasn't too hard."

"Modest, aren't we?" he says with a chuckle.

I shrug. "Just honest. I'm sorry you're stuck with me tonight while everyone goes out to celebrate."

"It's no biggie," he says. "I was at Toxic last week."

My head snaps to him. "They're taking him to a strip club?"

Vinnie grimaces. "Didn't you know? Fuck."

Fuck is right. I send a text to Rake.

Faye: Where you taking Dex tonight?

Rake: Why?

Faye: 'Cuz I wanna know.

Rake: Wind Dragons' night out—don't ruin it.

Faye: #$!&^&^&^

Rake: Give the man his balls for the night!

Rake: Faye!

Faye: Fine.

Rake: Love you.

Faye: Fuck you.

I tilt my head back against the seat. It's just a night out. Seeing hot naked women who aren't pregnant and fat.

Fuck. I'm feeling insecure.

It's not a good feeling, and it doesn't look good on me.

"He won't do anything. They'll just drink and shoot the shit," Vinnie tries to assure me.

"Fine, let him have his fun," I reply, trying to keep my tone neutral.

While I sit at home studying and stuffing my face.

I see Jess and Trace sitting in the living area when I walk into the clubhouse. Trace is one of the brothers I never really talk to. He isn't friendly and outgoing like the others. He's very standoffish, and we generally steer clear of each other.

"Hey, Jess," I call out, nodding my head at Trace.

"Hey, honey," she replies. After the night we lost Mary, I no longer feel like an outsider among the women. I belong here, by Dex's side.

"How was the exam?" she asks.

"It was good," I tell her. "I have another one tomorrow."

Allie walks in behind Tracker. "Hey, baby mama," he says to me, kissing me on the cheek. I see Allie's eyes flash as he does so, but she doesn't say anything. Instead, she smiles at me in greeting, a smile I return.

"Excited for tonight?" I ask Tracker, unable to mask the anger in my tone.

He shakes his head at me, lip twitching. "Like you have anything to worry about. The man's not stupid."

"I know," I lie.

"Do you?" Tracker replies, tilting his head to the side.

I sigh. "Yeah, I won't allow myself to be *that* woman."

"What woman?"

"The woman who doesn't let her man go anywhere or do anything alone. She tags along even when he's with his friends. . . . I will never be that woman. That woman is insecure and codependent."

"Looks like you've thought about this a bit too fuckin' much," Tracker replies, scrubbing a hand along his jaw. "What I can tell you is that you have nothing to worry about. Believe me."

"I know. I'm just tired, I'm going to go to bed," I reply, mustering a small smile for him. The man did just listen to my stupid rant.

"What's happening tonight?" Allie asks, staring up at Tracker.

"Men are going out. Women are staying their asses at home," he says, opening the fridge and scanning its contents. "So don't wait up."

Allies eyes narrow, but again she stays quiet.

"There's lasagna in the oven," I tell Tracker as I exit the room. "Cindy made it today."

He calls out thanks. I climb into bed and close my eyes, letting sleep take over.

~

I wake to kisses on my face. "Wake up, sleeping beauty, dinner's ready."

I smile before I even open my eyes. "What time is it?"

"Seven. You slept for five hours," he says, kissing down my jawline.

"Happy birthday," I murmur drowsily. "Did you enjoy your present this morning?"

A deep chuckle. "Babe, there is no better way in the world to wake up. Trust me on that."

"Hmmmm," I hum as he continues his soft, chaste kisses.

"Tracker said you wanted to talk to me about something?" he asks, voice getting lower.

"What?" I ask.

"He said I should talk to you. What's going on?"

Dammit, Tracker. "Nothing. Just that I found out you were spending the night at a strip club."

He stills. "Is that where we're going?"

"You didn't know?" I ask, turning my head to look at his face.

"No, but I shouldn't be surprised. It's not a big deal. You know I would never cheat on you, right?"

"Yeah, I know. To be completely honest with you, it just hit me that you'll be seeing all these beautiful girls while I'm here with a double chin and swollen feet."

He makes a strangled noise, then breaks out into laughter.

"Oh my god! Don't laugh at me! I'm being serious," I snap, pulling on the ends of his hair to get his attention.

"I happen to love your double chin," he says, kissing it. "You have nothing to worry about. I think you're sexy as hell, pregnant with our daughter. Besides, it's you I'm in love with. I'll love you no matter what you look like."

"Even if my chin turns triple?" I ask, batting my eyelashes.

A chuckle. "Even then."

"Good, because I'm hungry," I say at the same time my stomach rumbles.

"Come on, then, let's get my woman fed. You know, I can stay home tonight. . . ."

"No, no, go have fun," I instantly say.

"Good, because they would have given me a lot of shit if I canceled," he says, looking amused.

"Is Arrow going?" I ask as Dex helps me sit up.

"Yeah, he's coming out."

"He needs to have some fun," I say, sliding off the bed. "And I need to eat and study some more."

He rests his palms on my belly. "Three months to go."

"Are you excited?" I ask him.

"Excited, nervous, curious, impatient—I'm a whole lot of different things," he admits. I look down at his tattooed knuckles on my stomach and smile.

"Time is going so fast," I say, taking his hand and walking with him out the bedroom.

"I know."

We sit down at the table and have dinner, then I study as Dex gets ready to go out. I try not to sulk, but I find myself doing just that. Rake walks out of his room first, wearing jeans and a long-sleeve shirt folded up to his elbows. His leather cut is worn over it, and his blond hair is damp from the shower. His green eyes are dancing with excitement.

"Why the hell are you so excited about tonight?" I ask him, raising a dark brow.

He plays with his lip ring. "One of the girls at Toxic—she's a fuckin' angel. Blonde. Huge-ass tits." He cups his hands in front of his pecs, mimicking the universal gesture for huge boobs. "I wanna bring her home."

"To your torture chamber?"

He grins. "Don't diss it till you try it."

Dex walks out next, and my breath catches. Dark jeans, tight black shirt stretched across his muscles. I lick my bottom lip as I take in his appearance.

"Stop looking at me like that or I'm staying my ass home," he growls. He checks his pockets for his cigarettes and wallet. Rake pulls out a bottle and starts pouring himself a drink.

"If you're drinking, you better be going in a taxi," I tell him.

"It's just one drink. I'm not rocking up in a fuckin' maxi taxi," he says, scowling. I laugh at his expression. Tracker walks in, his tattoo sleeves on showcase tonight with a white T-shirt.

"Everyone looks hot tonight," I grumble, staring down at my textbook.

My life sucks!

Dex kisses the top of my head. "I'm going out for a smoke."

"Okay." I sniff.

"Babe," he says.

"Yeah?"

"Stop pouting, yeah?"

Three sets of amused eyes stare at me.

"I'm not pouting. I hope you all enjoy your night. I'll see you at what? One a.m., maybe?"

Laughter ensues.

Dex kisses my lips, then heads out the front door. I look at Tracker, who winks at me when he sees me staring.

The rest of the men arrive, and they all get on their bikes

and ride out. Dex is the last one to leave, because he kisses me for about ten minutes before I can finally get him to go.

He kisses my stomach and then he leaves.

I study for two hours, then fall asleep.

≈

I wake up in the middle of the night to laughter. My door opens and Dex walks in, stubbing his toe on my new dressing table.

"Motherfucker!" he growls.

I stifle a laugh. He flops down onto the bed, his hands searching the sheets for me. When his fingers finally touch my arm, he says, "Yes!" like it was a big feat to find me, then rolls right next to me. He wraps me in his arms and kisses the back of my neck.

"I missed you," he says when he realizes I'm awake.

"Did you have fun?" I ask him drowsily.

"I did."

"Good," I reply.

"But I still missed you," he says, turning me to face him. "Next time you're coming with me."

"To a strip club?" I ask incredulously.

"Anywhere," he replies, his hands now roaming all over my body. "You're a million times sexier than those girls."

"So the grass isn't greener on the other side?" I ask a little breathlessly as his thumbs graze my breasts.

"No, and I never for one second thought that it was," he says quickly, claiming my mouth.

We make love, and I fall back asleep with a smile on my face—insecurities fading away.

# TWENTY-THREE

EXAMS pass in a blur, and then I get a two-week break. After more baby shopping, I'm about to pull out of the parking lot, when I see Renee.

And she's not alone.

When I see her with a man, my interest is piqued. When the man turns around, my eyes widen in shock.

What the hell is Eric doing with Renee? I take a photo of the two of them and send it to Dex. Sometimes a picture is all the evidence you need. I notice Vinnie staring in their direction too. He has his helmet on, so I can't see his expression.

We drive home, and Vinnie opens the door for me, not looking me in the eye.

"What's wrong?" I ask him.

"Nothing," he says, opening the back door and grabbing all my shopping bags out. Dex walks out of the clubhouse looking agitated, all coiled muscles. He slaps Vinnie on the back and takes the bags from his hands. Vinnie leaves, and I'm left feeling confused.

"Is everything okay?" I ask him, placing my hand on his chest.

He looks down at me, still radiating tension. "Everything's fine; we just need to talk about something."

That sounded ominous.

I suck in a deep breath. "Okay."

"Let's go into our room," he suggests. Or more like demands. He needs his own word. Deggests, or sumands.

I hold my hand up. "Is what you're going to say going to piss me off?"

He bobs his head. "More than likely."

"Maybe we should sit in my car? Then I can just drive off when I lose my temper."

I'm carried to my room.

"I'm having déjà vu," I say as I watch Dex pace before me.

"You can't get upset over this—you're pregnant," he finally says, his tone pleading.

I gape at his audacity. "Yes, I realize I'm pregnant. Now, tell me. What have you done?"

He looks down at the floor with his hands on his hips. "You know Renee cheated on me, yeah?"

"Yes," I say. I knew that part. Stupid-ass woman.

"But I didn't tell you who she cheated on me with," he says, risking a glance at me.

I shake my head in confusion.

Until it hits me.

My throat burns.

The picture I took today.

Eric and Renee?

He reaches out to touch me but his hand stops mid motion. "My brother slept with my wife. While he was dating you."

What was this? Fucking *Wife Swap*?

I swallow hard. "Okay, Eric is a douche lord, and I might even hate him, but why would I get mad at you over this?"

He stares at me, not giving anything away. "I kept it from you. I didn't want to hurt you. Then you sent me that photo today, and I knew you were going to ask questions. Maybe they're together now. I personally don't give a fuck. I didn't know how you would feel about it."

I scrub my hand down my face. "It's the past. It just shows that I've made the right choices since leaving Eric. Let them have each other—hell, they deserve each other."

He exhales, then smiles shakily. "You took that better than I expected."

Something else hits me then. "Wait a minute. . . ."

He freezes.

"You knew that Eric had slept with Renee when we first slept together," I say, my mind working. When it hits me, I grit my teeth. "You used me to get back at Eric!"

He rubs the back of his neck. "At the time, maybe. But I wanted you. You're fuckin' beautiful, babe—of course I wanted you."

"I was living a fantasy that night . . . and you were just doing it to get back at him?" I ask, my face falling.

"A fantasy?"

"You were the first boy I ever noticed . . . in that way. It was a childhood crush that turned into a teenage fantasy. I've always wanted you. I just never thought it was possible to have you," I admit.

"Faye, I ran into you, I didn't go looking for you. You were there, and you took my breath away. I couldn't believe my eyes, how sexy you were. I remember thinking how much of a dumb fuck Eric was to cheat on someone like you with someone like her."

I stare at him as my mind races.

"So it was more than just getting back at Eric? Because if you didn't find out I was pregnant, I'm not sure we would have ever seen each other again," I say, crossing my arms over my chest protectively.

Silence. Then, he surprised me. "I came by your school once. It was a week after we slept together, and I wanted to see you. You were standing there wearing all black, holding an animal-print folder, and your hair was down and sticking out in every direction."

He smiles, like it's a fond memory.

"Really?" I ask, my voice gentling.

"Yes. You need to understand, babe, you were doing well. Going to law school, making something of yourself. And you're young. I didn't know what I wanted, but I knew I wasn't exactly good for you. You'd gotten rid of Eric, and for that I was fuckin' happy. You had a chance at a fresh start. Sure, you fascinated me, but I didn't really know what I was feeling, so I just watched you—and then I left."

His eyes plead with me to understand. I was trying to get over Eric, and Dex was trying to get back at Eric. This whole thing is stupid and messed-up.

"You know what?" I find myself saying. "Who cares how we got together. We're here now, in love, and about to have a child. As long as you don't screw up again, I don't care about what happened before."

I laugh at his shocked expression. "I can be reasonable, Dex. Unless you cheat on me. That's another story," I say, my gaze going to his crotch, the threat visible in my eyes.

He cringes and cups himself. "I won't fuckin' cheat; I already told you."

"Just making sure, honey," I reply, smiling at him, the evil in me gone.

"You can be a psycho sometimes; you know that, right?" he says, getting down on his knees in front of me. I sit on the edge of the bed, now at each other's eye level.

"But I'm *your* psycho," I whisper, bringing my face closer to his.

Our foreheads touch.

"I want you to be my wife," he whispers.

"Did you just call me a psycho, then propose?" I ask, my eyebrows hitting my hairline. Now who's as romantic as Shakespeare? Not.

He grins playfully, leaning in for a quick kiss. "Marry me."

"Okay," I reply, kissing him and wrapping my arms around his neck.

"Yeah?"

"Of course. I love you, and I'd love to be your wife," I say, smiling with watery eyes.

He showers kisses all over my face. "It's like . . . I breathe you, babe. There is no other way to explain it."

That line is much better.

"I breathe you too, Dex," I say, our mouths touching briefly.

"You know you're the only one who I let call me that," he says, grinning.

"Dex?"

"Yeah, everyone else knows to call me by my road name."

"Why do they call you Sin?"

I stare into his amused gaze. "Why do you think they call me Sin?"

"Because you sin on a daily basis? Or maybe because you're sinfully sexy?" I guess.

He kisses my lips. "You think I'm sinfully sexy?"

I bite his bottom lip. "You know I do."

"And I think you were made for me . . ." he whispers.

I have to agree.

TWENTY-FOUR

PICK up my sandwich and take a bite, chewing thoughtfully as I stare at the man sitting opposite me.

"Can I ask you something?" I say to him after I've swallowed.

"You just did," he replies, looking up at me. Irish and I aren't that close, but we get along.

"How did you get the scars?" I ask, looking at his neck and jawline.

He puts down the newspaper he is reading and stares. "Knife fight."

"Hate to see the other guy," I joke, trying to lighten the mood.

He chuckles. "Me either. Skeletons freak me out."

Okkaaayyyyy, then. Next topic.

"Have you seen Arrow?" I ask. I haven't seen him since Dex's birthday, and I'm starting to get a little worried. I don't know what happened when they had negotiations with the Wild Men. I wonder if Arrow thinks that the club paid enough for the death of the men who killed Mary, or if he still needs them to suffer more. I don't know what's going on in his mind, and his eyes are so dead now that I can't tell what's working behind them. And that scares the shit out of me.

"He's gone away for a few days to clear his head."

I like listening to Irish talk in his accent.

"I miss him," I admit, looking down at my plate.

"He'll come around," he replies.

"How do you know?" I ask him.

He just shrugs. "I'm just hoping, is all."

Dex walks into the room, his eyes instantly searching for me. "I have something to show you."

"What?" I ask, standing up.

He takes my hand and leads me outside to his car. He opens the door for me and helps me get in.

"Where are we going?" I ask, placing my hand on his thigh.

"Surprise," he says, grinning excitedly. What is he so excited over?

When we pull up to my all-time favorite jewelry store, I give him a curious look. He tells me to wait so he can open the door and then once on my side gives me his hand to get out from the car.

Hand in hand we walk into the store. As we enter, the lady working there gives Dex a smile and then changes the sign from OPEN to CLOSED.

"What on earth—"

"Choose any engagement ring you want," he says, kissing me on top of my head.

"What?" I gasp, dazzled by all the rings set in front of me. A princess-cut solitaire catches my eye immediately. It has one very large diamond in the center of a gold band.

Simple. Classic. Stunning.

And I want it.

"Can I try that one on?" I ask the woman, who picks up the ring and hands it to Dex, who slides it on the correct finger. It fits perfectly and looks beautiful.

"I love it," I whisper, touching the diamond.

"We'll take this one, please," Dex calls out.

"Certainly," the woman says, more than happy to make a sale. "How will you be paying for it, sir?"

"Cash," Dex replies.

"C-certainly," the woman stutters. "Umm, that's twenty thousand dollars."

I gape. Twenty thousand dollars. That's way too expensive for a ring. "Dex—"

"It's yours, babe," he says, pulling out a stack of money. I send him a look. How dodgy does this look? The woman probably thinks he robbed a bank or something.

We leave the store with a pleased-looking Dex and get back into the car.

"Thank you," I tell him. "You really didn't need to spend so much."

"Babe," he says, chuckling.

"What?"

"That ring isn't going to bankrupt me," he replies, stifling laughter.

How rich is he?

"Good to know," I mutter, staring down at my ring and smiling. I feel like doing my happy dance right now.

"That smile on your face is worth much more than twenty grand," he says, reaching out and taking my hand in his.

That was really sweet. "Where are we going now?"

"We're going to my mom's to tell her we're getting married," he says in a careful tone.

My hand goes to the door handle.

"Don't be so dramatic. We'll stay there ten minutes, max."

"This is kidnapping! Is that why you were buttering me up with the ring and being all sweet?" I ask, wringing my hands.

"Babe."

"Dex, I was dating her other son for years. Oh my god, this is going to be so awkward," I say, staring out the window.

"She knows you're with me now, and we're having a baby girl. She won't look at you the wrong way, trust me. She doesn't want to jeopardize the relationship with her first grandchild," he explains patiently.

"She won't?" I ask, nibbling on my bottom lip.

"You think I'll let anyone say anything to you? I don't care who it is, Faye. No one disrespects my old lady. No one."

I puff out a shaky, shallow breath. "Okay, okay. Let's get this over with."

~

"Hey, Ma," Dex says, kissing his mother on the cheek. "How have you been?"

"Better now that my firstborn has finally come for a visit," she admonishes, then turns to me. "Nice to see you, Faye. How's your pregnancy coming along?"

"Hi, Gretchen," I say. "Coming along really well. She's due on September fifth."

"How exciting. I bought a few things, I hope you don't mind . . ." she trails off as I see her staring at my ring.

"You're getting married?" she asks, looking to Dex.

"Yeah, Ma, that's why we're here. I wanted to let you know," Dex replies.

"Well, congratulations," she says, trying to hide her shock. "Is your divorce finalized, then?"

Fuck. I completely forgot about that. I look to Dex, who grins at the look on my face.

"All sorted. I'm a free man as of this morning," he says, eyes smiling at me. He bought me a ring the day his divorce was finalized. I love that he didn't want to waste any time.

"When is the wedding going to be? Will you be having a big one?" she asks.

"Anything Faye wants," Dex replies, winking at me.

"I see," his mother replies, smiling. "This is a surprise, but I have to say, I'm happy for you. I know we all started off on the wrong foot, but I don't want to be let out of my grandchild's life."

"You can see her, Ma," Dex replies. "I wouldn't do that to you."

His mom nods, her eyes suspiciously wet. "Thank you, son. I know I haven't always done right by you."

I'm tempted to scoff, but I keep my mouth closed.

"Faye, I spoke to your parents the other day."

Great, just great.

"I'm not on speaking terms with my parents," I reply without emotion.

"Really? They didn't mention that. Just that you had moved out."

Of course they wouldn't, because that would make them look bad. My mother wouldn't allow that.

"I told them that you were dating Dexter. They didn't seem to be pleased about that," she says, leaning back on her white couch.

I shrug. "It doesn't matter what they say."

"I'm having some people around tonight, if you want to stay for dinner," she says, turning to her son.

"No, thanks, Ma. Faye and I have plans. Maybe next time," he says standing, to leave.

"I wish you would talk to Eric; he is your baby brother, after all," she quickly says, standing and smoothing down her dress suit.

"We've been through this. . . ."

"He's your brother!" she snaps, then clears her throat, lowering her voice. "I just want all of us to get along for once. We're a family. At the end of the day that's all that matters."

"I know, Ma, but he's also a fuckin' asshole. I have a bunch of brothers at home, and none of them would betray me. I wouldn't ever turn my back on a man like Eric," Dex growls, grabbing my hand and leading me out.

"This is just because of her." She sniffs. "You shouldn't fight over a woman, Dex. Eric will have to deal with this. But don't let that be the reason you throw away your relationship with your baby brother."

I assume I am the *her*.

Dex stops in his tracks. "It has nothing to do with her. Eric and I have never gotten along, and as much as it sucks, it is what it is. Don't try blaming Faye for this. Faye is the best thing that's ever happened to me."

It's then I see Eric out of the corner of my eye, leaning

against the door, listening. He bobs his head, gives me a sad smile, and then walks away.

I think he finally gets it. Dex loves me.

He breathes me.

Eric knows what we had wasn't that. It wasn't even close.

We say good-bye to his mother and get the hell out of there.

TWENTY-FIVE

I PUT my hand on my stomach as Clover moves around, kicking me. The banana I placed on my belly for safekeeping wobbles with one hard kick. I shake my head. I can't wait to hold my little girl. I'm now seven months pregnant. Dex moved us into our new house, but I still spend some nights at the clubhouse. Tonight is one of those nights. Dex has gone somewhere with Jim, and I'm hanging out with the rest of the brothers.

"Faye! Your huge ass is blocking the TV!" Rake calls out, the jerk. I throw my banana at his head as he cackles with laughter. Allie sits on Tracker's lap, his arms resting on her hips. He sees me watching and winks at me. I think those two are finally getting serious. I give him a thumbs-up. He shakes his head and mutters something about me being goofy. Arrow walks into the room and sits down next to me. I stare into his brown eyes and tug on his beard.

"Nice to see you, stranger," I say with a smile.

"Nice to see you too," he replies with a lip twitch.

"You look much better," I blurt out, taking in his freshly cut hair and circle-free eyes.

"I feel better," he replies.

"So I have my best biker back?" I whisper, not letting anyone else hear.

"You never lost him, little girl," he replies, flashing me his white teeth. "You've gotten so big."

I gasp. "You did not just say that!"

"I didn't mean it in a bad way," he quickly says, trying to cover up his blunder.

"So I've gotten big in a *good* way?"

I look down at my boobs. Okay, so those have gotten bigger, from a B cup to a C, but so has everything else too. My already huge ass has gone from J.Lo to Kim Kardashian.

Arrow turns to Rake. "Someone could have warned me."

"About what?" I ask, looking at Rake in confusion.

"Nothing," Rake adds, throwing me back the banana and turning his face to attempt hiding his smile.

"I'm not that bad," I sulk, peeling my banana and taking a bite out of it. Irish and Trace walk into the room.

"Is the beast in a good mood?" Irish asks as he sits down.

My mouth drops open. "I *was* in a good mood!"

To be honest, I have been grumpy the last few days. My back hurts, my feet hurt, and I have heartburn, but I totally thought I was suffering in silence.

Apparently not.

"When does Dex get back?" I ask, rubbing my stomach absently.

No one answers me. *Game of Thrones* is on, and almost everyone is watching it in fascination. Allie and Tracker start making out, his hands groping all over her ass. Feeling uncomfortable, I turn to Arrow, who is watching me in amusement.

"Still a prude?" he asks quietly.

"I'm not a prude. I just prefer that kind of stuff to be private. I'm not judging anyone, but I'd be lying if I said it didn't make me uncomfortable to see free live porn," I reply, just as quiet.

"Trust me when I say, before you moved in it was a lot worse. Naked women walking around twenty-four/seven," he says, looking wistful. "Those were the days."

"Ahh, the pre-Faye glory days," Rake adds in.

"Well, excuse me, I don't live here anymore, so on the days I'm gone feel free to return to those glory days," I huff, crossing my arms over my chest.

"Oh, trust me, we do," Rake says, tipping back his ice-cold beer. "Just yesterday I had this one woman bent over the—"

My banana peel hits him right in the face.

Everyone bursts out laughing, except Trace, who looks at us like we're all insane.

Rake is about to shout out some smart-ass remark I'm waiting for, when the front door slams open.

Everyone stands. Arrow stands in front of me, shielding me.

"Club room! NOW!" Jim yells as he enters with Dex. Everyone heads into the office. What the hell is going on? Why do they need a club meeting?

All of them on alert, they exit the room. Dex walks over to me and gives me a quick openmouthed kiss.

"Stay here," he demands, then walks off. I look at Allie, who looks just as shocked. I sit down, knowing it's not my place to get involved.

"I wonder what happened," I say, looking to where Dex was just standing.

Allie puffs out a breath. "Guess we'll have to wait and see."

≈

They all walk out about thirty minutes later. Dex storms up to me and wraps me in his arms. "Clubhouse is on lockdown. More people will arrive within the hour; do you think you can help with food and sleeping arrangements?"

"Of course," I say, my concern growing. "What's happening?"

He looks like he doesn't want to tell me, but then he speaks. "We got even with the Wild Men, then had negotiations."

I don't ask how they got even. I can only imagine.

"We still fuckin' hate each other, but we called a truce. Just found out Arrow killed their president in broad fuckin' daylight two days ago. Their MC members just found out who did it and are going to want revenge."

"But Arrow—"

"I know, babe, he looks like he has his shit under control finally," Dex says on a sigh. "I think that's why. He killed their president and feels like Mary's death has been avenged. However, we now have a war on our hands."

Arrow walks up to us, his lip bleeding. Wonder who hit him. He looks at me, at my stomach.

"I didn't want to put you or anyone else in danger . . . but fuck. He knew those men were going to come here that night! They were *his* men; he fuckin' sent them! He needed to pay," he grits out, his face going red.

I have no idea what to say.

"I can't put my daughter in danger, Dex!" I whisper. I love this man more than my own life, but not more than the life of my child. Dex nods his head, scrubbing a hand down his face.

Arrow looks ashen. I don't want to hurt anyone, but what can I do? Stay here and be a sitting duck, waiting for this "war" to finish and hoping Clover and I will be safe? Jim walks over and pulls Dex away.

"I'm sorry it had to be this way, but I'm not sorry that fucker is dead," Arrow says again, his voice hoarse.

"I know," I whisper. "I know."

What am I going to do?

Cindy storms in and starts barking orders, which I appreciate, because she saves me from standing here looking stupid. She knows what to do, what to say, and shows me just what it takes to be the president's old lady.

You need to keep your shit together.

A test that I'd passed at the shooting but just failed big-time this time around.

I went through it once—could I do it again? I don't want to. I guess the bottom line is that I shouldn't have to.

We organize food, places to sleep, and send the men on a store run to stock up on things we need. Apparently these lockdowns can last a few days. More men arrive, ones I've never met before. I feel Dex's eyes on me, watching, but he doesn't say anything. He's worried about me—I know it. I can feel it. See it in his expression.

I can't comfort him right now though, because even I don't know what I'm feeling.

# TWENTY-SIX

DON'T know what to do with myself. So I pace. I feel like I'm a sitting duck, just waiting for something to happen. Who are we going to lose this time?

Arrow?

Dex?

The baby girl I haven't even met yet?

I keep seeing Mary's face in death. Over and over again.

The thought makes me stop in my tracks and cry. Tears drip down my cheeks until I cover my face with my hands.

"Faye," Dex says, pulling me back into his warm body. "Don't cry."

"This isn't good for the baby," Cindy says from behind him. "She's stressed out, Sin. I think she's having a panic attack."

"I fuckin' know that," Dex growls. "What am I supposed to do? She's safest here, where I can watch over her. I won't let anything happen to her. And when this bullshit is over, she'll be safe. I'll kill every one of those fuckers if I have to!"

I feel like shit. They have bigger issues on their hands, but here they are, standing around me watching me lose my shit and trying to help.

"Dex—" Jim starts.

"NO!" Dex yells in reply, cutting off whatever Jim was going to say. "No, no, no."

No, what? I try to pull myself together, wiping my eyes and straightening my spine. "I'm fine; I'm sorry."

"She needs to leave," Jim says in a strong voice. "We need your mind on the club right now, not on her!"

"I'm sorry," I whisper.

"Don't apologize," Dex sighs, sounding resigned. "Everyone get out!"

The room clears.

"Babe, until this whole mess is cleared, you need to be somewhere safe," he starts, his face falling.

"What do you mean?"

"I'm sending you somewhere safe," he says. "I don't want you to leave my sight, but everyone's right, it's better for you to leave here for a few days. I'm being selfish in wanting you to stay."

"Can't you come with me?" I ask, taking in a few shallow breaths. I don't want to leave him. But I need to think of the baby first.

He looks regretful. "I need to be here for my brothers. I wish I could, babe, but I'm their VP. They need me right now."

I bite the inside of my cheek. He's right. "Where will I go?"

"Jim said his baby sister and her husband will look after you. They live a few hours away, and he's ex-army. They'll take good care of you," he says, looking down at the floor.

"Okay, I'll go," I tell him.

"Pack your bag."

"Dex . . ."

"Yes?"

"Promise me you'll come and get me in a few days," I tell him.

"Fuck, babe. It's going to be hell without you," he croaks. "But I need you safe. You need to take care of yourself and our little princess."

I nod and silently start packing a bag. "Who's driving me there?"

"It's going to have to be Vinnie," he says, looking apologetic. "I wish I could take you."

"It's fine," I reply, sliding my feet into my flip-flops. "It's going to suck, but we need to do what we have to."

"It's just for a few days."

Yeah, a few days while I'm wondering who is dead and alive?

Sounds like hell on earth, but at least my little girl will be safe.

"You need to go now so you get there before it gets dark," he says, cradling my cheeks in his hands. "We can do this."

I don't know who he's trying to convince. Me or him.

"I love you," I tell him as he kisses me with a desperation so thick I can taste it. His hands tangle in my hair as he shows me how much he's going to miss me through this kiss. Dex has become everything to me. He understands me; he lets me be me and appreciates it. I know how lucky I am to find someone like this, someone who doesn't want me to change any aspect of myself. Someone who makes me feel things, feel alive and wanted.

"Be safe, Dex," I whisper. "I'll be waiting for you."

"And I'll be fighting for you," he says, kissing me on the forehead. "Now, get out of here before I change my mind."

The drive starts out blissfully uneventful. Vinnie treats me like I'm fragile, making sure I'm fine the whole way. Apart from my swollen feet, I feel okay. I tell myself everyone will be fine so many times that I begin to believe it. Clover kicks me, reminding me that I'm here for a reason. Worrying isn't going to help Dex. I need to concentrate on what's going on here and just have faith that everything back home will be okay. I can't be mad at anyone. At Dex or Arrow. I knew what I was getting into here, and this is just one of the things I'm going to have to deal with as Dex's old lady.

We're about halfway there when Vinnie says, "Don't look now, but we're being followed."

I sit up straighter in my seat. "Are you sure?"

"Positive."

"What do we do?" I ask, wringing my hands.

"I'm going to try to lose them."

"And if you can't?" I ask, peering into the side mirror.

"Then I'm going to stop somewhere. Can you drive?" he asks, in a completely calm tone.

"Yeah, I guess so."

"Good," he says, as he suddenly speeds up the car. Shots start firing from behind us.

"Holy shit, holy shit," I keep muttering, my heart racing. I could only imagine the horror etched on my expression right now.

Vinnie goes even faster. The car behind us tries to keep up but soon falls behind. We stop at the gas station and swap seats.

As we get back on the road, Vinnie pulls a gun out of his jeans and loads it.

I gasp. "Is that why I have to drive?"

"Yes, I need my hands free," he says, peering behind us. "Turn left here. I'm going to go a back way, and hopefully they'll keep going straight ahead and end up somewhere else."

I turn left, like he says. We speed up but still find them trailing behind.

"What are we going to do?" I ask, starting to panic. "This is much more fun in movies."

"Either we lose them, or slow down and shoot them."

Oh fuck.

"Lose them, please. I vote for losing them!"

"Turn here," Vinnie suddenly says.

I turn, and we take a longer route to the house, but at least we make it there safely.

Fuck. That was close.

After sitting in the car with Vinnie and calming myself down, I meet Jim's sister, Paula, and her husband, Matthew. They are both lovely and make me feel welcome into their house from the get-go.

"Thanks for driving me here, Vinnie," I say, kissing his cheek. "Be safe."

"Always. See you soon," he says, lifting his chin in goodbye. I watch him drive away.

"Come on, honey, I'll show you your room," Paula says. She doesn't look anything like Jim, with her fair hair and features.

"Thank you so much for letting me stay," I say.

She waves her hand. "No bother at all. In fact I could use the company. It gets a little boring out here."

She shows me to the guest room. A large room with yellow walls and a big bed covered in white sheets. "It's gorgeous, thank you."

"I don't know about that, but it will do. Are you hungry? I'm just about to make something to eat," she says kindly. Matthew carries my bag in and places it on the floor. He's an older man, but he still has his army physique.

"Thank you," I tell him, mustering a smile for him.

"No problem," he says, walking away.

Paula sighs. "A man of few words, my Matthew. Come on, I'll give you a tour."

She shows me the house, an older two-story brick farmhouse, and the huge land that surrounds it. They have horses, sheep, and cows.

"I wish I could go riding!" I sigh when we pass the stables.

She grins and looks down at my stomach. "Maybe after the baby comes."

I laugh. "I'll hold you to that."

"You're welcome here anytime, honey, even when you aren't being chased by crazy bikers."

I look around and smile.

It really is a peaceful place, with fresh air and scenic views.

I could learn to enjoy my time here.

# TWENTY-SEVEN

CHECK my phone obsessively for the first two days. Dex messages back whenever he can and tells me everything is okay. I get a call as he wakes up, and a text before he goes to sleep, which is much later than me, but I don't mind. Days three, four, and five pass the same. Calls and messages, but no mention of what's going on or when I'll be going home.

> Faye: I miss you.
> Dex: Miss you too.
> Faye: What's going on over there?
> Dex: Trust me. Will call when I can.
> Faye: Okay. I want to come home.
> Dex: When it's safe.

How long is that going to take? I don't think anyone is ever going to be safe.

Paula takes me to see a local doctor for a checkup. I feel depressed that Dex wasn't there with me.

Selfish, I know.

When I don't hear from Dex on days six and seven, I call Cindy, who tells me Dex is okay—just busy.

But something doesn't feel right.

I call Arrow, Irish, and Tracker. No one answers.

I start to panic.

The next day I ring Jim and demand answers. "Little girl," he sighs.

"Just tell me!" I yell into the phone. Is he dead? In the hospital?

"He's in jail. Cops came to search the clubhouse. Dex was armed."

Jail?

"When will he get out?" I croak, clutching the phone so hard it might break.

"We'll find out soon. I sent the lawyer, Greg, to try and get him out. Stay strong, okay?"

"I will," I mutter before we both hang up.

Jail.

At least he's alive.

When I finally get his call a few days later, the tears refuse to subside.

"Faye," he says quietly as a greeting.

"Oh my god, Dex!" I sob into the phone. I start to pace as we talk.

"How are you and the baby?" he asks.

"We're both fine. When can you get out?" I ask him, rushing the words out.

He sighs. "My lawyer is trying to get me out on bail. Should find out soon."

"I miss you," I whisper.

"You too," he replies. "I don't have much time."

"Is it safe for me to go home?" I ask. "Fuck, I wish you were here."

"Wait there until I come and get you" is all he says in reply.

"Okay. I love you."

"Faye," he murmurs, so much emotion in that one word.

"Dex?"

"I breathe you, baby, don't give up on me."

"I won't."

We hang up.

≈

The next day I'm lying in bed when there's a knock at the door. "Come in, Paula!" I call out.

The door opens, and I turn my head. Then I scream. "Dex! You're here!"

He walks over. "Don't get out of bed for me."

With my size, it's kind of hard to anyway.

He takes me into his arms, kissing my forehead, my nose, and finally my lips. "Missed you so fuckin' much, Faye."

He kisses my stomach twice.

"I missed you too. I was going crazy. What happened? And how are you here?" I ask him, not letting go of him for even one second.

"Lawyer got me out on bail this morning, I stopped at the clubhouse first, then came straight here," he says, nuzzling my neck. When he starts to trail kisses down my collarbone I struggle to breathe.

"I'm not done questioning you yet," I tell him.

"What do you want to know?"

"Everything."

"Cops raided the clubhouse. I was armed, they took me in—possession of a firearm," he says, kissing my mouth before I can say anything in return. He pulls down the strap of my white sundress and brushes his thumb over one of my nipples. I moan into his mouth.

"I want you," he says against my lips.

"Then take me," I reply. I thread my fingers through his hair and grip on the ends. His lips don't leave mine as his fingers start to explore my body. I start to pull his T-shirt off, gripping the hem that sits just above his ass and sliding it upward. He pulls away from me for a second to tug it over his head and throw it on the floor. I admire his chest for a few seconds, before he lies back.

"I don't want to squash you. Can you ride me?" he asks, lifting up my dress.

I grin and undo the button on his jeans. He lifts up his hips as I pull his pants down. His arousal stands up proud, begging for attention. I kiss the head of him, then pull down my panties and straddle him. He plumps my breasts with his hands, then leans forward to taste. Unable to take any more, I slide his length inside me, slowly, inch by inch. We both moan at the same time as I start to ride him slowly. Our eyes stay connected as I take my time with him, showing him with my body how much I missed him and how much he means to me. We finish together.

"What aren't you telling me?" I ask him after we catch our breath.

"Is this our pillow talk?" he asks, stroking my hair.

"Dex . . ."

"I have to go to court in a few weeks. Because I have a record, my lawyer thinks I might have to do some time," he says hesitantly. His eyes flash with uncertainty.

"Possession of a firearm. You'd have to do about six months," I gasp, sitting up on the bed.

"Babe, it'll be okay," he soothes, rubbing my back. "You'll be safe. That's all that matters."

"What happened with Arrow?" I ask him, turning to face him.

"He's fine, and it's all taken care of."

"Dex—"

"You don't want the details, Faye, trust me on that."

I sigh. "Shall we drive back now? Or tomorrow morning?"

"Paula insisted we stay for dinner," he says. "How have you been feeling?"

"Tired, but everything else is fine. I saw the local doctor here," I assure him.

"Good," he whispers. "Do you know how happy you make me? You're all I could think about. If something happened to you . . ."

"I'm fine, it's you who was in jail," I say with an eye roll. And has to go back there for six fucking months. What the hell do I do with that information? He might be going away as soon as Clover is born.

"What are you thinking?" he asks, wrapping me in his arms.

"You aren't going to be here for Clover and me," I whisper. "I know it's selfish to even say, but . . ."

"It's not selfish. I'm sorry, Faye. Let's not think about this right now."

How am I supposed to not think about it?

TWENTY-EIGHT

W E can't keep our hands off each other on the drive home. Even if it was just my hand on his thigh, or him kissing my fingers, we stayed in contact as much as we could. We didn't talk about his possible jail time.

I just wanted to enjoy the moment.

"How did you get involved with the Wind Dragons?" I find myself asking him.

He glances at me before answering. "After I left home, I went in search of my dad. Eric and I have different fathers, which I assume you know."

I nod my head. Eric's dad is a dentist who lives on the east coast.

"Turns out he was a member of the club but had died a few years back. My mother and he weren't serious. I'm pretty sure they met and hooked up a few times, and that was it. Jim and him were best friends," he says, sadness lacing his tone. "That's how I met Jim. And the rest is history."

"They became your family," I say, looking down at our intertwined hands.

"It felt like I was close to my dad, even though he wasn't there. It turned out that he wanted to be a part of my life, but Ma said no. She didn't want me growing up around the club, so he sent her money and that's it. Jim did tell me that he came to my graduation, and he was proud as hell," he says, the tone of his voice letting me know that it did mean something to him. His dad had loved him, even though he wasn't able to be a part of his life.

My throat starts to burn. "Your mother did to him what I almost did to you."

Clover would have gone to find her father and ended up hanging around the MC anyway.

He squeezes my hand. "All in the past, babe. I've forgiven you; you should forgive yourself."

"Did anyone get hurt?" I ask hesitantly. He doesn't want to talk about it, but I need to know what went down while I was away.

"Trace got shot in the arm; Rake is a little black and blue," he says, looking straight ahead.

"Okay." That's not bad, I guess. "And then the cops raided the clubhouse?"

"Yeah, we had just let everyone clear out, lockdown being over, when they busted in," he replies. "People heard gunshots at the Wild Men clubhouse, and I don't know, I guess they must have seen one of us around there. Both clubhouses were raided. Unlucky for them they were found with drugs, guns, and women who were there against their will. We were only caught with a couple of guns."

"So they're in big shit, then?" I ask, unable to stop the slow spreading smile taking over my face.

"Bloodthirsty woman," he mutters, but I see his lip twitching, giving away his amusement. "Now where are we going? To the clubhouse or to our house?"

I think about it. "Clubhouse. I think we should move into the house after Clover is born."

"I love that you love it at the clubhouse," he admits.

I shrug. "Those guys have grown on me. Everyone has, even Allie, that bitch."

Dex laughs. We're silent for a few minutes, lost in our own thoughts.

"I miss Mary," I whisper. "She didn't deserve to die."

"I know," he replies. "She was a good woman."

"Too good," I say on a sigh. I hope she's in a better place. They say death is easy; it's living that's hard. I love my life, and I wouldn't say it was hard. But people who pass away don't have to live with the pain of losing someone.

When we arrive at the clubhouse, my mouth drops open as I see the women standing there with pink balloons. "Surprise!" they shout in unison.

"What the hell is this?" I ask, excitement coursing through me.

Dex wraps his arms around me from behind. "Baby shower. This is my cue to leave. Brothers and I will be at the bar."

Then anyone with a penis promptly flees the clubhouse without a backward glance.

I walk into the living area, which has a table full of wrapped gifts. Tears well in my eyes. "You guys!"

Allie smiles sadly. "Mary was planning it before . . ."

I give her a shaky smile, then look to Cindy, Jess, and the others. "Thanks, all of you."

"You're welcome," Cindy says. "Now, let's eat, then play some baby-shower games."

I looked heavenward and sent a thank-you to Mary. I

should have known she would have been at the heart of this. "I can't believe you did this," I whisper, taking in all the effort they'd gone into.

"Come on, Faye!" Cindy calls. "Look at the cupcakes we made."

Cupcakes?

I grin and follow them into the kitchen.

≈

"Where's Arrow?" I ask Dex later that night when all the guys came back to the clubhouse.

Everyone goes deathly silent. "What?"

"You didn't tell her?" Jim asks Dex.

"Tell me what? Oh my god! What happened to him?" I ask, walking up to Dex and grabbing on to the lapels of his leather jacket. "Is he okay? You said he was okay!"

"He's in jail, babe. I didn't want to stress you out any more," he says, putting his hands on my stomach.

"Why is he still in there?" I ask. "What priors did he have?"

All the men exit the room. What the fuck?

"He didn't get taken in on gun possession; they charged him with murder," Dex says, his eyes betraying the casualness of his tone.

"What?" I whisper, shaking my head no. "No. No, this is not happening."

Arrow? He can't go to jail. My mind races.

Flashbacks.

Him cooking breakfast naked. Him smiling at Mary. Him staring at my stomach like I was contagious.

"Club lawyer is on it," Dex says. "Let Greg do his job."

"I'm going to call him and get all the case details, see if I can help."

Dex nods. "Okay."

"When I'm the official club lawyer, no one is going to fucking jail," I mutter, my voice cracking.

Dex grips my chin. "When?"

"When."

He lowers his head and gives me a possessive, lingering kiss that makes my head spin. "Baby shower's over, yeah?"

"It can be," I reply against his lips.

"Good," he replies. His eyes touch every feature on my face. He pushes his hips against me, letting me feel how hard he is. "See, triple chin, and I'm still hard as a fuckin' rock."

I gasp. "You ass—"

Another kiss cuts me off. He walks me backward into our bedroom, mouths still attached.

Soon, our clothes are on the floor, and Dex is right where he belongs.

TWENTY-NINE

I LIKE this whole waddling thing you've got going on," Tracker says, eyes laughing at me. I'm now almost nine months pregnant, and the whale jokes are getting old.

"You guys are such jerks," I say around a mouthful of ice cream.

"And I can see why Sin is so whipped," he says, watching my tongue lick the spoon.

I pause. "You're a sick bastard, you know that?"

"I don't get any complaints," he adds, rubbing his chest with his palm.

"How's Allie?" I ask nosily, wiggling my eyebrows.

His expression doesn't change. "Why don't you ask her?"

I lick my ice cream and pout. "Fine, don't have a deep and meaningful conversation with me."

"You want it deep?" he replies in a low tone.

"Is that your sex voice? Hot!" I reply, fanning myself.

He doesn't look impressed, but I think I see a lip twitch. "There's a danger in loving someone too much. . . ."

"That's a song!"

"What?"

"That line is from a song," I say, shaking my head. "I'm a hundred percent sure it is."

He stares at me for a few tense seconds. "I'm going to get a drink."

As he walks out of the living room, I feel something dripping down my legs.

Shit.

I walk into my bedroom, looking for Dex. I hear the shower on, so I open the bathroom door. The room is filled with steam, and he's singing the lyrics to an Incubus song.

"Dex . . ." I call out. The shower curtain opens and his head sticks out, still covered in shampoo.

I look down my legs, to where my water's just broke. "I need to go to the hospital. It's time."

I speak to him in a calm tone, but as soon as the words penetrate I can see the panic fill him. "Now?"

He turns the shower off and jumps out.

"Babe, wash the shampoo out first." I stifle a laugh.

He runs a hand through his hair, then jumps back in, not even waiting for the water to get warm. I grab my already packed overnight bag, and the smaller bag that is packed for Clover. When he runs out and starts to get dressed, I get into the shower and breathe through a contraction. Dex slides open the curtain. "How are you doing?"

"Okay. Can you call the hospital and let them know we're on our way?"

He nods and leaves the bathroom. I turn the shower off and dry myself. I'm putting lotion onto my skin when Dex stops in front of me.

"Really? Do we have the time for this?"

I hide a smile. "I'm ready; I just have to put on my dress and some panties."

He helps me dress, then we walk out of the room. Tracker walks toward us, drink in hand. "You okay?"

"She's having a baby; no, she's not fuckin' okay," Dex growls.

"Dex," I snap.

Tracker's eyes go wide, and he starts to stare at my crotch like the baby is going to drop out at any second. "I'll go get the car ready."

Rake walks over and holds my other side. "Say good-bye to your tight—"

"Do not even finish that sentence!" I bark at him. "Dex, please hit him for me."

"I will afterward," Dex replies, opening the front door for me. Tracker is standing by the car, doors wide-open and the engine running. Dex helps me into the front seat and fastens the seat belt over my bulging belly. Rake and Tracker both kiss me on the forehead and wish me good luck.

"You okay?" Dex asks as he reverses.

I breathe in and out. "So far so good. Lucky the hospital isn't too far away though."

Dex reaches over and takes my hand in his.

We're almost at the hospital when I cry out. "Fuck!"

"What?" Dex yells, panicking.

"That contraction hurt. Oh my god! It hurts!" I say, trying to breathe through the pain.

Dex starts cursing. "We're almost there, babe."

"This is all your fault!" I yell, looking for someone to blame for the pain I'm in.

"Babe, we're here. You can yell at me all you want; let's just get you in there."

And yell at him I did.

———

Thirteen hours later, I hold Clover Mary Black in my arms. With her father's black hair and my hazel eyes, she is absolutely adorable. She's eight pounds, with chubby cheeks and little pouty heart-shaped lips.

She's perfect.

"You were amazing," Dex tells me, blue eyes sparkling. "That was . . . something else."

"Scarred for life, are you?" I ask, trying not to laugh.

He scrubs a hand down his face. "You didn't see it! A thick head of black hair stretching the shit out of your—"

"Dex!" I growl when the nurse starts to give him dirty looks.

He takes Clover from me, holding her in his large arms. "She's so tiny. Is she supposed to be this small?"

"She's very healthy," I tell him. "Everything is as it should be, don't worry."

I roll my eyes as he fiddles with the Wind Dragons baby beanie he had made for her. "Everyone wants to come in and see her; is that okay? Or do you want to wait?"

"Send them in, I don't mind," I reply, covering my breasts with the sheet. In fact, I can't wait to show her off. How did I create something so perfect?

Cindy, Allie, and Jess rush in first while Tracker, Rake, Jim, Trace, and Vinnie trail in behind. The women ooh and aah, and the men stare at Clover like they have no idea what to do with her. Then the nurse comes in and chases half of them out of the room.

"You did well, baby mama," Tracker says. I notice he and Allie are holding hands.

"Did you expect otherwise?" I ask with a raised brow.

He grins and shakes his head. "I think we know not to underestimate you."

Dex gently drags a tattooed finger down Clover's rosy cheek. "I'm screwed, aren't I?"

Tracker puts his hand on Dex's shoulder. "We have your back, brother, always."

Rake puts his hand on his other shoulder. "You think anyone's going to want to touch the Wind Dragons' princess?"

I roll my eyes at their protectiveness. "Give the girl some room to breathe."

Clover starts to cry, and Dex starts fussing over her. We all watch with wide eyes as he gently rocks her back to sleep.

"I've got this." He grins smugly. Jim looks amused, wrapping his arms around Cindy and watching on.

Dex's eyes find mine. "I've got this," he repeats, kissing Clover on her forehead.

~~

We have six weeks of bliss before Dex has to go to court. Six weeks of nothing but family time. It was amazing.

"Where's my little princess?" Dex coos to Clover as she stares up at him. "Such a beauty; look at those eyes."

I smile. He's so amazing with her, I can't even believe it. He's so in love with her, she has him wrapped around her little finger. I suddenly smell something and wrinkle my nose.

"Shotgun-not!" I yell out before he can.

He turns to me and frowns. "I changed the last one."

I smirk. "And I shotgunned-not yet again. It's the rules, Dex, you can't change the rules."

His lip twitches at that.

Just as I had guessed, Dex got six months behind bars.

Six. Fucking. Months.

The day before he had to leave, I cried. I cried so much that Dex begged me to stop.

"Don't cry, Faye. I need to know that you're going to be okay or I'm gonna go fuckin' crazy in there," he says. He slides down onto his knees before me. "I need you to be strong for me."

We make love. Slow and gentle.

In the morning before I wake up—he's gone.

That day, I move back into the clubhouse. No way am I staying alone in our house for half a year. I'd drive myself crazy in no time. Clover helps to make time go quicker than I thought. I miss Dex every day, but Clover is my shining light.

She gets me through the darkness.

~

"She's looking more like you every day," Tracker muses, staring down at Clover.

I look down at her angelic face. "Do you think so?"

He peers down at her again and bobs his head. "Yeah, she's your mini me."

We're silent for a few seconds.

"How are you holding up?" he asks in a low tone.

I exhale heavily and lean back on the couch. "I'm okay, because I have to be, you know?"

"You're fuckin'—" He looks down at Clover and then starts over. "You're strong, you know that? Who would have thought that you, walking into the clubhouse with no clue, wearing cupcake pajamas, and staring at us all wide-eyed like you had no idea what to do with us . . ."

He laughs and shakes his head. "You turned out to be the best thing to happen to Dex, and you're more than old-lady material. You don't just take care of Dex . . ."

"Hey, love the man, love the club, right?" I add when Tracker trails off. I yawn, bringing my hand up to cover my mouth.

Tracker grins. "Let Allie and me watch Clover. You get some sleep."

"Okay, if you two don't mind," I say, the exhaustion of being awake all night catching up to me.

"Just 'cuz Dex isn't here—we're gonna look after you," Tracker says softly, running his hands through his blond hair.

"I know," I reply. "So are you and Allie together?"

He tilts his head to the side. "I guess we are, yes."

"Good. You deserve to be happy," I tell him, meaning every word.

"For the record, we could have been fuckin' amazing together," he says, stretching his arms above his head lazily.

I can't stop the blush that makes an appearance. "Is that right? I've heard about your piercing. . . ."

"Oh, this," he says, unbuttoning his jeans. "Do you want to see?"

I elbow him in the ribs, laughing. "I'm curious but not that curious. Dex would kill you."

He smiles. "Good to hear you laugh again."

I watch as he gently takes my daughter from my arms, then kisses the top of my head. "Sleep. Clover will be fine."

"Thanks, Tracker," I mumble, my eyes already closing.

My last thought is of Dex before I fall asleep.

THIRTY

DEX has been gone for four months when Jim dies from lung cancer.

Everyone is devastated.

I sit by the hospital bed and watch as Cindy cries. The woman who didn't even cry the night Mary died right in front of her is bawling her eyes out. Something about seeing such a strong woman shatter makes it hard for me to try to stay strong.

I cry silently, holding Clover close to my chest.

The men stand around Cindy, helping her from the room. She wails, screaming Jim's name. We all leave the hospital and go back to the clubhouse. The place is unusually quiet, and extremely depressing. The men drink.

And then drink some more.

Jim's good friend Jack Kane and his son Xander come to help us with the funeral. Apparently Jack was once a member of the club, and I guess, officially, still is.

Since the new president of Wind Dragons is still behind bars, Trace takes over until Dex gets back. The club gets three new prospects; Ronan and Zack I like, but the other, Pill—not so much. I don't know why exactly, but I just don't trust him. Something about him doesn't sit right with me. I guess time will tell.

I refill Trace's drink and get a chin lift in thanks. Allie is sitting on Tracker's lap, whispering in his ear, so I don't intrude. Instead, I walk up to Rake, showing him the bottle of scotch. He lifts his glass up for me to pour.

"How are you holding up?" I ask him so only we can hear.

He gulps his drink, replying with a question of his own. "Where's Clover?"

"She's asleep," I tell him, pointing to the baby monitor sticking out of my jean pocket.

He nods his head, then stands up. "I need a woman and some more alcohol."

"I can provide the scotch, but unfortunately, I'm not a pimp."

That earns me a small smile. He cups my face and kisses me on the forehead. "Why don't you and Clover go home for a few days? This place isn't going to be any fun to be around."

I feel a little hurt, but I realize he's right. "That's probably a good idea."

I stay at home for a week.

Each day they send someone to check on me. It's not necessary, but kind of nice too.

When I return, the place is a mess, and there are women sleeping out in the open.

"Did they throw a party?" I ask Allie when I see her in the kitchen.

She nods. "It's been like this since you left. Few members from other chapters are here too, so it's not safe to just walk around here anymore."

Tracker walks into the kitchen, wearing nothing but a pair of boxer shorts. He smiles when he sees me. "You're back."

"Yeah, but I'm not staying," I reply, eyeing the place with distaste.

Tracker looks around and grimaces. "Place has kind of gone to hell."

"You think?" I reply dryly. Clover stirs in my arms.

"Can I hold her?" Allie asks.

I nod my head and gently pass her to Allie. "I'm gonna try and clean this place up a bit."

I get a large garbage bag and start picking up all the trash. After finishing the inside, I head out the back. I'm throwing bottles into the recycling bin when I hear steps behind me. I quickly turn and come face-to-face with the man from the first party I saw. The one Dex spoke to who wanted to "share" me. My pulse races as fear shoots through my system. There's something not right about this guy.

"How nice to see you again, and without your man," he says, staring at my breasts.

I force a smile. "I'm just trying to tidy the place up."

He takes a step closer and grips my wrist. "Dex isn't here, so I guess I should take care of you for him. I'm sure he doesn't want his old lady going without."

"Dex will kill you if you touch me," I grit out, trying to pull my wrist from his hold.

His grip tightens. "Dex isn't here."

He forces his mouth on mine, gripping my head with both his hands. I can feel him pressed against me, and he's hard. Hell no, this is not happening to me. I reach for one of the bottles in my trash bag, lift it, and hit him in the head. When he pulls back, his face contorting with rage, I whimper. He backhands me and I fall onto the ground.

I scream.

I scream for Tracker at the top of my lungs.

The man grabs me by the hair and yanks me up, just as Tracker runs out, still half-dressed.

"What the fuck!" he growls, running up and punching the man across his face. "Have you lost your fuckin' mind, Shame?"

Shame? How fitting.

I rub my hand along my jaw, grimacing at the burning pain. Tracker punches him in the stomach, then knees him in the head.

Shame falls to the ground.

"You're fuckin' dead when Dex gets out," Tracker spits out, kicking him in the head for good measure.

Suddenly Rake is behind me, picking me up like I weigh nothing and carrying me into the house.

"I want to go back home," I whimper against his chest. He puts me on his bed and touches my face, checking the damage.

"It's just a bit swollen. He hits like a bitch," Rake says. "Fuck, I can't believe he'd be so fuckin' stupid."

"I'm fine," I mumble. I stand up, ignoring Rake's demands. I find Allie and take Clover from her, then we both go home.

I cry as I drive, needing Dex.

I can't do this alone anymore.

≈

Two days later, I hear the rumble of motorcycles. I walk outside, Clover in my arms, to see Rake, Vinnie, Trace, Tracker, and the prospects all there.

My first thought—something has happened.

Tracker gets off his bike and walks to me.

"Is everyone okay?" I ask him, looking into his eyes for a hint of why they are here.

"Everything is fine. Are you okay?" he asks, a callused finger touching my jaw.

I flinch at the contact. "I'm fine; what's going on?"

"We came to bring you home. Everyone's cleared out, the random women are gone. It's all cleaned up. We want you back there. What happened the other day never should have fuckin' happened. We don't hurt women, and especially not you," he says, staring down at me. "Dex is going to gut all of us for not protecting you better."

I swallow hard. They were all here for me? "I don't know—"

"Get in your car, Faye, and bring that beautiful girl with you. We'll follow you," he says, crossing his arms over his chest, letting me know he wasn't going anywhere.

I smile. "Fine, let me pack some stuff."

Tracker helps me pack, and then they all follow my car home.

~

"Hi," I say into the phone, staring at Dex through the glass.

I see his throat work as he swallows, his gaze darting to every part of me that he can see.

"How are you? How is Clover?"

"We're fine, Dex, don't worry about us. We miss you so damn much though," I say, my voice catching at the end.

I clear my throat. I wasn't here to make him feel like shit; I needed to be strong.

"You have no idea how much I miss the two of you," he replies. "No fuckin' idea. I'm never leaving you again."

I was happy to hear it.

"Tell me," he says. "Tell me everything about her. I want to know everything."

"She has the cutest little laugh . . ."

~

Back at the clubhouse, everything goes back to normal. Without Dex, it isn't the same, but we make do and try to continue on like he wanted us to. The men do their business and make sure everything is running smoothly and look after the women.

Me, I count down the days until I get to see my man again.

I talk to my daughter about him, and I visit him in prison every chance I can get.

And then finally—finally that day comes.

The one I've been waiting for.

I wait for him, a few steps in front of the club members, Clover in my arms. I hear the rumble of an engine as his car pulls into the lot. The sun glints off the windshield so I can't make out his features—I shift impatiently, willing him to get out of the car quickly.

Then the door swings open and, at last, I see him. A plain white T-shirt clings to his muscled body, and his eyes solely are on me.

It's like no one else is here.

Just us.

He jogs toward me and grips the back of my neck and kisses me like . . . well, like a man just getting out of prison. I ignore the whistles and catcalls from the peanut gallery. Dex pulls back and our eyes connect. His are full of emotion, desire, need, and pain all at once.

"We missed you," I whisper, pulling him back down for another quick kiss.

"I missed you both so fuckin' much," he whispers, resting his forehead against mine, his voice thick. He looks away from me to Clover.

"She's so beautiful," he says softly, taking her into his arms, kissing her forehead and whispering to her, making her laugh. He looks at her like she's everything to him.

Like she's precious, like he couldn't look away even if he wanted to.

He holds her to his chest and kisses the top of her head.

Then, his daughter in his arms, he goes and greets his brothers. Many half hugs and shoulder slaps later, he comes back to me and wraps me in his arms.

"Time to go home, yeah?" he says, grazing his teeth across his bottom lip. "Fuck, it feels like it's been forever. Home. Now. We have lost time to make up for."

I go up on my tiptoes and kiss him on the lips. "Take us home, then."

THIRTY-ONE

H E walks out, his stride slow, dressed in that hideous green jumpsuit.

"Arrow," I whisper, and he sits down, his small smile and eyes for Clover and Clover only.

"She's gotten so big," he rasps, taking her in from head to toe. "Brother," he says, nodding his head at Dex, and then looking to me and giving me a warm look. "Faye."

Clover makes a giggling sound, and we all look down at her.

"She looks just like you," he says to me, flashing Dex a look that says *Good luck with that.*

It's so awkward making conversation with someone in prison. What do you ask them? *How are you? What did you do today? What are your plans for the week?* We let Arrow guide the conversation and answer him as he asks how everyone is and what he's been missing out on. We stay for an hour before we have to leave.

As we walk to our car in silence, I try to push away the miserable feeling of leaving him behind.

"Let's go home, babe," Dex says, his palm rubbing his chest, right where his four-leaf clover tattoo is.

I look back at the prison one last time before putting Clover in her car seat.

"How come you never let me drive your car?" I ask when we get on the road.

"Have you seen you drive?"

"Yes, and I'm awesome," I reply, my eyes narrowing.

He scoffs. "What were you wearing for your driving test? Something fuckin' short, I bet. With your tits out."

I gasp in outrage. "You did not just say that!"

I think back to what I wore for my driving test. Jeans. And okay, maybe a low-cut top, but that's not why I passed my test.

"See. You were, weren't you?" he says, sounding smug.

"No, I wasn't," I lie.

"Liar."

"Annoying," I mutter under my breath.

His hand rubs up my thigh. "Are you happy?"

I turn to him, taken off guard by the seriousness of his tone. "I'm very happy."

"Good," he replies, soft blue eyes on me for a second before turning back to the road.

"I'd tell you if I wasn't," I add. "Trust me, you'd know."

His lip twitches. "Good."

"Are you happy?" I ask.

"You're everything to me. You and Clover. I don't think I've ever been this happy in my life," he says quietly.

"Good answer," I mutter under my breath.

He grins. "I'm learning."

I lean over and kiss him on the cheek. "I breathe you, babe."

He turns his head and catches my lips in a quick kiss. "Right back at you."

I aim the gun like a pro and shoot at the target.

"Fuck, you're getting good," Dex says when I'm done.

"I'm a woman of many talents," I tell him, wiggling my eyebrows suggestively.

"Don't I know it," he adds, his gaze dropping to my mouth. "It's hot seeing you handle a weapon."

I love when he looks at me like he has to have me right then and there. I didn't exactly lose all my baby weight after Clover. My stomach is a little rounder and has a few stretch marks. Dex doesn't seem to mind one bit though.

"I feel confident with guns. Now we need to move on to something else. Knife throwing, maybe?" I propose. I'd just seen a movie in the cinemas with a hot-ass guy throwing knifes and now I wanted to try it.

"Knife throwing?" he asks, eyes dancing with amusement.

"What about fencing? That ought to be a good time," I suggest.

Now he straight out laughs at me.

"I want to learn how to ride my own motorcycle too," I tell him. I love being on the back of his bike, but I want the feel of steering a machine like that myself.

"That I can teach you," he muses, eyes turning hungry.

"Good, I'd hate to have to ask one of the other men," I tease.

His eyes immediately darken. "You don't get on the back of anyone else's bike, or let them teach you anything, you know this."

"I've only ever been on the back of your bike."

"I know," he says. "And that's how it's gonna stay. Isn't it?"

He leans forward and cups my chin in his hands. My breath hitches, and I feel my body respond to his tone.

"Only you, Dex," I assure him.

"Want to fuck you bent over my bike," he whispers into my ear. "Your ass sticking out, ready and waiting for me."

I rub against him, only to feel him hard already. Good, I'm not the only one getting turned on here.

"Take me home, prez," I whisper into his ear, nibbling on the lobe.

# EPILOGUE

DEX scoops some baby food onto the spoon, then makes an airplane sound, trying to get Clover to open her little mouth. She opens it but then closes it at the last second, making the food dribble all down her chin. Dex takes a bib and wipes it, then tries another trick, trying to make her laugh, then quickly putting the spoon in her mouth.

It doesn't work.

"Clover, you need to eat to become big and strong like your dad," he tells her, trying again. This time, she opens her mouth but then spits it all out. A blob lands on his face.

He sighs patiently and raises his thickly muscled arm to wipe the food from his face.

I start laughing; I can't help it.

He spins to see me, wiping the food from his face. "Thank f— Thank eff you're here."

"I've been here for a while. I was just watching you," I admit, unable to hide my smirk.

He puffs out a breath. "I need a smoke."

"Go have one; I'll give Clover a bath," I tell him, taking her out of her high chair.

"How was class?" he asks, slapping me gently on the ass.

"Same as usual," I reply, kissing my daughter's chubby cheek.

"So you're kicking ass then?"

"Of course," I reply. I'm one of the top students in my class.

He steps up behind me, wrapping his arms around me from behind. "That's my girl."

He kisses the top of my head, then Clover's.

I smile to myself.

This wasn't how I thought my life would turn out, but I'm glad it did.

Dexter Black twisted my world upside down, but then he gave me his.

And his world is where I want to be, as long as he's right there by my side.

$\approx$

My high heels tap on the floor, the clicking sound keeping me distracted. Holding my file close to my chest, I wait impatiently. Finally I see him walk out, carrying a bag in his hand.

"Took your time," he calls out as he walks toward me, looking in desperate need of a haircut.

"Sorry," I reply, throwing my arms around him. "I kind of had to get my degree first, then wait for you to be granted parole."

"Where's your husband?" he asks, looking around for Dex.

"Everyone is waiting for you back at the clubhouse," I say. "And we all know I'm your favorite person, so I came alone."

They have something planned for his welcome-home and

were busy getting it organized. I know it involved a bunch of strippers and lots of alcohol. Arrow's kind of party.

"Let's get the fuck out of here," he growls. "I've been in there so long, even you're starting to look good."

I gasp and punch him in the arm, ignoring his husky laughter.

"Still your charming self, I see. And you think I want to be here? I feel like I live here," I complain, shaking my head.

His lip curves slightly. "Comes with the territory."

"I'm going to practice at the shooting range, want to come?" I ask.

"Very fucking funny."

I grin and take Arrow home.

# ABOUT THE AUTHOR

New York Times and *USA Today* bestselling author **Chantal Fernando** is twenty-seven years old and lives in Western Australia.

When not reading, writing, or daydreaming, she can be found enjoying life with her three sons and family.

Chantal loves to hear from readers and can be found on her Facebook author page or her website.

Being the younger sister of a Wind Dragons MC
member isn't as great as you'd think it would be . . .

Find out how Anna deals with the bad boys of the
Wind Dragons Motorcycle Club and paves her
own way in the second book in this sexy new series
from bestselling author Chantal Fernando!

ARROW'S HELL

Coming summer 2015 from Gallery Books

CHAPTER ONE

Anna

D O you have any plans now?" Damien asks as we walk out of the
lecture.

I turn to him. "My ride will be here soon. I'm just going home.
I have a lot to do."

"Oh, okay. How about this weekend?"

Damien's a nice guy, but I don't feel anything when I look at
him. He is just a friend; not even that, more of an acquaintance.

"I'm going out with my best friend, Lana, this weekend," I reply,
forcing a smile. I don't want to lead him on, but I don't want to hurt
him either. I am horrible in these kinds of situations.

"Maybe I could take you—"

I roll my eyes as I hear the rumble of a motorcycle, stopping
Damien midsentence. Sliding my phone into my bag for safekeeping, I say, "Gotta go, Damien. I'll see you tomorrow, okay?"

"'Bye, Anna."

Right on time—like clockwork.

I glance around the courtyard, then walk toward the parking lot.
You would think at my age I could catch a bus home to my apart-
ment without any drama, but that isn't the case. I don't have a car,
but I'm saving up for one. However, my brother makes sure I have
a lift home after class, especially if I finish in the late afternoon. I'm
still not sure how I feel about it. It does feel good to have someone,

my brother in particular, looking out for me, but at the same time, after doing my own thing for so long I feel a little claustrophobic.

My brother is one of my favorite people in the world, and after not having seen him for some time, I am happy to be getting to know him again. I just moved back to the city, and am finding the move easier than I had anticipated, mainly because my best friend, Lana, is here. We'd stayed in touch ever since I moved away, so I'm psyched to be so close to her now. My brother has changed, but I know that he still loves and cares about me. I'm the only family he has, after all. His overprotectiveness, however, needs to change. I know he means well and is trying to make up for lost time, but the constant escorts are beginning to drive me batshit crazy. He keeps an eye on my every move and sometimes tries to dictate them. I feel like I'm in a damn prison. I love my brother and I'm trying to make this work for the both of us, but we're both still on shaky ground, not 100 percent comfortable with each other yet. We're feeling each other out, seeing how we've both changed and how we've stayed the same.

I don't miss the curious stares from the other students on campus, but I ignore them. I can just imagine how it looks, my getting picked up every day by a different man on a motorcycle, each one of them sporting a Wind Dragons Motorcycle Club cut. Luckily for me, I'm not a young, insecure girl anymore and there's only a handful of people in the world whose opinion I actually care about. Likely they think I'm a biker groupie, or something along those lines. In reality, I'm just a twenty-five-year-old PhD student and a girl who happens to be the younger sister of a Wind Dragons MC member. If people want to judge me, that's their prerogative, and I couldn't care less.

I'm proud of my brother. He is who he is. He means well and I know he loves me. Yes, he's a biker, belonging to a motorcycle club that is well-known in these parts, but he's also a good man.

Adam's always been a good man.

He also happens to be a huge pain in my ass, a total man-whore, and overprotective to the point of stupidity. Ever since I was a little girl, he'd taken his role of big brother very seriously. It probably had to do with the fact that we didn't know who our father was, and our mother was . . . absent. That was putting it nicely—in fact, our mother was a junkie who left us to fend for ourselves ever since I could remember.

My brother also made it his business to scare off any potential dates, and that hasn't changed. If anything, it's gotten worse. It seems when most men around here find out who my brother is, they decide I'm not worth the ass kicking they'll get—but in a way it's almost like a screening test. I don't want a man who's a pussy and afraid of my brother. I want a strong man who'll tell my brother to fuck off and smile while doing it. The thought makes me grin to myself.

I wonder who my babysitter will be today.

Seeing the sexy beard and the broad, wide shoulders encased in tight black fabric, I smile widely, pleased with my escort for today. I walk straight up to his idling bike, sashaying my hips with each step.

"Good afternoon, Arrow," I say, grinning cheekily.

He narrows his eyes on me. "You gonna give me trouble today, Anna?"

Probably.

But only because he needs it. The man hardly smiles, so I find myself being more playful around him than I am around anyone else, just to get a reaction out of him.

"Anna?" he repeats, staring at me weirdly when I don't reply as I continue to study him, lost in my own thoughts.

Fuck, but I love the way he says my name. Arrow must have a good ten years on me, but he doesn't look it. Not to me. He has a better body than most of the men my age and a beard that looks badass on him.

I do love a good beard.

You can tell that under the beard is a strong, square jaw. I wonder if he has a dimple in his chin.

He also has soulful brown eyes that you just know have seen the world at its worst, but he's still survived. He has faint crinkles on either side of his eyes, letting me know he once used to laugh a lot. His mouth is full, firm, and entirely lickable.

"I have no idea what you're talking about," I tell him with a shrug. I push my blond hair off my face and flash him an innocent look. I have the same green eyes as my brother, and while his incite lust from the opposite sex, mine don't seem to be doing the same. Arrow's face turns grumpier, if that's even possible. What the hell is he so moody about all the time? Yes, I heard he did time in jail, but most bikers do at some point, don't they? At least the ones I've heard of. Okay, I guess I shouldn't stereotype like that. But Arrow did do time, although I don't know what for. I overheard my brother talking with Tracker, another member of the MC. I've been around these bikers for a month or so now, and out of all of them, Arrow is the one who keeps both his distance *and* his guard up.

He's also the one I can't stop thinking about.

Quite a conundrum.

Well, for me anyway.

Have you ever seen someone for the first time and just *wanted* them? Something about them attracts you, like a moth to a flame, without rhyme or reason. Every time I look at Arrow I feel that pull. That want, that need. There is something about him, something that draws me to him. Sure, he is gruff and rough around the edges. He is also temperamental, broody, and usually pretty damn grumpy. He is a man of few words—the strong, silent type. The more time he is forced to spend as my babysitter, the more I've gotten him to open up. Slowly, little by little, he's started speaking to me. It is progress, but still, I know I am stupid to hope for anything more. Sure, my heart races whenever he is near, but I try to ignore that little factor as best as I can. It doesn't change anything. Arrow is my guilty pleasure, something I know I shouldn't want but want anyway. The thing is, I've seen little glimpses of him that make me believe he is more than he shows the world. I've seen him playing with Clover, the MC president's daughter, and sneaking her strawberry candy. I've seen him tickling her, her loud giggles echoing throughout the room. I then overheard him telling her that if any boy messes with her, to let him know and he would take care of it because no one hurts the princess.

She's five.

No one can tell me the man doesn't have a heart.

"Get on the bike and hold on," he demands, turning away from me. It frustrates me that he never looks at me for longer than he has to. Is he not attracted to me at all? I'm not vain, but I know that I'm not completely unfortunate in the looks department. Adam has even said I'm too beautiful for my own good, but as my brother, I guess he's a little biased.

Maybe Arrow sees me as nothing more than Adam's baby sister. But that doesn't explain why he always seems so eager to leave my presence. I like to think I'm easy to be around, and sometimes even a little fun.

"Where are we going?" I ask as he hands me my helmet.

"Rake wants to see you at the clubhouse," he replies distractedly.

"Then why didn't he pick me up himself?" I ask. Not that I'm complaining, since I secretly covet being around Arrow, but still.

"I was closer to campus, so it just made more sense. Now are you getting on the bike or are we gonna sit around while all these stuck-up assholes stare at us?"

I look around.

Yeah, people are still staring. If he didn't want the attention, maybe he shouldn't have worn his cut today. Who am I kidding? People would stare either way. Arrow is imposing. It is in his build, the breadth of his shoulders, the way he carries himself. The sharpness of his gaze. He just commands attention around him, and there is nothing he can do about it. He couldn't fade into the background if he tried. I slide onto the back of his bike. Wrapping my arms around his waist, I grip the leather in my hands and lean into him. He smells like leather and . . . strawberry candy? I want to ask, but before I can he starts the engine and pulls out of the lot. I hold tight, enjoying both the ride and the feel of my body pressed against his.

I'd never been on a motorcycle until I moved back here. It was a new experience, and one I found that I loved. Nothing felt more freeing, and I found myself wanting to get my own motorcycle license. If being on the back feels this way, I can only imagine how good it feels to be in front, in control of the bike.

I wonder what my brother would think about that idea.

Adam and I didn't have the best childhood growing up. Neither of us talks about it much, to each other or to anyone else—at least that's how it used to be before I left. After I turned eighteen, I moved to the other side of the country for college. That was the year Adam—or should I say Rake—joined the Wind Dragons MC. We kept in touch here and there, messages, phone calls on birthdays and holidays, but for the most part we grew apart. He was busy, I was busy, and we were too far away to be of any real use to each other. I know he's proud of me. He used to tell me every time we spoke on the phone. He was happy I was making something of myself—starting from scratch to become someone statistics prove I shouldn't be. I also know he wants the best for me, he always has, but it almost feels like he doesn't know how to act around me anymore, how to be himself. He's changed over the years, I guess being in a motorcycle club will do that, but underneath he's still my Adam. A mix of protective, sweet, and goofy, and usually found with a grin on his face or a woman on his arm.

That definitely hasn't changed. My brother has always been, and will always be, a ladies' man. However, he's gotten even more protective of me than he was before I left the city, which makes no sense, because I'm not a girl anymore, I'm a grown woman. I'm his baby sister, by a year, but he's acting like I'm seventeen and trying to keep tabs on my every move. It was cute at first—but now it's getting damn annoying and he and I are in need of a good chat. I can't imagine he's any better at compromising than he was growing up, but maybe I can use my puppy-dog eyes to let him loosen the reins a little. The truth of the matter is I love being around Rake and his MC. I just don't like being controlled. I want to be there on my terms, not his. I want to be given choices and know that I'm being heard. Being around a group full of alpha males isn't easy.

I sigh against Arrow's back, enjoying the sensation of being pressed up against a man I should be glad wouldn't give me the time of day. He's dangerous, I know it and so would anyone who saw him. It is more than his physical appearance. You can almost feel the menace radiating from him, the raw power. It also doesn't take a genius to see that he has an extra-large chip on his shoulder, weighing down on his muscular build. My breasts rub against his back and I feel him tense, so I move away slightly, my fingers gripping him with more pressure than before.

The ride is quick, and Arrow's bike soon skids to a stop. I climb off, handing him back his helmet.

"Thanks, Arrow," I tell him quietly.

He grunts in response and takes the helmet from my hands, but doesn't bother to look me in the eyes.

"How's your day been?" I ask, tilting my head to the side and studying him as he gets off his bike.

He glances up at me, finally, and rubs the back of his neck. "It was okay. You gonna ask about the fuckin' weather next?"

"If I have to," I mutter, rolling my eyes. "In case you were wondering, my day was kind of awesome."

He grins then, his eyes softening on me slightly. "Good to hear, Anna, good to hear. Now get your ass inside."

He is trying to get rid of me. How predictable.

"Arrow," I say, taking advantage of his attention. "Do you think Rake will tone down the whole escort thing?"

He licks his top lip, then follows through with his teeth. I stare at his mouth, mesmerized by the action.

He clears his throat. "Don't look at me like that, Anna."

"Like what?" I ask, still staring.

"Anna," he snaps. I lift my gaze, my cheeks heating. "Go and ask Rake, but I don't think so. He just wants you safe. Bad shit has happened before, and he's going to make sure that nothing bad touches you. And I agree with him. Now get your ass inside before he calls me asking where the hell you are."

"Okay," I reply, puffing out a breath.

He steps to me and touches my cheek in an almost-there caress. Okay, this is new. He's never shown this type of affection to me before.

Our eyes lock.

I swallow hard.

He pulls away and turns his back to me. Looks like I've been dismissed.

"Nice chatting with you as always," I call out as I walk into the clubhouse. The scene before me is a familiar one. Rake is sitting there with a woman on his lap, blissfully unaware of the rest of the world. Faye, the president's wife and queen bee of the clubhouse, is talking with Tracker, another MC member and a friend of mine. Sin, the club president, is nowhere to be seen. Faye turns when she notices me, her auburn hair framing her pretty face. I nod my head at her, giving her the respect she's due as Sin's old lady.

I know Faye is a badass chick, I've heard all the stories about her. I tend to stay out of her way—we don't really interact, even though she's close with Rake, Tracker, and the rest of the guys. I think in any other situation, we'd probably really get along well. I've heard nothing but good things about her, but I still have no plans to befriend her anytime soon. I'll never admit this to anyone, but I envy her. She has all the men wrapped around her finger, but more important, they treat her like an equal. No one tells her what to do or orders her around. They listen to her and respect her. And it pisses me off that while I'm treated like a child, she can do as she pleases.

I know the men keep a close eye on me only because of Rake's commands, and I hope that will ease up when my brother realizes that I'm a woman who can take care of herself. I think he needs to figure out that he never let me down when we were younger, and he has nothing to make up for. He's a great brother, even though he can be a tad excessive when it comes to me. I know it's because of how much he cares about me, but I don't think he knows what to do about it. Or me.

Tracker walks over to me when he sees me, a smile playing on his lips, and wraps an arm around my shoulders. "Anna Bell!"

"Don't call me that," I reply, raising an eyebrow at him. Tracker is friendly, easy to get along with, drop-dead gorgeous, and completely fuckable. Shoulder-length blond hair frames a handsome face with bright blue eyes and full lips. His body is impressive, lithe and toned, and covered in tattoos. Why he's with Allie, I have no idea. I think it's one of those things—like how good girls always finish last, because the bitch definitely won when she got her paws on a man like Tracker. The first time I came to the clubhouse, he approached me and made a comment about breaking in the fresh meat. I replied with a joke about how I was harder to get than Rake, and we both found that amusing. We've kind of become friends since then. Tracker is very easy to be around, and he's a good listener. I just bonded with him from the very start.

"It's a very cute name, for a cute lady," he says, squeezing my cheeks, shaking my head left and right.

"Fuck off," I tell him with a smile, slapping away his hands.

"How was class?" he asks, pulling on a lock of my blond hair. Could he be more annoying? He treats me like the sister he never had yet didn't want, so I make sure to return the favor.

"It was okay," I reply. "Still thinking about quitting and becoming a club whore though. It seems to hold a certain appeal."

He laughs, a deep rumble. "Don't let Rake even hear you joke about that."

"What would he do? Treat me like a kid and have people escort me everywhere?" I ask, voice full of sarcasm.

"And that," he says, smirking, "is the reason you will never be a club whore."

"What?" I ask, confused.

He chuckles. "Your sharp tongue. We like the club women to be pliable and—"

"Stupid? Easy? Flexible?" I offer, waggling my eyebrows sleazily.

He laughs harder. "I was going to say accessible."

My lip twitches and I shake my head. "I can't believe we're having this conversation right now."

"It's a normal conversation for me," he adds.

"I'll bet."

"Where's that sidekick of yours?"

I narrow my eyes on him and purse my lips. "Why do you want to know?"

I saw the way my best friend, Lana, stared at Tracker when she met him. Like he was fucking Superman or something. I caught Tracker studying her too, but didn't think much of it until now.

I know that Lana would never be someone's side chick, but Tracker has this way about him . . . I hope he just leaves her alone. Lana is smart, bookish, and doesn't have much experience with men. If Tracker shows interest in her, that's not a good thing. Allie is his woman and is so crazy—legit crazy, not just crazy in love—she'd probably claw Lana's eyes out. I don't miss the looks she gives me when I talk to Tracker, and I'm just a friend.

Of course, Allie might have to watch her back. Lana can be quiet and unassuming most of the time, but she has a serious temper on her. Trust me, I've seen it firsthand. It hardly ever comes out, but when it does, everyone is in trouble.

He shrugs like it doesn't matter to him either way. "Just making conversation. Put those claws away, Anna Bell."

Rake walks over to me like he's only just realized I've been standing here. Which he probably did.

"Hey, sis," he says as he rubs his scruffy jaw. Blond hair and green eyes the same shade as mine, my brother has an eyebrow piercing and lip ring that suit him. He's good-looking and knows it.

Yes—he's one of *those* men. He uses his good genes to his advantage and no woman is safe in his presence. I wonder when he'll settle down, and the type of woman it would take to make him do it. I'm thinking she would have to be pretty freaking phenomenal, because Rake seems to like a lot of variety and never stays with one woman long enough for me to even get to know her. Okay, that's not exactly true. Rake started acting this way only after he broke up with Bailey in high school. She was the only woman I've ever seen Rake pay any real interest to. I wonder what Bailey's up to these days.

"Hey. Why did you want me to come here?" I ask him, getting straight to the point.

He looks confused. "I thought we could hang out; I haven't seen you in a couple of days."

I blink slowly.

"Okay. Will she be joining us?" I ask, pointing to the woman who is now standing behind him wearing a pouty expression.

"Fuck, no," he replies, turning back and telling his tag-along something.

"Cut him some slack," Tracker tells me softly so no one else can hear.

My mouth drops open. "But . . . but . . ."

He grins. "I know, but he's trying."

I know he's trying; I do. He isn't used to me in his space, I'm not used to being in his space, but I'm getting there. It is a lot to take on, being thrown headfirst into the MC lifestyle. I am adapting though, and know it means a lot to Rake that I try to fit in here.

When I see Rake walk past Faye and kiss her on the top of her head, my throat burns. How can he be so loving and affectionate with her but not his own sister?

I pretend his casual affection with her doesn't hurt.

Rake says something to Faye, and she throws back her head and laughs. "What have you done now?"

Rake grins boyishly. "Nothing . . . yet. Just need some legal advice on something. Make some time for me, woman."

Faye looks amused. "Come see me tomorrow."

My brother nods and says something to her in a low tone that I can no longer hear.

"He doesn't wanna fuck things up with you, so he's being careful," Tracker muses from beside me.

Thank you, Dr. Phil.

I sigh and lean my head on Tracker's arm. "I know he cares about me. I just wish he wasn't so . . ."

"Slutty?" Tracker adds with a wolfish grin.

I laugh, shaking my head. "No. It's almost like he's scared to be himself around me."

"I think he just wants you to be proud of him and not scare you off with his bikerish ways."

"I am proud of him," I say, cringing when he slaps the woman's ass as she leaves. "Okay, he can be a pig sometimes."

Tracker's loud laugh gets us looks from everyone in the room.

"What's so funny?" Rake asks as he walks over and moves me away from Tracker. He sends Tracker a look that says *She's my sister, asshole.*

I roll my eyes. Rake has the protective big-brother thing down pat, that's for sure. He's always looking out for me, always has.

Tracker raises his hands, proclaiming his innocence. "We're just friends, man, you know I wouldn't go there."

"And why not?" I ask him in a sweet tone. "Is there something wrong with me?"

I put my hand on my hip, cocking it to the side, and give him a look that dares him to say anything other than how I'm one of the most beautiful women he's ever seen. I try and keep my face serious, not wanting to break out in the smile that's threatening my lips.

Tracker tilts his head to the side, taking me in from top to bottom. "You kind of look like Rake if you squint your eyes, so yeah, no, thanks."

He doesn't expect the punch in the gut. "Ow! You're strong for someone so little."

Rake grunts. "Come on, Anna, stop bullying my brothers."

Tracker laughs and rubs his rock-hard stomach. Like that even hurt him.

Arrow chooses that moment to walk in, and as always, he garners my full attention. I watch as he storms into the kitchen and comes out with a bottle of Scotch in one hand, a cigarette in the other.

He plops down on the couch and starts to drink straight from the bottle.

He doesn't look up, or pay attention to anyone around him, until Faye walks over and starts to talk to him in a hushed tone. I follow behind Rake as he leads me toward a long hall, forcing myself not to look back at Arrow. We stop at a door, and he grins boyishly at me as he opens it.

"This is your room. So, you know, you always have somewhere to stay, no matter what," he says, gesturing for me to enter. The room is bare except for a stunning black leather bed.

"It's new," he explains as I turn to stare at him.

"I have my own place," I tell him, feeling confused. Growing up, we didn't really have a house. We moved around and stayed wherever we could, couch surfing or living with our mother's latest boyfriend. We didn't have a stable life, or many other things that most people took for granted. We didn't come first to our mother; the drugs did. Maybe that's why he wants me to feel as though I have a home here? That no matter what, I'll always have a place to go? A place that I will be welcome?

My heart warms at the sentiment, but it isn't necessary. I am no longer that scared little girl; I am now a woman who knows how to take care of herself.

"I know you do, but you also have a place here. With me. You will never have to worry again."

Looks like I was right.

"Rake—"

"You don't have to call me that," he says, not for the first time.

"I know, but it's weird when I'm the only one calling you Adam and no one knows who the hell I'm talking about. Although I still call you Adam in my head," I try and explain.

His laugh makes me smile. I like seeing him laugh. "It's weird having my baby sister calling me Rake."

I raise an eyebrow. "So you're nicknamed after a man who lives in an immoral way and sleeps around a lot."

I used the dictionary for that one. It says a rake is another name for a womanizer, or a libertine.

The flush that works up his neck lets me know he isn't exactly pleased to be having this conversation with me. "Maybe I just like to . . ."

He searches fruitlessly for another reason to be called Rake.

". . . get rid of leaves?" I suggest in a dry tone.

"You always were a smart-ass," he says with good nature. "Fine, I like women. Sue me. I'm the perfect example of a man you shouldn't date. Learn from it."

"Surely there are some good men around this clubhouse . . . ?" I say casually, pretending to look around.

Like Arrow.

That's what I really mean.

Rake's laughter isn't what I was expecting in response. "No one will go near you, Anna. They know you're off-limits."

"How would they know that?" I ask him suspiciously, my hackles rising.

"Because I told them," he replies, unable to keep the smugness out of his tone.

My mouth drops open. "Why would you do that?"

"Because you're my sister," he says, crossing his arms over his chest.

"Yes, but I'm not asexual," I reply dryly, walking farther into the room and sitting on my new bed.

"To me you are," I hear him mutter. "Look, Anna, now that you're back here . . . I want to be here for you, like I haven't always been in the past."

Ahh, the infamous Jacob incident.

"That wasn't your fault," I say for the hundredth time.

He ignores me.

"Do you wanna get a drink?" he asks, the conversation clearly over. "You can tell me how your week has been."

"Sure, I could use a drink."

I wonder if Arrow will share his bottle.